the grave

of

god's daughter

ALSO BY BRETT ELLEN BLOCK

Destination Known: Stories

WILLIAM MORROW

An Imprint of HarperCollins*Publishers*

BRETT ELLEN BLOCK

the grave

of

god's daughter

HarperCollins books may be purchased for educational, business, or sales promotional use. For information please write: Special Markets Department, HarperCollins Publishers Inc., 10 East 53rd Street, New York, NY 10022.

FIRST EDITION

DESIGNED BY JUDITH STAGNITTO ABBATE/ABBATE DESIGN

Printed on acid-free paper

Library of Congress Cataloging-in-Publication Data

Block, Brett Ellen.
    The grave of God's daughter / Brett Ellen Block. — 1st ed.
    p. cm.
    ISBN 0-06-052504-5 (hc.)
        1. Polish American families—Fiction.   2. Allegheny River Valley (Pa. and N.Y.)—Fiction.   3. Allegheny Mountains Region—History. 4. Iron and steel workers—Fiction.   5. Mothers and daughters—Fiction.   6. Girls—Fiction.   I. Title.

PS3602.L64G73 2004
813'.6—dc21   2003051260

---

04 05 06 07 08 WBC/QW 10 9 8 7 6 5 4 3 2 1

For my mother and father,

always

ACKNOWLEDGMENTS

―――――――――――――――――

I am indebted to my parents for their unflagging support and encouragement. Thanks is also due to my friends—Ruth Foxe Blader, Grace Tseng, Ann Rollert, Heather and Gavin Frater, Amy and Brad Miller, Alex Parsons, Alice Dickens, Sarah Gegenheimer, Anne Engelhardt, Sue Zwick, Maureen Squillace, Matthew Vaeth, and Barbara Sheffer.

I would also especially like to thank Jonathan Pecarsky, my literary agent, as well as my editor, Clair Wachtel.

I am deeply grateful to James Michener and the Copernicus Society of America for their grant, without which this book would not have been possible.

the grave

of

god's daughter

CHAPTER ONE

I WAS ONCE TOLD that the distance between a lie and the truth is like the distance between thunder and rain—the latter is never far behind. But now, even as darkening clouds crest the hillside above the cemetery where my mother will soon be buried, I know it will not rain, not today.

It is almost winter and the grass is brittle underfoot, though it remains a vibrant, almost vehement, shade of green. My mother's simple coffin rests on planks of wood, suspended above her open grave, while a handful of mourners gather along either side. The few elderly men and women stand around solemnly, unspeaking, like people waiting for a bus. I recognize no one, but to them, I am the stranger.

"Are you the daughter?" a voice asks.

It is the priest. His skin looks pale against his long purple vestments and his back is severely hunched beneath his overcoat. It is as if years of ministering to the people of this town have buffeted him into the humble pose, the way a tree can be permanently bent by the wind.

"Yes," I say. "Yes, I am. I'm sorry I—"

"No matter. You're here now," he says, with the firm manner of a doctor rather than the kind or careful demeanor usually ascribed to a priest. That may be the very reason my mother chose him to perform her service.

I imagine her planning this funeral the way one might plan a wedding. Making a guest list, choosing the church, handpicking songs for the organist to play. More important still would have been the location of her burial, Saint Ladislaus cemetery. Set on a low knuckle of the Allegheny Mountains, it is an old community cemetery, full of generations of coal miners and steelworkers who saved what little money they earned to buy marble tombs and detailed headstones, the only memorial to their existence they would ever have. What no one knew when the cemetery was founded was that an underground stream flowed deep beneath the property and, over time, the moving water has buckled the land. The once-smooth sprawl of earth is now rolling with knolls, the grass undulating like sand dunes. All of the delicately carved headstones list and pitch as if riding a heady sea. The sculptures of angels with their eyes upturned to heaven are now tipped and gazing off like bored schoolgirls. Undermined by what secretly pulsed below, this cemetery speaks more about the condition of life than that of death.

"You made it."

I turn and find my brother, Martin, plodding up the dirt path toward the grave site. Were it not for his voice, I wouldn't have known him. His face looks as if all expression has been beaten out of it. His clothes are rumpled like he has just been in a fight and was lucky to have escaped unscathed.

Martin hugs me roughly. In that brief embrace, I can smell the liquor on him.

"I'm glad you're here," he says.

His eyes linger on my face for a moment, a flicker of grateful recollection, then he pulls away, uncomfortable being so close. I know better than to ask him how he's been. It will only invite an argument about how I haven't called or written or visited, about how I have abandoned my old life, this town and him. It is neither the time nor the place for a conversation about my failings. To spare him the silence, I ask softly, "Who are these people?"

"Couldn't say for sure. All from the church, I s'pose."

We are my mother's only living relatives, the only remnants of her family.

"Priest's about to start," Martin says, ending the conversation before either one of us can say something that might make us feel more than we have to.

I approach my mother's coffin and Martin positions himself at my side, though he is more in front of me than anything else. There is a rip in his jacket that starts at the shoulder and carves down over the ribs, a jagged gash that makes it seem as if my brother has been stabbed in the back. The long, fraying tear is a reminder of why I am here and why I left.

What I know about my brother's life now is scant, almost cryptic, like the bottom of a page torn out of a long, inscrutable book. He hasn't worked in years and has never married. For him, home is a room in a boardinghouse and the only regular thing about his life is the welfare checks he receives monthly in the mail. Decades of heavy drinking have taken their toll. It is as though the liquor has literally diluted my brother's blood, leaving his spirit limp, like a bedsheet on a clothesline in a gale. He is not the person I once knew nor, I doubt, will he ever be again.

The priest clears his throat and bows his head ceremoniously. Martin drops his eyes, then buries his hands in his pockets, hiding them from the chill of the rising wind. It appears to be an effort for him to stand straight. I can't be sure if he is drunk or if it is true sorrow that has rendered him unsteady. When he was a child, my brother was precocious, eager, resolute. He was the child I would have liked to be. But since that one spring in our childhood, when everything in our small world unhinged itself from what we knew it to be, my brother has never been the same. From then on, Martin was a ship set adrift, never able to maintain course. Years later, his drinking served only to snap the few sails he had onboard. I fear that with my mother's death Martin's ship will run aground and become hopelessly moored on shore, never to set sail again. It is a fear that stings my heart.

"In the name of the Father, the Son, and the Holy Ghost," the priest intones, then he repeats himself in Polish:

Imie ojciec i syn i swiety duch.

I understand the words instantly, though I have not heard the language in years. All of the mourners reply with a sonorous refrain:

I pozwalac wieczny swiatlo jasnia nadje.

The meaning floods my mind: *And let perpetual light shine on the dead.*

The priest crosses himself. One woman dabs the corners of her eyes, preempting any tears. Behind a neighboring headstone lies a roll of sod tied with twine. The breeze rustles the bound blades, leaving them quivering. It is the grass that once covered my mother's grave. The notion that this tidy bundle will soon be unfurled as a final, burgeoning shroud sends a pang of sadness through me, but I do not have the will to cry.

I feel my mother's death the way one might feel a cut on the tip of a finger. The pain is not severe, but it makes me aware of that tiny stretch of skin and all that touches it, awakening the memory of what I have long ignored. I alone know the reason my mother lies here in this very spot and that knowledge makes gravity seem somehow lighter. It is as if my body is full of air and I am floating silently behind the mourners, like a balloon tied to my brother's wrist, weightless but not free.

The site of my mother's grave is as deliberate as a kiss. Situated atop a lonely rise, it has a view of the river and the town below as well as of a potter's field, which lies in the shadow of the mountains at the edge of Saint Ladislaus property. It is a pretty vista marbled with fields and tracks of fir trees, and it is almost picturesque in spite of the other cemetery, a swath of land dotted with tiny dimples of stone.

My mother's most precious secret lies buried in that flat, unhallowed field, her lone treasure so long entombed. From this spot, she will always have it close and in her sights. For this reason alone, I do not grieve for her, only for myself and all that was never mine and never will be.

The priest continues his eulogy, but I lose the somber words in the sound of the wind.

CHAPTER TWO

IT WAS THE YEAR that the girl drowned in the river. She was the first that spring in 1941. The opening casualty of the Allegheny's fierce current was usually a boy, caught in the coursing tide while trying to impress his friends, or some fisherman in a rowboat who'd been swept over the dam and pinned beneath the falls. But this time it was a young girl of five who had waded out into the fast water to show her brothers that she was as brave as they were. Her body was found a mile downstream. Afterward, the steel mill's whistle blew eight times, the way it always did whenever somebody drowned. That was how we knew.

I cannot recall the girl's name, though I can remember her face. The town of Hyde Bend was not large, just over two thousand, and most of the children attended Saint Ladislaus Catholic school. Though I was twelve that year and many grades above her, I could not help but notice the girl in the school halls. She had light brown hair and a delicate face that seemed to be made only for smiling. Sister Bartholomew, the head nun, could often be heard chastising her for giggling after class. "What are you smiling about, girl?" the sister would snap, her Polish accent bowing the words. "If God wanted you to smile all the time, your mouth wouldn't be able to frown." Despite her reproaches, the nun's remarks could never wipe the grin from the girl's lips for long. She was, it appeared, incapable of any permanent unhappiness.

The day after the girl's body was fished from the river, the nuns made us all say a decade of the rosary for her, one Our Father, and ten Hail Marys. Then they warned us not to play by the river, that doing so invited trouble. It was possible to beckon bad luck, of that they were sure. We had heard these warnings before, though they did little to dissuade us. The river was our one and only temptation.

A half-mile strip of the great Allegheny ran along the far edge of Hyde Bend, and its banks were too enticing to resist. They were a place of adventure, ripe for a thousand games with sticks and rocks and hollow reeds, the toys even the poorest of us could afford. Although the water was thick and silty, making it the color of tarnished silver, and the temperature was a constant, burning cold, there was no lure like its shores. We called the river's edge "the beach," though it was merely a spit of land covered in mud and slippery stones. Still, it was ours, the only definition of a beach we knew.

To get to the river, you had to brave the teetering wooden

stairway that led down nearly twenty feet to the bank. The wood creaked and groaned louder with every passing winter, yet the stairs remained, more a testament to our need to be connected to the river than the strength of the stairs' construction. Like the River Styx, the black border dividing hell from the land of the living, our river was all that separated us from what we did not know. As a child, I could not be sure which side I was on. And it took years for me to figure it out.

THE CLAPBOARD HOUSES that were built along the river were considered prime real estate in spite of the fact that, by virtue of their very location, those homes caught the brunt of the biting wind that came off the river from early fall until far into spring. Nevertheless it remained a privilege to live by the water, like a front-row seat. So if it was cold, those people were proud to lay claim to getting cold first. The men who owned those homes were not the sort who wore coveralls or hard hats to work. They were the ones who wore clean, pressed shirts and wool suits. These people were the minority in Hyde Bend. They were the ruling class, families whose names I knew but at whose houses neither my family nor myself would ever be welcome.

River Road, as it was aptly named, marked the town's perimeter on one side and at the other end was Field Street, which, also appropriately enough, faced a lettuce field that had long gone fallow. Field Street was Hyde Bend's main drag. Stores and businesses lined the road, while just beyond the backs of the buildings on one side a wide expanse of weedy land stretched for miles and petered out into nothing. Bracketing the far side of town was Consolidated Steel, a hulking mill that churned out massive slabs of metal as consistently as it churned out sooty smoke into the sky. On the opposite side of Hyde Bend squatted a long, low plant called General Salt. Though the name was vague, everybody knew what was made in the factory; they produced salt-based chemicals, mainly pesticides. Years later the plant would go on to create a top-selling product, a fine, pink powder known by the initials DDT.

The three towering smokestacks from the mill and the rows of chimneys that topped the plant were the tallest things for miles except for the enormous neon cross that stood on top of the mountain across the river. The cross had been erected in 1938, a gift to Saint Ladislaus church and the people of Hyde Bend from both of the factories that bookended the town. The towering cross stayed lit from five in the afternoon until five in the morning, its peak rising high into the sky above the mountain, a constant, glowing reminder that nothing was higher.

Hyde Bend was an enclave of Polish immigrants, entirely Catholic. Most knew at least a little English; however, since everyone's first tongue was Polish, that was all that was heard. Signs in store windows were written in English. Inside, Polish was what was spoken. It was as though the whole town was pretending to be something it wasn't, keeping up an American facade in order to retain the privileges that came with the country. Yet the customs, the traditions, the food, and the morality, they were vestiges carried straight from the villages outside Warsaw and Kraków.

When it came to outsiders, Hyde Bend was as friendly as a fist—hard and tight-knit. Those who moved into town for jobs at the mill or the plant but who weren't either Polish or Catholic soon moved away. They relocated to neighboring towns and took the bus run by the steel mill in to work. Visiting strangers never stayed and outsiders who commuted in for their jobs at the factories stuck together once they got there. They sat at their own tables during lunchtime and kept to themselves. They had little choice. The men from Hyde Bend purposefully spoke only in Polish on the job. It was their own form of segregation, a way of staking their claim and asserting their position. It was the one slice of power they had and they took as much pleasure in it as pride.

The town was named for the unforgiving crook in the river on which it sat. The shallow, rocky shoals below the water had ripped the bottoms from so many boats and steamers that they no longer passed that way. Even after the dam was built to regulate the river's depth, few would attempt to navigate our cursed corner of the Allegheny. The reputation of Hyde Bend was sealed simply by its location.

The town was laid out in a tidy rectangle, and it hardly seemed like coincidence that there was only one exit onto the road that met the highway, making Hyde Bend a sort of cul-de-sac, a bottle with only one way in and one way out. Stocky, brick one-story houses and saltbox cottages covered in pine siding lined the four main streets that connected each end of town. Most of the homes were painted white—the least expensive color—though they never remained that way. Because of the soot from the mill and the never-ending wind off the water, the crisp, white paint quickly turned gray. Some people would go to the trouble of washing their houses by hand come summer, but the paint would soon fade back to a dull shade of dust. It was as if the color white was unattainable, if not impossible, in Hyde Bend.

There were no trees in town. They had all been cut down to make room for houses when the mill went up. There were no lawns either, not even a narrow collar of grass at the sidewalk. There was no room for nature it seemed, not even in the town's margins. Without trees, birds were a rare sight, except for the occasional seagull coasting on the breeze and the crows, which stood constant watch on the phone wires, always scouting for scraps and carrion. The only time we would see birds was in flight or when they would briefly settle on the ground, but we never heard them sing, so the idea of having a bird as a pet was a fantasy for most of us children. Boys would form hunting parties to try and trick the crows down from the lines with bits of bread. When one came down to feed, the boys would attack, hurling themselves at the crow, arms outstretched. But the birds were too quick. They always got away. It didn't matter though, because none of us had a cage in which to keep the prized catch. The real thrill was the chance to touch one of the birds, to touch something that had the ability to leave that place, to leave and never return.

BETWEEN THE FOUR MAIN ROADS that crisscrossed Hyde Bend were three alleys. They had once been merely paths, but as the town grew, strings of shacks cropped up along the alleyways, squeezing in like weeds within the town's cracks. These places became home to Hyde Bend's poorest residents. The first alley was simply called "First" and it was closest to River Road, so even though it was an alley, the people there took pride in the relative position, as though the proximity somewhat softened their circumstances. The second alley was one street farther in. And the last alley, "Third," was slumped up behind the Silver Slipper Tavern and the police station. The unpaved alley was flanked by a row of ramshackle, two-room apartments that listed up against each other, as close as teeth. There were no gutters, so mud was a virtual constant. Trash was collected only at the far end of the alley, so the lingering smell of garbage was as persistent as the mud. Most townspeople often avoided that alley altogether and forbade their children from crossing through even as a shortcut. Third was the opposite of haunted. It was achingly empty despite its inhabitants, a place to which everything in Hyde Bend that was wrong, unacceptable, or ugly sifted down. That was where we lived—me, my brother, my father, and my mother.

My father called the stunted clapboard shack where we lived "our house," though it was closer to a shed than anything else, like a place for tools, inanimate objects, certainly not a place meant to be lived in. The walls were stuffed with newspaper for insulation, and at night, when the wind wasn't whistling through the gaps in the siding, we could hear mice nesting in between the boards.

Like much of the rest of Hyde Bend, most everything on Third was gray. The shingles, the stoops, and the tar-paper roofs were all covered with a layer of soot. Things seemed an even darker shade of gray on Third than anyplace else though, as if all the color had been leeched out by the cold and the stench. However, there was one tiny patch of dirt from which life sprang. It was a small rose garden with a few struggling bushes that, come summer, were all crowned by a single, vivid flower. The roses, as with everything else on Third, were owned by the woman we knew only as Swatka Pani. It was Polish for "sweet lady."

Though the nuns had always told us that no picture could ever do justice to the devil, I was convinced that he couldn't be a far cry from Swatka Pani. She did not speak, she hissed, and she didn't walk, she thundered. Because she was a widow, the only color Swatka Pani ever wore was black, and she had wiry hair that she dyed a rusty red, but the color usually grew out, leaving gray roots, so she looked like she was aging, transforming, before our very eyes. Though she was only in her late forties, Swatka Pani walked with a cane. Some unknown infirmity had stiffened her hips and made her shoulders cave. She had also gone deaf in one ear. Despite her ailments, Swatka Pani had the keen ability to whip around in an instant, tipping her head to tune in with her good ear. The fierce, feral motion was almost more frightening than anything she could say or do. Like the rest of the children on Third, I feared even a glance from her.

Swatka Pani's husband, long dead, had left her as landlord of the apartments on Third, a vast fortune in those days, especially for a woman, and she reigned over the shambling alley like a tyrant. There were no toilets in the apartments, only outhouses between every other building, and Swatka Pani would charge extra for using the toilets and even more if she found them too filthy for her taste. The families that shared them would then be charged a fine. "A slop tax," she called it. Swatka Pani was also merciless when it came to the rent, always threatening to throw out anyone who didn't pay on time. It was her habit to bang on doors with her cane at one A.M. on the day the rent was due, shouting, *"Drisiaj-zaplata mnie co ty winiensz mi."*

It meant, "It's time. It's time to pay what you owe."

 ⸱ *That is what the devil will say to me if I am a sinner*, I would think whenever I heard her speak that phrase.

A sin was like a debt, and a debt to Swatka Pani was indeed like a debt to the devil. She would always collect, one way or the other.

Everybody on Third could recount the story of the man named Lubiak who'd lived at the end of the alley. After his wife had died in childbirth, he was inconsolable. Lubiak would not eat or sleep or work. All he did was pace the street outside Saint Ladislaus church where he and his wife had been married. When the man's rent came due and he could not pay it, Swatka Pani simply smiled at him and quietly went away. The next day, she waited on her porch until Lubiak left for the church, then she used her key to go into his apartment. She paid a few of the older boys from the alley to break all of the man's furniture then throw the splintered pieces into the alley and grind them into the mud. It didn't matter that the man might have been able to sell some of the furniture to get her the money. All that mattered was that Lubiak and the rest of us learned the consequences of a sin against Swatka Pani. For her, the lesson was worth the sum of his rent. No one ever saw Lubiak after that nor did we ever learn what became of him. However, he remained in our minds, a punished spirit that revisited Third each month and spoke to us in the rapping of Swatka Pani's cane on our doors.

Swatka Pani loved nothing except her money and feared nothing—except the river.

Her fear and hatred were born nearly two decades before my birth, yet everyone in Hyde Bend knew the tale. It had been handed down as both folklore and fact. For years, Swatka Pani would go to the riverbank to collect dirt for her rosebushes. She claimed that the dirt was special, that it was what made her roses so radiant and hearty. Something from those inimical waters nourished the flowers and, with inconceivable alchemy, gave them life, and Swatka Pani refused to go without it. Whenever she went to the riverside for her precious dirt, she would always take her young son, Joseph, who was a toddler at the time. While she filled her buckets, Swatka Pani allowed the boy to stand at the water's edge and play with a wooden boat she had bought him, a handsome hand-carved ship that was painted red and topped with a paper sail and a string for guiding it. One day, Swatka Pani turned her back for too long, spent a moment more filling her buckets, and when she finally looked up from her digging, Joseph was being swept downstream, his head sinking beneath the water's surface while the red toy boat bobbed along after him. Joseph's body was never found, but the boat was. The river had released it onto the shore and into a tangled nest of branches, safe and intact.

Shortly after her son had drowned, pneumonia took Swatka Pani's husband, leaving her utterly alone. With the money her husband had left her, she easily could have moved away from Third, perhaps even to the coveted River Road. Nevertheless, she stayed, rarely leaving her house at the end of the alley, the only decent-sized structure nearby. People said that all of that tragedy had made Swatka Pani's heart dark. She grew cruel and, most would claim, insane. People refused to cross her, afraid that the punishment might be to suffer her same fate.

Since her son's death, Swatka Pani had refused to go anywhere near the river. If anyone even mentioned it in her presence, she would spit on the ground. The word alone was a hex. Yet Swatka Pani still needed her precious dirt, so she paid Leonard Olsheski to go down and fill her buckets, then bring them to her garden. Olsheski was in his twenties, built like a bull, with strapping shoulders that dwarfed his neck and head, but he was also slow-witted. He stopped attending school after the third grade, though it was mainly because the nuns wouldn't have him. He couldn't keep up and was prone to outbursts. One minute he was quiet and docile, the next no one could hold him down. However, as Leonard grew older and his father, his only caretaker, died, the people of Hyde Bend had taken pity on him. He was allowed to clean the barroom at the Silver Slipper Tavern in exchange for a cot in the back, and to make money for food, he carried people's groceries or moved boxes or shoveled snow. It was Swatka Pani who kept Leonard busiest. Once a week, like clockwork, I would see him lugging two heavily-laden buckets along Third, then empty them into Swatka Pani's garden. Later, he would return with two more buckets, unfazed by the weight or exertion, content to have a task.

Leonard spoke only Polish, but his was so broken and stunted it was nearly unintelligible. Worse yet, he often stuttered out of shyness. Leonard's two front teeth were long and prominent, so much so that they slid out over his bottom lip even when his mouth was closed, like a rabbit's. It was another reason he rarely talked or smiled. Most people couldn't understand him and would ask him to repeat himself, which only made Leonard more ner-vous, so he usually wound up walking away in embarrassment. But I could understand him.

Once a week, Leonard would go up and down each of the alleys, knocking on doors and asking, "You need me work?" Whenever he got to our apartment, his eyes would grow eager at seeing my face. My parents always instructed me to tell him to go away. Even if we did have work that needed to be done, we couldn't afford to pay him. Nevertheless, when Leonard would come by, I would slip him a sliver of cheese or a small apple if we had one and hope my mother didn't catch me. Then Leonard would break into a broad, elated grin, which he quickly hid behind his hand. He would thank me with a nod and go on to the next apartment in hope of work or some other kindness.

On Third, Leonard usually had little luck. Most of our neighbors were as bad off as we were. Many were widows or women whose husbands had run off and left them with nothing except children to feed. Though we were as poor as the rest, my mother kept Martin and me apart from the other children on Third, the same way a mother in a wealthy family might keep her children away from us. She never said we were better or different than the other people on the alley, but her actions implied as much. So neither the children nor the adults paid Martin and me much interest. If they did, it was to whisper about how haughty we acted and that we didn't have the right to—we lived exactly where they did.

The insults and gossip came mainly from the women because there were so few men who lived on Third. My father was one of just five and one of only two who had a steady job. He worked at the steel mill on the late shift that went from ten at night until six in the morning. The mill ran twenty-four hours a day and every eight hours the whistle would blow, signaling a shift change. It was a low, doleful wail and the sound would expand and drift over

Hyde Bend like a haze that lingered in the air. Afterward, dozens of men would file out of the mill's main door, their faces and hands and coveralls coated with grimy soot, as if they'd all just walked out of a burning building.

My father was a ladle liner. The ladles were the giant vats into which the molten steel was poured, and the mill had nine of them altogether. Each was ten feet across and nearly twice as deep. The ladles were lined with bricks to insulate them and keep them from cracking under the heat of the molten steel. The bricks crumbled quickly and wore down from the scorching temperatures. It was my father's responsibility to climb into the massive ladles and chip out the old bricks by hand with a hammer and chisel, then replace them one by one. It was grueling labor that left his muscles sore and his hands permanently chafed, the nails etched with black.

My father arrived home from work around the same time the sun rose. Our apartment had only two rooms, so even if any of us were asleep when he came home, we couldn't stay that way for long. Of the two rooms, the main one housed a deep porcelain sink, an icebox, and an oven that also served as a coal stove, as well as our table and chairs, a radio, and a single cot where my brother and I slept. Martin was small for his age, so we managed to share the bed, sleeping back to back, me against the wall to keep him farther from the cold that constantly seeped through the siding.

The other room, which my parents used as their bedroom, was in the rear corner of the apartment and was barely wide enough to hold their sagging mattress. In the front corner of the apartment was a washroom, which held a narrow tub and a tiny washbasin, with hardly any room left over. The apartment floors were made of wooden planks that creaked under even the slightest weight, and the walls were a brownish tackboard. The only decorations to grace the apartment were a wooden cross, mounted over the cot where my brother and I slept, and a small painting of Matka Boska Czestochowska, the Black Madonna. In it, the Holy Mother was cradling a swathed baby Jesus, their faces soft yet unflinching despite the fact that the skin of both mother and child was nearly black, the color of burnt flesh. It was said that when the church where the original painting hung was set ablaze by nonbelievers, the painting survived despite the ravaging flames. Stranger still, the colors of Mary's robes and the baby Jesus' swaddling clothes remained bright, unharmed, while the skin had darkened, as if mother and child had indeed been burned alive.

The painting of the Black Madonna was a miracle in and of itself, a symbol of the power of faith. My mother had paid eleven dollars for the nearly miniature copy, an enormous sum for us, but to her, it was worth it. She cherished the painting and prayed to it daily, locking eyes with the Madonna and whispering to her, pleading almost conspiratorially. For what, I did not know. My mother would gaze at the painting with such desperate, unrivaled adoration that I grew to fear and hate it. That flat, lifeless object had what I never did—her devotion.

The Black Madonna hung over the table where my brother and I sat with my father every morning when he returned home from work, the eyes of the Holy Mother and child peering down on us vigilantly. While we ate our bowls of oatmeal, my mother would fix my father his dinner, usually a few slices of bread and a thin soup made with vegetables and whatever meat we had. We weren't allowed to play the radio in the mornings. After hours of working in the deafening din of the steel mill, the noise of the radio hurt my father's ears no matter how low the volume. He would drink exactly three bottles of beer with his meal and smoke while he ate. Crumbs of bread would stick to the end of his cigarettes though he was too tired to notice or care. He was also usually too tired to speak, or had no interest in talking, so we ate together in silence and all that could be heard was the sound of our collective chewing.

As soon as my father finished his meal, he would go straight to bed and shut the door behind him. That meant that no one, not even my mother, was to bother him or to enter their bedroom. We never did. My brother and I would quickly brush our teeth and put on our school uniforms, shabby sets of blue sweaters, pants, and skirts that had been given to us by the Benedictine nuns because we couldn't afford to buy them. I had to pin my skirt to hold it on and Martin had to cuff his pants to keep from tripping. Each day we donned our ill-fitting uniforms and readied ourselves for school as quietly as we could. Any noise was liable to send my father flying out of the bedroom screaming curses. Though we spoke only Polish at home, these were words I did not know, words so sharp the sound alone would make me wince. So we learned how to step lightly on the ever-squeaky floorboards and how to speak in silent gestures rather than words.

We could tell when my father had finally fallen asleep by the sound of his snoring, then my mother would order us into our coats with a nod and guide us out the door, closing it soundlessly behind us. Every morning, she would walk us to school, not because she chose to but because she worked next door, at Saint Ladislaus church. She was the cleaning lady. Given the church's size, hers was no small task, hardly a job for one woman, however, asking for additional help would have cut into her pay, so she did it all by herself.

Saint Ladislaus church sat in the center of town, a towering stone building topped with a brick dome. Though it was hardly as large as either the mill or the plant, the church somehow felt bigger than both of those buildings put together.

Ground was broken in 1903, and to save money, the townspeople dug the hole for the foundation themselves with shovels and buckets. That way they could put every last cent into the church itself, making it a place of majesty and splendor, their own glimpse of heaven. Inside the church, soaring vaulted ceilings were held high on the shoulders of finely carved columns, and the vast dome rested on chiseled limestone arches. The interior of the dome was painted with lavish frescos depicting the apostles, all hovering benevolently in a sky festooned with clouds. A choir loft crowned the back of the church along with a massive organ whose bronzed pipes rose far into the rafters. Row after row of dark mahogany pews created the ribs that led up to the large center altar, which was adorned with painted statues of the saints, each with a doleful face and flushed cheeks, making them seem overly alive. The life-sized statue of Saint Ladislaus stood by itself in the left-hand corner of the church, near a side altar. Like a worshiper arriving late to Mass, the statue had a conspicuous air about it. The stone version of the saint carried a staff and wore a white cape detailed with gold and robes painted in rose. He was clean shaven with a kind expression, yet his eyes were distant, perpetually preoccupied. Unlike other saints, Ladislaus was not martyred nor was he holy. He was a bureaucrat, a man of high birth who brought the

Catholic faith to the people of Hungary and Slovakia. He then Christianized and colonized Transylvania, uprooting pagan traditions and building churches throughout the land. Afterward, he was made king of Hungary for his gift of religion. His acts were more businesslike than saintly, and the distracted look on the face of his statue appeared fitting. It was as if he were aware that he was unlike the other saints, perhaps unqualified, and afraid of being found out.

Keeping the church clean was a colossal task. The floors were swept daily and mopped once a week. The wax that dripped from the votive candles constantly had to be scraped. The pews required a special oil that had to be massaged into the wood once a week, and each statue was to be dusted with diaper cloth. The process was overwhelming. Though that was only the half of it. My mother was also charged with tending to the rectory and its sole occupant, Saint Ladislaus's head priest, Father John Svitek.

The rectory was a drafty, ignoble house that huddled near the rear haunch of the church, cowering in its shadow, clearly an afterthought on the part of the builders. Despite its inglorious location and plain construction, Father Svitek ran his home like a mansion.

For a man of the cloth, Father Svitek had an air of hardness that made people treat him more like a dignitary than a priest. He was a stern man in his sixties, tall and lean with the posture of a stone pillar. His long hands and severe chin made him look even more elongated, as though he was the same height as his own shadow. Father Svitek's manner was as rigid as his comportment. He was always curt and to the point, even in his sermons, and he spoke in crisp, meticulous syllables. Words were a commodity he didn't want to overuse. However, he had a habit of whistling softly whenever he wasn't speaking. It was a cheery sound that was incongruous with his persona, and it was the only gentle thing about him.

When he wasn't in the pulpit, Father Svitek would sequester himself in his study. He would leave lists of chores for my mother to do, duties in addition to washing all of his laundry by hand and cooking every one of his meals. The priest also demanded that my mother keep the house so impeccably clean that dust had no time to settle. The windows and floors were done weekly and the sheets changed three times per month.

Father Svitek earned only a meager stipend from the church, but because his family was wealthy, they provided him with whatever extra money he needed and Father Svitek preferred to live up to his means. In spite of his vow of poverty, he had a new radio, leather-bound books, and a down mattress. Though the priest's possessions were common knowledge around Hyde Bend, no one ever complained about the comforts he awarded himself. No one would dare. They would never speak out against a priest.

Another extravagance Father Svitek indulged in was having fresh meat delivered regularly, a luxury my family would never know. Besides her pay, the only other benefit my mother received from her job was being allowed to take the priest's leftovers home for us, and that was simply because he refused to eat the same thing twice. Father Svitek worked my mother the way a farmer would a mule, then acted as if giving away his uneaten food was more than generous recompense, yet my mother never complained, not once.

In school I had been taught that a priest was not only a man of

God, he was the closest thing to God on earth that I would ever know. Like God, he could listen to our prayers, but a priest could answer in a human voice. To me, Father Svitek was as cold as the statues he made sure my mother scrubbed clean, and I found it hard to believe, if not ironic, that God would consider such a man kin. Even as a child, I was well acquainted with the concept of irony. Though I didn't know it by name, irony was the thread that ran through everything the nuns taught us. Faith was a double-edged dagger that only the brave embraced. God loved us unconditionally. However, it took courage, if not madness, to love Him back. *The Book of Saints* told tales of righteous men having their eyes put out. The tongues of the pious were cut out at the root. Injustice, like irony, was commonplace, a consequence of living. So it seemed fitting that Father Svitek was, presumably, as close to God as I might ever get and it didn't seem unfair that my parents spent their days scratching out a living cleaning two of the most important places in Hyde Bend while we lived in a place that would never be anything but dirty.

About a month after the little girl drowned in the river, my mother woke us early one morning and told us to dress as fast as we could. She left my father's food on the table covered in a cloth and hurried us into our clothes.

"What's happening?" Martin asked as my mother forced him into his school shirt and buttoned it quickly. Martin was seven that year, though his tiny body and spindly limbs made him look even younger.

"Your father's still at the Silver Slipper and I'm going to get him," she answered flatly. Her anger had boiled down to fact.

I pulled on my sweater and, just as I'd gotten it over my head, my mother was on me with a comb, running it through my hair and yanking out the knots. This was a ritual for her, and I'd given up protesting. She would stand in front of me, carefully part my hair and tuck it behind my ears as if I was incapable of doing it on my own. She never braided my hair or put any ribbons in it, but there was a certain way she wanted me to look, one in which I had no say. Once she was satisfied with my appearance, my mother would stop and admire my face and hair without looking into my eyes, as if I were a mannequin she was dressing for a shop window.

We had one mirror in the house, over the basin in the wash-room, but I rarely stood before it. I knew what I looked like and I knew I was not pretty. Not like other girls I'd seen. And not like my mother. Even though she wore her weariness like a heavy mask, it could not blunt her fair features or hide the hint of the flexibility for a smile in her lips. In spite of her old clothes and the kerchiefs that covered her hair, my mother was still a woman that men glanced at and admired. I saw them do it. I also saw them look at me, only briefly. I did not share that incalculable currency of beauty with my mother, though I found that a comfort. I could conceal myself, go unnoticed. My plainness was a kind of camou-flage, one that allowed me to decide if I wanted to exist or not. Yet when it came to my mother, there was no hiding.

"You'll take your brother to school this morning," she in-structed, wrapping a scarf over her head with a flourish, then knotting it under her chin as if she were strapping on a helmet.

"And hold his hand when you walk with him. The roads are slippery from the rain."

Because my mother had woken us unexpectedly and hustled us into our clothes, it was only when we were walking out the door that I noticed that her painting of the Black Madonna was gone.

"Where's your picture?" I asked, surprising myself as much as my mother with the question. Her face deflated into a wounded stare.

"Yeah," Martin chimed in. "Where did it go?"

In that agonizing instant, I sensed that my father must have sold the Black Madonna. Most likely, it was for money to buy alcohol. The realization made my chest feel like it was filled with sand.

"Come on," my mother told us, her voice wavering just above a whisper. "It's time to leave."

Outside, a steady drizzle was falling, making the air feel dense, almost solid. I took Martin's hand and together we watched my mother walk toward the end of the alley, the mud sucking at her boots as she went, her shoulders hunched against the chill. As she neared the corner of the alley, I willed her to look back at us, maybe even to wave, something that would take the edge off the morning. She didn't. My mother rounded the corner and disappeared, leaving the road empty except for the growing puddles, as if she had never been there at all.

"Should we follow her?" Martin asked.

"No," I said. "We can't go where she's going."

The Silver Slipper was open twenty-four hours a day to cater to all the different shifts that clocked in and out of the mill and the salt plant. The tavern was owned by the Pierwsza brothers, Edgar and Clement, who took turns manning the bar. Both were sturdy, wide-faced men, though neither stood far above five feet. What they lacked in height, the brothers made up for in menace. Fights would often break out in the Silver Slipper, but if either of the brothers was forced to get involved, someone would end up needing a doctor. They were notorious for keeping baseball bats behind the bar, but these were no ordinary bats. They had hammered nails into the ends, and the brothers were said to come out swinging if there was any sort of commotion. Most men knew that if they wanted to brawl, it was in their best interest to do so outside.

Though the Silver Slipper was almost as inhospitable and dangerous as the steel mill, it was the only place where my father could go to see his brother, William. An undeclared but bitter war had been waged years ago between my father's family and my mother, and though I was never told the reasons behind it, it was clear that this was why we were never allowed to see our relatives. When Martin was still a baby and I had learned that the other children in my school had cousins, I asked my parents if I had cousins too. My mother and father swapped a fast glance, then he stormed out of the apartment. Afterward, my mother pinched me on the arm and hissed at me, "Don't ask those kind of questions. Do you want to start trouble?"

I never raised the subject again. Once Martin was old enough to start wondering, I told him of the incident and warned him not to bring up our relatives. Normally, such a suggestion wouldn't have been enough to curtail his curiosity, but something in the way I recounted the event must have convinced him that his questions weren't worth the risk.

To talk of family was forbidden in our house, though occasionally the topic would creep into my parents' conversation. What I could glean from those exchanges was meager, a threadbare history patched together with scraps of dialogue and innuendo. For my mother, love and loss were synonymous. They could have been the same word. Her father had died during her youth. A heart attack sent him to his grave when my mother was just half my age.

Then her younger brother, Stephen, died a year later of scarlet fever. Shortly afterward, my mother lost her own mother to pneumonia. The litany of loss spanned most of her lifetime. My mother would never speak of the deaths, not any of them, not to lament them nor to question them. I couldn't help but think that God had turned against my mother, that He had forsaken her. But I had been taught that you didn't have to be a sinner to suffer undue misfortune. That was simply our lot. Still, I wondered if it was luck or some other force that had conspired to keep the people she cared for from her.

My mother had watched each member of her family consigned to a grave, then she had buried each of their memories along with them. Though all of my father's siblings were still alive, his brother and two sisters, he saw his brother only from time to time and that was at the Silver Slipper, a place my mother would not normally set foot in. There seemed to be an unspoken deal between my mother and father—he could see his family as long as the rest of us didn't. For my father, it was an unfair arrangement, but he agreed to it nonetheless.

In those weeks that April after the little girl drowned, things had begun to change. My father hadn't been coming home for breakfast. We would hear the mill's whistle blow and wait for him at the table, our food growing cold, but he would not appear. My mother would tell us that he must have been working overtime and not to worry, to go ahead and eat without him. Martin believed her, but I knew better. The money my father spent buying drinks at the Silver Slipper was money that never went to buy groceries or to pay the rent, so in my mother's mind, it was money lost. We had too little of everything to waste anything, not food, not clothes, not time, and, least of all, money. The fact that my father would spend even a nickel more than necessary was a slap in the face for all of the effort my mother put in trying to support us. Pawning her beloved painting was worse than if he'd quit his job altogether.

"So where did it go?" Martin asked as we trudged through the alley toward the schoolhouse. He and I spoke in English when we were alone. Most other children did too, though not around their families. At home, everyone spoke Polish. In private, however, Martin and I chose English, as if it was our private language, a secret code we kept to ourselves.

"What?" I asked, hoping to bluff my way out of having to answer his question.

"The painting."

I couldn't tell my brother what I believed. I couldn't bring myself to say the thought aloud. "The hook on the back was broken," I answered. "He probably just took it to a handyman to fix it." It was true that the hook was broken, but it had been broken since my mother bought the painting.

Martin nodded, easily persuaded for once, and I was thankful for that much.

"So why is he at the Silver Slipper?"

"I don't know. Drinking, I guess."

"But he can drink at home with us at breakfast."

"Maybe he doesn't want to drink with us."

"Why wouldn't he?" Martin persisted. He was holding my hand harder, trying to press out the answer he wanted to hear.

"I don't know."

My tone was enough to convey that anything else I might say

would be more than he wanted to know, so Martin let the subject drop and we walked in the opposite direction my mother had gone and into the rain.

THAT DAY IN CLASS, Sister Bernadette gave a lecture about the martyrs of North America. She told us the story of Father Lalemant and Father Breboeuf, two French priests who had come to this country as missionaries and who had spent years with the Huron Indians preaching the word of the Lord. One day, a rival Iroquois tribe attacked the Huron village, and Father Lalemant and Father Breboeuf were seized and tortured. Red-hot hatchets were applied to their bodies, heated spear blades hung around their necks, belts of bark soaked in tar and resin were tied around their waists and set ablaze. Because he continued preaching to them throughout these tortures, the Iroquois gagged Father Breboeuf, cut off his nose, tore off his lips, and poured boiling water over him as a parody of baptism. Finally, large pieces of flesh were cut off the bodies of the priests and roasted, then their hearts were torn out and eaten along with their steaming blood.

Sister Bernadette recited the account with firm purpose and without a hint of disgust. All of the nuns took rare pleasure in recounting such horrors to us. Like soldiers who never saw combat, the gory tales of the saints were their adoptive war stories, and the nuns reveled in the fear they stirred in our souls.

Sister Bernadette spoke English, but like the rest of the nuns, her first language was Polish. So if the students wanted to whisper in class or talk about her behind her back, we spoke as quickly as we could in English. The jumble of words was impenetrable to Sister Bernadette and often made her angry enough to bring out the dreaded twin rulers from her desk drawer. When held together back to back, a pair of rulers made a formidable weapon, especially when slapped across the top of the hand. Children bore scars for weeks at a time from ruler blows. Most wore them as badges of honor. I'd never done anything in class to warrant a lashing with the rulers and had no intention of doing so. I only spoke when questioned and never raised my hand. That way I remained inconspicuous, hidden, and that made day-to-day life at school bearable.

Later that morning, Donny Kopec came to class sporting a broken arm tied in a sling made of rags. He impressed everyone, including Sister Bernadette, with the story of how he'd broken his arm while riding the bicycle he used to make deliveries for the butcher, Mr. Goceljak. Donny had hit a rock and was thrown over the bicycle's handlebars and into the middle of Field Street. He described the bicycle rearing up and tossing him through the air, then he claimed he'd heard the bone in his right arm break and mimicked the sound for everyone to hear. Unlike the gruesome stories of martyred saints told to scare us, this was the sort of gore we couldn't get enough of and Donny was forced to repeat his story—which grew grander and more life threatening with every telling—throughout the school day.

At lunchtime, I sat with a few other girls who talked about the boys they had crushes on while I ate quietly and pretended to listen. Those sorts of conversations were always beyond me. It was like listening to my father talk about church taxes; the subject did not pertain to my life and seemed as if it never would, so I simply nodded when it appeared I was supposed to nod. I was just happy that the girls let me sit with them.

In between their giggling, I overheard Donny tell some other boys that he was glad he wouldn't have to make deliveries for Mr. Goceljak anymore and that the butcher would have to find somebody else to do the job. Those words rattled through my head like seeds until an idea blossomed in my mind, an idea so radiant I had to close my eyes in order to determine if it was possible.

There was only one shop in town where my father could have pawned my mother's painting, the Savewell Five'n'Dime. It was a regular store, but the owner, Mr. Sekulski, also bought and sold personal items out of his back room. It was supposed to be a secret, but like most secrets in Hyde Bend, everybody knew. If I could get Donny's old job making deliveries, I thought I could earn enough money to buy back the painting. I believed that if I could return the Black Madonna to my mother, then she might look at me the way she looked at it. Hope crystallized in my heart like a diamond.

AFTER THE SCHOOL BELL RANG, I bolted to Martin's classroom and shoved him into his coat just as my mother had done that morning.

"This isn't the way home," Martin groused as I dragged him toward Field Street. "Where are we going?"

"No place."

"Then why aren't we going home?"

"Because we're not."

"Then what are we doing?"

"You'll see," I told him, pulling him by the hand. Martin had a book in his arms, a collection of illustrated Bible stories with a drawing of a lamb on the cover, and he was holding on to it for dear life. The younger children were allowed to take only a single book from the library per week, so books were a treat, especially for us because the only one we had at home was the Bible. Martin had just recently begun to read, but he was the fastest reader in his class, a fact I took great pride in. If he could have, Martin would have read all day instead of playing with the other kids or the meager toys we had. My father had made us a set of wooden blocks, and Martin and I would stack them into teetering towers, but there were never enough blocks to build anything that resembled a structure. My mother had bought me a rag doll at a church rummage sale, yet no matter how many times it was washed, the doll's face remained dark with dirt and age, just as the Black Madonna's had grown dark in the flames. We had little in terms of material possessions, but Martin's ability to read seemed to suggest that what we lacked in wealth, we made up for in other ways.

"I don't want to *see* where we're going," Martin declared. "I want to *know*."

This was a game we played, a tugging match to see how long I would hold out on him and how long it would take for him to wear me down. Martin was not content unless he knew the whole story, the whole truth. By the tenor of my voice alone, he could distinguish a fact from a lie, and he would pester me with questions until he got an answer he believed. Sometimes his incessant questioning would bother me, but usually I enjoyed it. Martin wanted to discover things, to acquaint himself with every facet of the unknown, unlike my father who was happy to forget his life as well as ours and rushed to erase it all by drinking.

Field Street was quiet. None of the shifts had let out yet and the housewives had finished their shopping and gone home to wait for their children. I guided Martin to Savewell and boldly led him inside.

"Are you crazy? We can't buy anything in here," Martin whispered.

"We're not buying. We're just looking," I said, guiding him down an aisle of linens and toward the back.

"I don't want to look at things I can't have."

"Then close your eyes."

I made sure nobody was around, then checked to see if the door to Mr. Sekulski's back room was open. It was and there didn't appear to be anyone inside.

"Stay here," I instructed Martin.

"I will not. Not alone."

If the painting was in the back room, I couldn't let Martin see it. I had to think of a way to make sure he wouldn't want to tag along.

"Okay, then you're going to have to sneak into that room with me."

"I will not," Martin insisted. "That would be a sin."

"Looking into a room isn't a sin."

"Well, sneaking sounds like a sin. Sneaking does not sound good."

"Fine, then stay here."

Before Martin could pipe up again, I left him at the end of the aisle to go peek into Mr. Sekulski's back room. It was a cluttered space the size of a large closet and it was lined with shelves, each overflowing with everything from a phonograph to a silver tray to a life-sized figurine of a cat. My mother's painting was propped up on the top shelf between a candelabra and a dented teapot. Sitting there among the odds and ends, the little painting looked lost, the Holy Mother and child unquestionably out of place.

"What are you doing in here?"

I spun around to find Mr. Sekulski behind me, blocking my way out. He was not a big man, but his stomach hung out in front of him like a shield. He wore glasses, which rode low on his nose as though he was inspecting everything he saw. I sputtered for a few seconds, trying to come up with an excuse.

"You trying to steal something? I'll call the police, missy. Have no doubt." His Polish was choppy and riddled with flattening slurs.

Though I had been trying to sneak a glance into his back room, the suggestion that I would steal from him gave me enough fire to respond.

"No," I replied in Polish. "I wasn't going to steal anything. I came to see if you had my mother's painting."

"What painting?"

"That one. The little one. The Black Madonna."

Mr. Sekulski studied my face until he was satisfied I was telling the truth, then he started barking questions at me again.

"Well, what do you want? You can't just come around here visiting the thing."

"I want to buy it back," I told him.

"Buy it back? With what? Paper money?"

"I said I want to buy it back. How much will it cost?"

He squinted at me skeptically and rolled his response around in his mouth for a minute, savoring it before spitting it out. "Fourteen."

The word *fourteen* came at me like a fist and caught me right in the middle of the forehead. It sounded like an unattainable sum, a sum so high it might as well have been a fortune.

"Why?" I demanded, the question exploding from my mouth. Anger had made me bold. "My mother paid eleven dollars for it. Why is it more now when it was ours to begin with?"

"That's the price of business," Mr. Sekulski pronounced with an unsympathetic shrug, as though the policy had nothing to do with him.

"Promise me you won't sell it until I bring you the money."

Mr. Sekulski let out a laugh, amused by my attempt at a threat. "Don't worry. Nobody will want that thing."

That should have made me feel better. Instead, all that registered was the impact of the insult rather than relief. Nobody wanted the most valuable thing we had.

"I'll get the money," I told him.

"Okay. Sure."

"I will," I assured him. I wanted to convince myself as much as him.

"Then I guess I'll be seeing you," Mr. Sekulski said as he moved out of the doorway, leaving me just enough room to slip by.

I was fighting the urge to run out of there, but forced myself to walk, to make sure Mr. Sekulski saw me striding out of his store, unafraid. After Mr. Sekulski had shut the door to the back room, Martin peered out from around the end of the aisle. He had witnessed the whole scene and his eyes were wide with panic.

"I told you not to go in there. I told you."

"It's okay. Nothing happened."

"But you got caught."

"Yeah, but he didn't do anything to me."

Martin cleared his throat, expecting a further explanation.

"What? I was only looking." He exhaled a small snort, his usual way of telling me he knew I was lying. "Fine. Believe what you like."

"No, I only believe the truth."

"Okay, then try this one: we're going home now."

Martin snorted again and rolled his eyes. "All right. Where next?"

"The butcher's shop."

"At least that's not a lie."

THE BUTCHER'S SHOP sat in the middle of the block on Field Street, on the same side as the field. The storefront was painted a bright yellow and through the large picture window I could see the butcher, Mr. Goceljak, standing behind the counter talking to a customer, an older woman in a red felt hat.

"Stay out here," I instructed Martin.

"Why? I got to go in last time."

"Because I said so."

"What's inside that's so special?" He went to look in the window and I yanked him away harder than I'd intended to.

"You hurt me." Martin rubbed his arm, more to make me feel guilty than because I'd injured him.

"I'm sorry, but you have to stay out here. And don't talk to anybody. And don't touch anything. And don't move."

"Why?"

"Just stay here."

Martin looked sad and wounded; it was the face he made whenever he thought he was being excluded.

"Please," I begged.

"Okay, but don't take long."

"I won't."

"If you do, I'm coming in."

"Fine," I conceded, then I positioned him between the picture window and the door so he couldn't be seen from inside. Martin stood against the wall and stiffened like a toy soldier, then flashed me a salute.

"Remember: don't move."

"I'm not moving," he said between gritted teeth, trying not to open his lips.

I took a deep breath and entered the butcher's shop. A bell above the door sounded my arrival. The walls were the same chipper yellow as on the outside of the building and it was cool inside, as if the back door had been left open, but I knew that the air was chilled because of the iceboxes hidden in the rear of the store. I'd only been in the butcher's shop once before, on an errand with my mother for Father Svitek. The delivery boy at the time had brought him the wrong kind of kishke and Father Svitek wanted my mother to exchange the sausage. This was before Martin was born and it was summertime. I remembered asking my mother why it was so cold in the butcher's shop when it was so hot outside. That was when she told me about the iceboxes. When I asked her what was inside them, all my mother said was, "Ice." I couldn't be sure if she had said that to spare me the explanation of where meat came from or to avoid telling me that it was something we would rarely have the money to buy.

Mr. Goceljak laid a thick cut of marbled beef on the counter for the woman in the felt hat to inspect. She scrutinized the piece of meat as if it were a gemstone, eyeing it from every angle to make sure she'd gotten the best cut. Mr. Goceljak waited patiently, letting the woman have her look. He was a thin, tightly muscled man with black hair and a hawkish face. He was so slim he had to tie the strings of his apron around his waist a number of times to make it fit. The apron itself was pure white from the neck to the chest, but from the midsection down, the fabric was stained brown with drying blood. After the woman nodded her approval, Mr. Goceljak swiftly wrapped the meat in a sheet of paper and presented it to her like a present. The woman counted out her coins and bills to the cent, then thanked him and walked around me and out the door.

Mr. Goceljak hadn't appeared to notice me until that moment.

"What do you want?" he said in a manner meant to say that if I was about to ask for money for the church or the children's choir, not to bother. His Polish was coarse, the accent irregular, and I had to struggle to understand him. I knew little about Mr. Goceljak other than the fact that his wife was gone. It wasn't clear if she'd died or run off or just disappeared. Some people said he'd had to commit her to a sanitarium, that she wasn't stable. Whether or not the story was true mattered little to me. All I hoped was that Mr. Goceljak would hear me out.

"I'm here because I heard about Donny Kopec, your delivery boy." I'd been holding my breath in anticipation, and it took all my might to get those few words out.

"What about him?"

Mr. Goceljak put his hands on his hips as if to say I was already wasting his time. I took another breath and began, "Well, he was your delivery boy, right? And now he's got a broken arm. So I figured you didn't have anybody to make your deliveries anymore."

"So?"

"I could do it. I mean, I want to do it. I want the job."

For a few painfully long seconds, Mr. Goceljak stared at me without a word. Then he came out from behind the counter and folded his arms purposefully. I had to resist the temptation to back away from him altogether.

"You're a girl, you know that?"

"Yes," I answered, somewhat tentatively.

"And you want a job like this? Delivering meat? You ever seen uncooked kishke or kielbasa? It doesn't look like paper dolls or anything."

"I know."

"Then why do you want this job?"

"My family needs the money."

The sentence prickled as it passed over my lips, as sharp as tiny chips of glass. Though this wasn't entirely a lie, it wasn't the truth either, and it was as close to sin as I had ever come. I silently prayed that God would understand, that He might sympathize.

Mr. Goceljak's expression changed. I prepared myself for him to yell at me, to tell me to get out and never come back, but he simply asked, "Do you know how to ride a bicycle?"

"I—yeah, I mean, yes, I do. Yes, sir."

This was a complete and unequivocal lie, and it seeped over my soul like a sudden spill. I'd never been on a bicycle in my entire life. Few children in town had ever touched one, let alone ridden one. I braced myself, waiting for a bolt of lightning to strike me down where I stood. But nothing happened.

"All right then," Mr. Goceljak said. "Follow me."

In a daze, still awaiting my punishment for lying, I let him lead me around the front counter and through a thin curtain into the back of the shop. It was less a room than an alcove full of scarred, wooden butchers' blocks, metal tubs, and a sink. Sharp, steel hooks dangled from the ceiling next to strands of flypaper. On one side of the room hung two pigs. The heads had been removed and the bodies were split from the necks down through the legs. The cut was so smooth, the sides so even, it was as if the animals opened like books. Beside them was a rack of cow's ribs laying on a chopping block. A stream of blood had collected beneath the ribs and the white spokes of bone were reflected in the pooling liquid. Mr. Goceljak was monitoring my face for a reaction.

This is your punishment, I thought.

I was so stunned by what I beheld that I couldn't even blink. Perhaps it was my penalty for lying; it was, however, also a test, Mr. Goceljak's test. It was my only opportunity to convince him to give me the job, so I looked the pigs up and down defiantly, biting the inside of my cheek until I proved I wasn't scared or squeamish.

"Good," he said. "Now I'll show you the bicycle."

I trailed him out the back door to a gravel alley. The bicycle was propped up against the steps and chained to a handrail made of used pipes. Its frame was old and rusted, and Donny's accident had left a deep indentation in the front fender. The royal blue paint was flaking and the metal basket was crumpled at the corner. But to me, the bicycle was beautiful. I couldn't take my eyes off it.

"You'll have to wipe down the basket," Mr. Goceljak explained, noting my interest. "The blood runs out of the packages and gets all over the metal. If you don't clean it, you'll have the flies chasing you. 'Em and the dogs."

"Dogs?"

"If you pass any houses and the dogs aren't chained up, they'll run after you."

The notion of being chased by dogs had never crossed my mind, and it truly terrified me. "Will they bite me?"

"You, probably not. But they'll get at the meat if you let 'em."

"What do I do?"

"Just ride fast," Mr. Goceljak suggested. "And don't fall down."

For someone who had never ridden a bicycle, those were possibly the worst instructions I could hear. Yet by then, there was no turning back.

"Come by tomorrow after school. I'll give you the route and you can start then. Pay's a penny per delivery. You work Monday through Friday. Got it?"

"Yes."

"All right then. See you tomorrow," Mr. Goceljak said and turned to go.

"Wait. Don't you want to know my name?"

"I know who you are. I recognized you when you walked in. I know your mother. Works for Father Svitek."

The fact that I was both known and could be recognized swept over me like a strange breeze. I hadn't imagined that either was possible.

"Well, all right then," Mr. Goceljak repeated, then he left me alone with the bicycle.

I gazed at its curves, only to discover that it was a boy's bicycle. The center bar was raised high in the frame. I knew there was a difference between bicycles designed for boys and for girls, but I had yet to find out exactly what that difference entailed. I chose not to think about it. All that mattered was that I had done it—I had a job. I was a delivery boy.

MARTIN WAS RIGHT where I'd left him in front of the shop. As soon as he saw me, he let out an exasperated sigh, as though he'd been holding his breath the entire time I'd been gone.

"Thank goodness," he said. "I thought the butcher had cut you up into pieces and was going to sell you for stew."

"Martin!" I was half-scolding him and half-laughing. He was pleased he'd gotten a smile out of me. "Let's go," I told him. "We're late as it is." I took my brother's hand and began leading him home.

"So what did you do?" he asked.

"Nothing."

"I waited outside for nothing?"

"No, not nothing. Something. But it's a secret, so you can't tell anyone."

"Not even . . . ?"

"No," I replied, knowing he meant our parents. "Not even them."

"What kind of secret is it?"

"A *secret* secret. If I tell you, will you promise not to tell?"

"I guess."

"No, not 'I guess.' You have to be sure, Martin. Absolutely sure."

"I can be absolutely sure. I promise. I won't tell."

"I'm going to make deliveries for the butcher. So I can make money."

"What do you need money for?"

"Everybody needs money, Marty."

"That's not the question I asked. I asked what you needed it for."

"Nothing. I just do."

"Then why can't you collect glass?"

Once a month, a truck from Harrisburg would come to town to collect broken glass to melt down and make new. They'd pay a penny per pound, so my father would send Martin and me out with a bucket and a hammer. We would collect bottles and smash them in the bucket, then turn them in for change.

"I can't collect bottles. It wouldn't be enough."

The pitch of my voice made Martin suspicious. "You're not telling me something," he groaned. "I can tell you're not telling me something."

Thankfully, as we neared Third, I was given a reprieve in the form of a distraction, one which Martin quickly spotted. "Look," he said, pointing happily. "It's Ragsoline."

Coming up the road was an old black man in denim overalls and a floppy hat, the man we knew only as Ragsoline. He was leading a tawny, swaybacked mare pulling a wooden cart. The cart was filled to the brim and teetering with a tall load of rags. We called him Ragsoline because that was the phrase he'd yell out as he traipsed from one end of Hyde Bend to the other asking for people's used rags, which he collected to sell to the paper factory a few towns over. No one knew where Ragsoline lived—it could have been miles away—all we knew was that he was the only black man we'd ever seen. He had come to town once a week for as long as anybody could remember, and over the years he'd picked up a few Polish phrases that he would say to the people who donated their rags to him.

"*Dobre jen, Pani,*" he would say to greet the women. Or he would say, "*Dejkuya, Pani,*" bidding them farewell with a tip of his hat.

"Let's talk to him," Martin insisted.

"No. We don't have any rags to give him."

"So? Maybe he just wants to talk for a change instead of always asking for rags."

Martin ardently tugged me down the street, waving and calling out, "Ragsoline! Hey, Ragsoline!"

Ragsoline slowed his cart. "*Dobre jen Pan i Pani,*" he said with a smile.

"We speak English," Martin said proudly. "You can speak English with us."

"Then good afternoon, sir and madame," Ragsoline intoned. "What can I do for you today?"

"We don't have any rags to give you, but if we did, we would," Martin said.

"Well, that's very kind, young sir. Very kind."

Next came a long silence during which Martin realized that he didn't actually have anything to say to Ragsoline.

"We're sorry to bother you. My brother only wanted to say hello."

"Perfectly fine. Perfectly fine," Ragsoline replied. "You can pet the horse if you like."

"Can I really?" Martin was asking permission from me as much as Ragsoline.

"Of course," Ragsoline said, then I nodded my approval to Martin, which Ragsoline noted.

Martin approached the horse cautiously. "How do I do it?"

"You just pat her. She's old and she won't mind it a bit. Like this," Ragsoline instructed, demonstrating for Martin. Ragsoline stroked the horse's shoulder and Martin mimicked him, rubbing the mare's side, which was as high as he could reach.

"We could use another hand here," Ragsoline told me with a wink.

The horse was standing perfectly still, her head slightly bowed. I stepped up to her and gently placed my hand on her neck. The short, coarse hide was smooth to the touch, the flesh warm. I ran my hand over her mane, letting my fingers slide through the thick hair like a comb. That was the first time I had touched any animal besides the stray cats that roamed the alleys, and it was like nothing I'd ever felt before.

"See, she likes it," Ragsoline said, though it was unclear if he meant me or the mare.

"Well, we should get going," I said.

Martin was disappointed but acquiesced after a final pat on the horse's hip. "Can we visit you and your horse the next time you come to town, Ragsoline?"

"Of course. We'd like that."

"Us too," Martin said, taking my hand, the one I'd been petting the horse with.

"Good day then, sir and madame," Ragsoline said with a tap to the brim of his hat, then he took up the horse's lead and headed on down the street calling out "Ragsoline" as he went, his voice echoing off the cobblestones.

"See," Martin said once Ragsoline was out of earshot.

"See what?"

"That wasn't bad."

"No, Marty," I said, letting him win. "That wasn't bad at all."

THAT AFTERNOON when Martin and I arrived home, we shucked off our muddy boots and left them next to the door the way my mother always insisted we do. My father, on the other hand, kept his boots on all the time, muddy or not.

The faucet was running in the washroom. My father was shaving.

"He's home!" Martin shouted, unable to contain his excitement. "I'm going to tell him about the horse."

He went to the door of the washroom but knew better than to open it. "Guess what?" he called, putting his mouth to the jamb and talking into it. "Today we touched a horse. We asked Ragsoline and he let us pet his horse."

"Don't talk to that nigger," my father ordered, his voice booming from behind the door. "And don't touch his damn horse neither."

The door to the washroom flew open, sending Martin jumping back so he wouldn't get hit.

"You understand?" my father demanded, wiping shaving cream from his neck with a towel.

"Yes, sir."

"And don't you let him go near that nigger either," my father said, eyeing me.

"Yes, sir," I said, echoing Martin.

My father went to the icebox and pulled out a bottle of milk. He poured himself a large glass, nearly emptying the container, then sat down, leaving the bottle on the table, unconcerned that it would soon get warm.

"Tomorrow one of Stash Nowczyk's boys is going to bring us over a catfish," my father told us between gulps. "Been catching them in the river by the bucketful and they've got more than they need. But we've got to keep it in the bathtub for a few days and feed it cornmeal to clean out its gut before your mother can cook it."

"Why?" Martin asked. His questions were not as welcome with my father as they were with me, something Martin was well aware of, though he simply couldn't help himself.

"Because," my father snapped. "Catfish are bottom feeders. They eat all the garbage from the bottom of the river. Do you want to eat that too?"

"No," Martin said sheepishly.

"When the boy comes by, you take the fish and put it in the tub with fresh water. You got it?" he said to me.

"Yes, sir."

He checked his watch, then swallowed what was left of his milk and put on his coat.

"Where are you going?" Martin asked.

"Work. Where'd you think I'm going?"

"But—" Martin began, then I shot him a cautionary glance. It was long before my father needed to be at the mill, but my mother would soon be home. He was trying to leave before she got back. From my look, Martin figured that out as well. His expression faltered yet he remained silent.

"Put that milk away," my father said, then he left.

AT SUPPER my mother was especially quiet. She prayed over her food, as did we, but hers was a fervent whisper. Afterward, she poked at her food and finally pushed it away half eaten. Martin and I kept eating and pretended not to notice. He was reading his book with the lamb on the cover, something my mother normally wouldn't have allowed at the table. That night she didn't seem to mind. Her silence was palpable and I scoured my mind for something to say, something that would draw her back to us.

"Tomorrow we're supposed to get a catfish," I announced. "One of the Nowczyks is bringing it."

My mother stared off as if she were processing the statement, letting it sink in. "I'll buy some cornmeal then," she said after a long pause.

Those were the only words she spoke for the rest of the evening. She took our plates and her own and left them in the sink, then retired to the other room without saying good night. Martin glanced up from his book to watch her go, then turned to me, his small face peeking over the top of his book. Before he could ask any questions, I took the book from his hands.

"Why don't you read to me, Marty." I pulled my chair close to his, put my arm over his shoulder, and held the book out in front of us so he could read in the shelter of my arms.

To keep his mind off what had happened, I made my brother read the tale of God's lamb until he was falling asleep at the table. Martin was already in his nightclothes, so when he could no longer keep his eyes open, I led him to the cot, laid him down, and watched him drift right to sleep, then went into the washroom to change into my nightclothes. I had a cotton nightdress, but because it was so cold in the apartment, even with the coal stove burning, I usually wore the sweater from my school uniform over it.

Once I'd pulled the sweater over my head, I inadvertently found myself staring eye to eye with my own reflection in the mirror above the washbasin. My hair crackled with static and a few strands stood out, floating buoyantly in the dry air. I surveyed my face as if it were a map. The curves of my cheeks and the sloping bridge of my nose seemed unfamiliar to me, my own features foreign. I was a stranger to myself. I didn't look like my mother, that had always been obvious, but I bore little resemblance to my father either. His forehead was wide and high and constantly furrowed while mine was short and narrow and split by a widow's peak. His eyes were big and persistent, as though nothing could escape even his view. My eyes were deep set, the lashes dark. Meeting my own image in the mirror was like catching someone staring at me in the street. Before long, I felt compelled to turn away.

After I brushed my teeth, I realized I had to go to the bathroom. The sensation sent a surge of panic through me for a single, piercing reason—it meant I would have to go to the outhouse. Nightfall brought the rats up from the river where they lived in the pipes that drained waste from the steel mill, the salt plant, and the town's sew-ers directly into the Allegheny. Under the cover of darkness, the rats came out to scrounge for food, and each night they would invade the outhouses on Third, tunneling in under the floorboards in search of any morsel or scrap. I made it a practice not to drink anything with dinner so I wouldn't have to enter the outhouse after nightfall, but the pressure below my belly left me no choice.

I slid on my coat and boots and peeked out the front door. Though people were often seen going to the outhouses in their pajamas, I was shy. The thought of someone seeing me in anything other than my regular clothes was nearly as frightening as the rats.

It was cloudy, yet the moon was bright enough to see by. The wind had died down but the cold night air was severe enough to prickle my skin within seconds. To reach the outhouse, we had to cut between the apartments, along a narrow path that led to an even tinier alley where the outhouses were lined up at the rear of the apartments, each flanked by rows of laundry lines. All the sheets and clothes and towels that were hanging out to dry on the lines hung still, iridescent in the moonlight.

I gently kicked the door to the outhouse and shook the handle. That was supposed to scare the rats away. I pounded on the door once again for good measure.

"Okay, if you're in there, please leave," I whispered, hoping that if the rattling wood wasn't enough to scare them off, maybe a human voice would.

The interior of the outhouse was pitch dark. There was no light, no window, only a ledge for a candle, which I didn't have. The stone slab that served as a floor was slick with mud. A wooden seat with a hole cut in the center served as the toilet, but the wood was often wet, so I never sat down. As I hiked up my nightdress and prepared to squat over the hole, a pale gray rat scurried across the floor, unintimidated by my presence.

A shriek caught in my throat. My brain seized the noise before it could escape. If I screamed, the sound would wake everybody on the alley and I would never hear the end of it from my mother or, for that matter, from anyone else. Fear kept my feet glued to the floor even as the rat edged closer to sniff at my boot. It sat up on its hind legs, drawing in a scent, then on reflex I punted it aside and threw open the outhouse door. I barreled down the pathway and whipped around the corner and into our apartment.

I hurled my boots from my feet and was about to climb back into bed when my bladder reminded me of why I'd gone outside in the first place. There was no way I was going back to the outhouse, but my stomach had begun to ache. I was trembling from the fright and the cold, which made the need to urinate even more urgent. I scanned the room, searching for some sort of inspiration, and my eyes caught on the kitchen sink. Martin was asleep just feet away, so I opted to go into the washroom instead.

A single bulb was the only illumination in the washroom and it was controlled by a pull chain that was long gone and had been replaced by a length of twine. I stood on tiptoe to tug on the light, then quietly closed the door behind me and studied the basin, unsure of exactly what to do. The white porcelain stood out against the sink's rusting underbelly. The tiny teacup of a basin was hardly built to accommodate an adult pair of hands let alone someone sitting on it.

I hoisted up my nightdress and pushed myself up onto the sink's edge. The porcelain was like ice on my skin, but that made it easier to go. Relief swept over me. My heartbeat slowed and my muscles began to relax. Then, without warning, the door to the washroom opened. It was my mother. She was in her nightclothes and robe, long strands of hair framing her face. Her expression upon seeing me was pure shock.

"What are you doing?" she demanded as I clambered off the sink, desperately yanking down my nightdress.

I couldn't explain myself. My cheeks burned with embarrassment. She looked beyond me and into the sink.

"I had to. I couldn't go outside. There was a rat. I'm sorry. I couldn't . . ." I was stammering, near tears, and a drop of urine was slowly running down my leg.

My mother was staring at me as if she had never seen me before, as if I were an uninvited guest who had barged in on her. She snatched a rag from behind the tub's faucet and hurled it at me. "Clean yourself up."

"I'm sorry," I said. "I—"

"Don't you ever do that again. Ever. And clean up the mess you made."

She left, shutting the door behind her resolutely. Then the tears came and wouldn't stop. I ran the water to wash away any trace of urine from the sink and scrubbed the basin with soap and the rag she had thrown at me. I scoured the sink for what seemed like hours, rinsing it again and again until my hands throbbed from gripping the rag. When I allowed myself to be finished, I looked up and found my reflection in the mirror again. My eyes were red from crying and my face was flushed with the heat of my mortification. Not only did I fail to resemble my family, I now failed to resemble even myself.

THE FOLLOWING MORNING, both my mother and I tried to act as if nothing had happened, but I still couldn't bring myself to look at her directly. To make matters worse, my father hadn't come home again. Martin kept a constant vigil at the window waiting for any sign of him. Even when my mother ordered him to the table to eat his breakfast, Martin positioned his chair to face the door and could hardly concentrate on his food. My father never arrived. We got ready for school and my mother prepared to go to work as usual. She tied on her apron, a plain linen one that Father Svitek had purchased for her, then wrapped her hair up in a thin, flowered kerchief.

"You're going to get him, right?" Martin asked.

My mother took her time to respond. "No," she said. Her voice was bitter, but her expression wavered. I couldn't tell if it was from disappointment or resignation.

"But—" Martin began.

"Get your things," my mother ordered, cutting him off. "I have to be at the church early today."

Martin waited for me to back him up, but I dodged his glance and busied myself making our bed. He accepted that his argument was a lost cause and did as he was told. After I'd finished making the bed, I noticed my mother gazing at the spot where the Black Madonna had hung. Her lips were moving in silent prayer and she was blinking hard to keep from crying. It was the one time I'd ever seen my mother close to tears, and it would turn out to be the first of only two occasions in my entire life that I would ever witness such an occurrence.

My mother walked us to school at a brisk clip and left us on the steps of the schoolhouse without a word.

"I think she's lying," Martin declared.

"Lying about what?"

"I think she is going to the Silver Slipper. She just doesn't want us to know."

"Why would you say that?"

"Because. She's like that."

Part of me wanted to believe that my brother, in his seven-year-old wisdom, was actually right, that somehow, because of his age and innocence, he had the ability to sense whatever truth my mother was attempting to conceal. Perhaps my mother was on her way to the Silver Slipper as we spoke. Perhaps she would march into the tavern and drag my father out of the bar or make a scene until he was too embarrassed to stay. We would never know. Maybe it was better that way.

I considered telling Martin what had happened the night before in the washroom so he'd understand why I hadn't taken his side that morning, but I was too ashamed to do so. That shame had lodged itself in my stomach and lay there like a brick. In the aftermath of my disgrace, I had forgotten what awaited me that afternoon. It was my first day as Mr. Goceljak's delivery boy. That sudden realization cleared the shame from my mind and made way for a pang of dread that was as potent as pain.

"What's wrong?" Martin asked. "You look like you forgot something."

"I did."

WHEN THE SCHOOL DAY was done, I hurried to Martin's classroom and waited outside for him. The instant he came out, I grabbed his hand and began hauling him down the corridor.

"Where are we going *now*?" he asked. "Back to the butcher's shop?"

I hushed him, glancing around to see if anyone had heard. "I told you that's supposed to be a secret. And no, you're not coming today."

"Then where am I supposed to go? Home? I'm too little to be left alone on my own."

"That's why you're not going home."

I led Martin to the school's library, and once he realized

where I was taking him, he ceased complaining. The library remained open for an hour and a half after school, but it was uncommon for children to go there. Most went home or out to play. Given the opportunity, Martin would have stayed there all night if he could have.

"Wait a minute," he said. "Sister Teresa isn't going to let me stay here without you around."

"She will if I say Mama asked me to ask her."

"But she didn't ask you to ask her."

"But Sister Teresa doesn't know that. And you're not going to tell her. Right?"

Martin hemmed his lips, uncomfortable.

"Just look at all of those books, Marty. Hundreds of them. Just waiting to be read."

The school's library was a narrow room with two study tables in the center, and it was lined from floor to ceiling with books, some teetering from the tops of shelves. For Martin, it was a paradise.

The library door was open and he leaned in, tempted. "All right. But I don't want to get in trouble."

"You won't. Not if you don't say anything."

Sister Teresa was the oldest of the nuns still working at the school. Due to a bad hip and her ever-worsening senility, Sister Teresa was relegated to the library, where her main job was to check out books, a task that only involved pressing a rubber stamp to the back page of each selection. The real labor of retrieving and reshelving the books was left to the other nuns who came in early in the morning and straightened up. As I entered the library, I prepared myself for what I was about to do—I was going to lie again. Given that I'd already lied to Mr. Goceljak about being able to ride the bicycle, it consoled me to think that this lie was necessary, but only slightly.

Sister Teresa's eyes were closed. She was napping. "Sister Teresa," I said. She gave no response. "Sister Teresa," I tried again. She stirred.

"Oh, good afternoon," she said in Polish rather than English. "I must have nodded off."

"That's all right, Sister. I've brought my brother in. My mother was wondering if it would be okay if he stayed here until the library closes. I've got to help her at the rectory and there's no one else who can watch him."

Sister Teresa and all of the other nuns knew who Martin and I were because they knew what my mother did. Anyone who did anything for Father Svitek was beyond reproach in their minds, so I had little doubt that Sister Teresa would not deny me this favor, especially since I said I was going to be helping Father Svitek as well.

"Of course, child. The boy will be fine here with me. But he's not loud or a troublemaker, is he? I can't have any troublemakers in here."

"No, Sister. He won't make a sound." Martin was watching me from the door. He'd heard my lie and put on a perturbed scowl. "Isn't that right, Martin?"

"Yes, Sister," he replied grudgingly.

"What did he say?" Sister Teresa asked, clearly deaf.

"Yes, Sister," Martin shouted.

"Okay," Sister Teresa said with a smile.

I guided Martin to a study table and waited as he got settled. "I'll be back before the library closes."

"You'd better be."

I checked the clock on the wall. It was nearly three-fifteen. I left my books with him and dashed out the door. I ran all the way from Saint Ladislaus to Field Street in what felt like a minute flat. I charged in the front door to the butcher's shop still panting as the bell sounded my arrival. Mr. Goceljak was waiting for me. He noted the time on his watch.

"Am I late? I'm sorry. You didn't say—"

"No, you're not late. You're here earlier than Donny was at least. That's a good thing."

Mr. Goceljak's sentiment made me breathe a little easier.

"Hope you came ready to work. I've got a lot of deliveries to go out today."

"Yes, sir," I answered, feigning full confidence in myself. Not only did I have to learn how to ride a bicycle in an hour and a half, I also had to make deliveries. The full force of that fact had yet to settle in my mind, and that was probably another *good thing*. If I'd really given it any thought, I might have fainted there on the spot.

"Come on then, I'll get you the packages and load up the bicycle for you."

I followed Mr. Goceljak into the back room where a stack of parcels wrapped in butcher paper waited on the wooden block.

"I put all of the names on them so you'll know who gets what. Go to Mrs. Zahorchak's house first. She can get nasty if she doesn't get her sausages on time. You can leave Mr. Beresik for last. He doesn't care when he gets his delivery, as long as he gets it. Got it?"

"Yes," I said. "I mean, yes, sir."

"I like that. 'Yes, sir,'" Mr. Goceljak said, repeating me. "Donny never called me 'sir.' Sounds . . . dignified."

"Okay, sir," I said. I was glad I had pleased him. Nothing I ever did or said at home seemed to please either my mother or my father. It was heartening to learn that it was actually possible.

"I'll help you with these." Mr. Goceljak took the packages in his arms and headed out the back door. He gingerly placed each parcel in the bicycle's basket, then twirled the dial on the lock.

"I don't give out the combination. At least I didn't give it to Donny. Afraid he'd steal the thing. But if this works out, maybe I'll give it to you."

I was taken aback by Mr. Goceljak's offer. He must have stunned himself as well because he grew bashful in the silence that followed.

"All right, then. Better be on your way." He removed the lock and freed the chain from the spokes of the bicycle's front wheel.

"Excuse me, sir. Could I ask you something?"

"Sure."

"Would it be all right if you didn't tell anyone I was doing this? You know, working for you."

Mr. Goceljak registered my request as an insult.

"I'm trying to save up money, but it's a surprise. For a present, sort of," I explained. "I don't want anyone to know what I'm doing."

Mr. Goceljak understood. "I won't tell anybody. But what if the people you're making deliveries to know you?"

Anyone who was well-off enough to receive deliveries at home probably wouldn't recognize me. However, Hyde Bend was relatively small, so there was a chance, albeit slight. "I didn't think of that," I admitted.

"I've got an idea," Mr. Goceljak said, then he disappeared into the store. He returned with a slouchy canvas cap in his hand and a pair of men's trousers draped over his arm.

"Donny left the hat here and the trousers used to be mine. I was going to cut them up for rags. You put these on and hide your hair up in the hat, then nobody'll recognize you, I bet."

I took the pants from Mr. Goceljak reluctantly. I was still wearing my school uniform, the sweater and pleated skirt, and couldn't imagine how this was going to work.

"You can pull the pants on over that school getup of yours and I'll get a rope to make a belt." My face betrayed my doubt as well as my discomfort. "Don't worry," Mr. Goceljak assured me. "Nobody can see back here, and I won't come out until you say it's all right. Okay?"

"Okay," I said, still reticent. Once Mr. Goceljak had gone inside, I opened the pants. They were far too long and the waistband was more than double my size. I put them on over my skirt, which took up a little of the extra room, but not much.

"You decent?" Mr. Goceljak called.

"Yes, sir."

When he popped his head out the back door and saw me in the trousers, he couldn't help but chuckle. "A little big, eh? This'll fix you up." He produced a long piece of twine. "You put this through the loops and it'll be like a belt. I had to do it like that when I was a kid too."

"But you weren't wearing a skirt under your pants."

"True."

I fed the twine through the belt loops, then pulled it tight and tied it into a knot. "What about the legs?" I asked. My feet had completely disappeared beneath the fabric.

"You got to roll 'em up. I had to do that too. Always had my brother's hand-me-downs, so nothing ever fit quite right."

I turned up the pant legs until I could see my shoes. "I don't think they're going to stay like this."

"I've got just the thing for that." Mr. Goceljak went inside, then came out again, this time with a roll of butcher's tape, then he got down on one knee and began to tape up the pant legs. "Now all you need is the hat," he said, holding it out to me.

I pulled the hat down to my ears and tucked my hair up under it. Mr. Goceljak studied my face, tugged the brim down farther, and pushed a few stray hairs beneath the brim.

"There," he said, satisfied. "I'd barely recognize you myself."

The twine was synched so tightly around my waist that it made the pants look enormous and the white butcher's tape stood out starkly against the dark trousers. Thankfully, the hat hid most of my face.

"Don't I look a little strange?"

"Hell yes, you look strange. Strangest-looking thing I've ever seen. But you said you didn't want anybody to recognize you. Now nobody will. They'll think you're, well, a boy."

"I don't know any boys who look like this."

"Neither do I, but I certainly don't know any *girls* who look like this neither."

"Won't people look at me funny?"

"I guess. But they'll just think you're poor."

"I am poor."

"Then you should be used to it."

From inside came the sound of the shop's doorbell ringing. "See you when you get back," Mr. Goceljak said, then he headed inside.

I was finally alone with the bicycle but baffled about what to do with it. First, I attempted to hoist my leg over the crossbar while steadying myself against the pipe railing. Before I could get my balance, the bicycle began listing from the weight of the packages in the basket. Next, I tried leaning the bicycle against the railing and scooting onto the seat from behind. However, the sagging crotch of my newly fashioned trousers got caught and I spent the following minute untangling myself. Already frustrated, I made one last-ditch effort to mount the bicycle by taking a running leap at the seat and swinging my leg over the top of it. I immediately slid off, nearly coming down hard on the crossbar, but managed to land on my tiptoes and steady the bicycle only to have the front wheel turn, causing the bicycle to take a nosedive. Fortunately, I caught the handlebars before the contents of the basket could go clattering to the ground. It was a losing battle and, I decided, another fitting punishment for lying about being able to ride a bicycle in the first place. The meat couldn't stay outside for long, but there was no way I could use the bicycle to make the deliveries, at least not yet.

Mr. Goceljak had a small curing shed a few yards behind his shop, and beyond that lay the empty field. Tall weeds and briar bushes that had grown unchecked for years had overtaken the land. The tops of the bushes were higher than my shoulders. No one, not even the most adventurous of children in town, would attempt to enter the field for fear of the prickling bushes and sharp weed stalks. If I could hide the bicycle in the field, there was no way it would be found.

I quickly packed the parcels of meat into the waistband of my makeshift trousers, tucking them securely between my skirt and the twine belt Mr. Goceljak had made for me. With the thick packets of meat around my waist, my body must have appeared to have doubled in size, adding to my disguise. All the better, I thought as I hitched up the pants and prepared to move the bicycle into the field.

No longer weighed down with the meat, the bicycle was much easier to maneuver. Getting it into the field would be the hard part. I pulled the sleeves of my sweater out from under my coat to cover the tops of my hands and hunched my shoulders to protect my neck, then forged through the threshold of briars and weeds. Thorns bit into my fingers and scratched at my face. The underbrush was as thick as mud, making it difficult to plod even a few feet into the field, but a few feet was enough. I stomped down the brush to clear a place for the bicycle and laid it on the ground as gently as I could. Even though it was stubborn, rusted, unconquerable, and ugly, I liked the bicycle. I wanted it to be safe.

Once the bicycle was hidden, I bounded out of the field as fast as I could, brambles snagging my clothes as I went. When I emerged, my coat was covered in nettles. I could feel them through the trousers, but I had little chance to care. There were eleven deliveries to be made, each at various ends of town, and since I had to make the journey on foot, there was no time to waste.

I couldn't run on Field Street without drawing attention, so I stuck to the alleyway along the field. I was moving my legs as fast as they would go, but the parcels of meat strapped to my sides started to slip and I was forced to clutch my hips as I ran. The regular percussion of my heart was replaced by a relentless pounding. My blood was drumming through my body and air was churning in and out of my lungs. At first, the sensation scared me. I'd run before, run until I was out of breath, but never like this. For a second, the feeling was akin to fear, a condition I was more than familiar with. Fear could creep along over your skin, climb its way up your ribs, or leap onto your shoulders without warning, I'd learned that much. I couldn't remember a time when my father didn't drink or a time when I wasn't afraid of what he could or would do. He might erupt in rage or laughter, angry about some unimportant incident or amused by some imaginary joke. Both were equally frightening, and the waiting, that constant waiting, was worse than any beating I could endure. The feeling that overtook me that day as I ran with all my might down the alleyway, the weeds quivering in my wake, was like nothing I'd ever known. My fear had turned inside out. It wasn't gone, but I almost didn't recognize it.

THE ALLEYWAY ENDED NEAR THE STEEL MILL, and my first stop, Mrs. Zahorchak's house, was only a half block over on Oak Lane. The homes there were sizable, but Oak Lane didn't carry quite the prestige of River Road because the houses faced the mill, which was hardly picturesque, and after each shift change, the road was flooded with a mass of men marching back to their homes in sooty coveralls. The street had once been lined with tall rows of oaks on either side of the block, hence its name, but once the mill went up, all of the trees were felled to widen the street. Each oak was lopped off at the trunk and leveled rather than dug up. The thick stumps were left in the ground like tombstones.

I tried to pick the nettles from my coat before I reached Mrs. Zahorchak's house. There were so many of them that I finally gave up. I doubted the nettles would make much of a difference given my already curious appearance. I was about to knock on Mrs. Zahorchak's door when I realized there was a doorbell. I knew what doorbells were and had seen them on other houses, but we certainly didn't have one and I'd never rung one before. The prospect of doing so was strangely exciting. I lightly laid my finger on the button, testing its feel, the smoothness and size, then pushed it and quickly withdrew. The high, clear chime of the bell floated through the door.

Footsteps resounded from inside the house and I pulled the parcel marked with Mrs. Zahorchak's name from the back of my waistband. Just as I had arranged my sweater to cover the rest of the packets, the front door swung open. Mrs. Zahorchak looked down at me with an imperious glare.

"You're late," she said, her English clipped by her accent.

She stood rigidly in the doorway. She was wearing a pale green cotton dress that seemed to have too much starch in it. It hung stiffly off her body and the collar pointed out at a harsh angle. The dress looked like it would hurt to wear it.

"You're not the regular boy," Mrs. Zahorchak proclaimed. "Where's the regular boy?"

"He broke his arm." As I spoke, I realized my voice sounded nothing like a boy's, but it was too late. Mrs. Zahorchak squinted at me, examining my face and clothes.

"What's your name?" she asked, her tone distrustful.

It was a question I wasn't prepared for. I scrambled to come up with an answer. I flicked back through my memory and plucked out the first name that came to mind.

"Nowczyk," I said. "I'm one of Stash Nowczyk's boys."

It was another lie, an echo of what my father had told Martin and me about the catfish, and it rolled off my tongue with credible ease. Mrs. Zahorchak appeared to be turning the name over in her head, then she promptly dismissed it as one that had no importance or bearing. She took her package of sausages and kielbasa from me with a quick jerk and said, "Since you're new, I'll make an exception about you being late. But I'm a very important customer. I expect to get what I pay for on time. So don't be late again."

"Yes, ma'am."

Mrs. Zahorchak shut the door on me, nearly clipping my toes. I stood on her porch for a minute collecting myself, but when I saw her peering at me through the curtains, I hurried off.

The next few deliveries were nearby, however after the scolding I'd taken from Mrs. Zahorchak, I ran all the way to each of the stops. When I knocked on the door at the following house, I was greeted by a teenage girl wearing wire-rimmed glasses and an irritated scowl. Inside, a baby was crying. As the baby began to wail even harder, the girl snatched the parcel of meat from my hands with a huff, then closed the door on me.

The woman who answered at my next stop was holding a toddler on her hip and smoking a cigarette.

"Delivery from the butcher," I said in as low a voice as I could muster.

"Thanks," she answered blandly, then she disappeared back into the house as the door lazily swung shut behind her.

It didn't cross my mind that these women were cold or unfriendly. That was what I was accustomed to. The fact that one had actually thanked me was more than I had counted on.

The next delivery was labeled with an address on River Road, but no name. When I got to the house, I recognized it instantly. Unlike all of the other well-tended homes along the river, this one had fallen into disrepair. The tall brick home rose three floors high and loomed over the street like a crumbling monument. Years of neglect had transformed the house into an ominous, hulking wreck.

The bricks had cracked as the house settled and the posts on the sprawling front porch had begun to bow. Too many harsh winters had forced loose most of the shutters. The roof sagged, as if the sky itself was pressing on it, making the house look as if it might topple with the slightest breeze.

The front steps felt spongy underfoot, liable to give way at any moment. There was no doorbell here, only a massive knocker that hung in the center of the door. It was nearly too high for me to reach. When I finally managed to get hold of the heavy, brass ring and knock it against the door, the sound reverberated in a low bellow. I waited for a few minutes with no response and was about to knock again when the lock turned. The door crept open to reveal an old woman, her thick, white hair disheveled, her eyes nervous.

The air that drifted out from inside the house was stale. The lights were off and all of the window shades were drawn. The rooms were brimming with clutter that overflowed into the hallway, where uneven piles of books and newspapers rose as high as the woman's hips.

"Delivery," I said hesitantly, more a question than a statement. "From the butcher's shop," I added, but the woman wouldn't respond.

She had two sweaters layered over a housedress, as if she were armored for a blizzard, yet the weather was mild that day. The woman didn't look up or make eye contact with me, but I could see her blinking rapidly, as if she were working up the courage for something. Then she held out her hand for me to give her the package. Her fingers did not extend beyond the door frame, not even the very tips of her nails, which forced me to reach in to her. Just as I laid the parcel in her palm, the woman jerked her hand back into the house. It was a sudden movement, a motion she hadn't appeared capable of.

The woman stood in the doorway for an instant longer and gave a single, short nod in thanks. It was as though she couldn't thank me out loud, that those words, any words, were petrifying to utter. She shut the door and rebolted the lock, as though she was trying to keep any more of the outside world from seeping in. I lingered there on her porch for a minute trying to place her. I scrolled back through my memory of faces that I'd seen in town or at church, but I was convinced that I had never seen this woman, not ever.

THE SUN WAS BEGINNING TO FALL and the breeze coming off the river was laced with a wet chill. It would be dark in an hour, if not less, and still I had one delivery left to make—Mr. Beresik. Him I knew, but only by name. He lived on the opposite end of Hyde Bend, beyond the salt plant on a lonely dirt road that didn't have a name. For years, he had made a living fixing people's farm equipment. However, when the steel mill and the salt plant went up, people stopped farming the nearby fields and Mr. Beresik was put out of his job. Few people in Hyde Bend had cars. There was almost no purpose for them. Most men worked only blocks from their homes. So in Hyde Bend, owning a car was considered an extravagant luxury, and having a new car was the ultimate in status symbols. A new car attracted as much attention as a parade. Children and adults alike would stop and stare whenever one of the brand-new Buicks or Fords rolled by with their burly frames, pearly paint colors, rounded features, and chrome trimmings. Those were the exceptions. Most of the cars in Hyde Bend were used and looked old beyond their years. They ran slow and loud. There were a handful of rusted mammoth sedans and the occasional two-door coupe, yet all showed the scars of age. Crumpled fenders, dented hoods, and missing hubcaps were common casualties. Even those metal bodies weren't immune to the ravages of the winters in Hyde Bend. Even they weren't safe.

I'd never ridden in a car and didn't think I ever would. Each time I saw a car bumping down the road I wondered what it would be like to sit inside, to feel the ground moving beneath me. However, I'd never considered what made a car run. I knew that automobiles had engines, a hidden heart that made them move, though I couldn't conceive of what else it would take to bring a car to life. That was until I strode up the road to Mr. Beresik's house. The scattered parts of disemboweled cars and tractors were heaped in the grass and burrowed in the dirt. The cast-off parts were strewn everywhere, most half buried, giving the place the feel of a ransacked cemetery where the earth has been upturned and scavenged. But it was the other way around.

Mr. Beresik's house sat on a flat plateau of land on top of a steep incline overlooking the nameless road that connected it to the only civilization for miles. It was a low-slung, rambling building made up of various lean-to-like additions, and it squatted along the hill's summit like a ramshackle castle. Behind it was a jagged wall of pines. These were the closest trees to town and they stood like a marker between our world and whatever lay beyond.

Once I crested the hilltop, I heard something that made my heart halt. It was the sound of barking, loud, fierce, unbridled barking. I froze and watched as more than two dozen dogs poured out of the listing barn behind the house. They charged over the grassy ridge in one clamoring wave, then hurled themselves at the high, chain-link fence that ran along the property, creating a sprawling pen. The dogs clawed the metal and stood up on their hind legs as if to scale the fence. I had never seen animals like these. They looked more like gargoyles than dogs, thickly muscled with skulls far larger than mine. As each savage bark erupted from their jaws, a cage of teeth would flash. I couldn't move. I could barely blink. Then the front door to Mr. Beresik's house opened. The shadowed figure of a man stepped out onto the porch. His very presence silenced the dogs instantly. Some trotted toward him while others stood guard, watching me.

"Quiet," the man commanded in Polish. The dogs didn't make another sound.

The figure took another step forward into the light. It was Mr. Beresik, a stiff cap pulled low on his head, a hunting jacket hanging loosely from his shoulders. His physical build was hardly imposing, but the sheer control carried in his voice gave him the supreme air of a king.

"Don't mind 'em," Mr. Beresik said, waving me toward the house.

I took a few tentative steps and the dogs retrained their eyes on me, following my every move, though they remained as still as statues. As I neared the house, they began to move too, to trail me. I could hear them sniffing the air, hard. They must have smelled the meat, but they knew better than to bark.

"You must be Goceljak's new boy."

I mounted the steps with the package of meat outstretched in my shaking hand. It was the largest one of the day, and because it was the last, the blood from the meat had seeped through the paper wrapping.

"They could smell you coming," Mr. Beresik declared, nodding to the pen. "You've got their supper."

The dogs were lined up along the fence, their clipped tails pulsing in anticipation. A few whimpered softly. Now they seemed almost docile.

"They're nothing to be afraid of," he said, taking the package from me. "As long as you're on this side of the fence, that is."

The fact that Mr. Beresik would pay for this much meat just to feed it to a dog was beyond my comprehension, and despite the weight of the parcel, it certainly wouldn't feed them all.

"I don't know if there's enough," I said hesitantly.

"Oh, it's not for all of 'em," Mr. Beresik replied. "Only for the good ones."

"How do you know which ones are the good ones?"

"Won't know till tonight."

"Tonight?"

These were bold questions for me. I was accustomed to listening and being talked to or talked at rather than speaking. My disguise had brought on a bout of courage.

"At the match," Mr. Beresik said. "A good pit bull wins. They get fed. A bad one doesn't."

I still didn't understand. "Why not?"

"A dead dog don't need to eat."

This time when I looked back at the pen, I noticed the scars on the dogs' bodies. Every one of them had deep gashes in their coats and scratches where the fur hadn't healed over. All of them also had thick, studded collars around their necks, which I hadn't noticed before.

"Why do they call them pit bulls?"

Mr. Beresik drank in the question. "You ever heard of a bull fight?"

"I saw a picture once. A man was waving a red cape at a bull with big horns."

"That's right. That man is called a matador and his job is to try to make the bull mad and make the bull charge him. See, bulls are attracted to the color red, makes them want to attack. So the matador, he teases the bull with the red cape, drawing him in closer and closer. Then the matador stabs the bull with a sword."

"The matador wants to kill the bull?"

"That's how he shows his honor and his skill."

"Is that what you do to the dogs?"

"No, not me," he said, as though I'd given him a compliment. "The dogs, they're meant to fight each other. But when they fight, they charge like bulls. 'At's how they got their name. That and because of the way they're built, big and strong. See 'em jaws? They can crush bone easy. And those teeth. Sharp as doctors' knives. Make short work a you or any man, that's for sure."

"Oh," I said, for lack of a better response. "Then what do you do?"

"Me?" Mr. Beresik asked, flattered by my interest. "I breed 'em. Find the best fighters and mate 'em so the pups'll fight even better and stronger than their folks. Like 'at one there." He pointed to the dog at the front of the pack. Its thick, black coat gleamed except on its front haunches, where long scratches and bite marks had yet to heal. "'At's Sally. She's the toughest bitch I ever seen. Nobody can beat her."

The name *Sally*, so gentle and familiar, seemed wrong at first, but the longer I looked at the dog the more it suited her. She had alert, knowing eyes, and in spite of the scars that crisscrossed her coat, she appeared sturdy, reliable.

"Sally's the best I've got," Mr. Beresik affirmed with fatherly adulation. "A lot of the studs I've sold have been her boys. Those 'uns fetch the most money too. People know she's a winner. You ask anybody and they'll tell you I got the best dogs around. Best bitches too. I only sell winners. The secret is, you got to keep the cream of the crop for yourself. That's why I'll never sell Sally. I'll fight her and breed her until the day she dies."

Mr. Beresik gazed out over the pen, and he appeared to be resisting a smile. I had seen this look before, the immense, unshakable love. This was how people looked at the cross during Mass. And this was how my mother looked at the Black Madonna. If I could step into her line of sight and be held there for one second, even a fraction of an instant, I believed I would know what happiness was. Mr. Beresik had gone quiet and I was holding very still, trying not to disturb him, when a strange compulsion swam through my body. Almost unconsciously, I raised my hand, higher and higher, until the tips of my fingers edged into Mr. Beresik's peripheral vision. In that moment when my fingers crossed into his gaze, I was sure I felt a tiny surge, like a bolt of warmth. Then Mr. Beresik blinked as though waking and the feeling was gone.

"You can come by and watch a match if you like," he offered. "It's a good time. There's betting and all, but I'm sure your father won't mind you seeing that. You're getting older and a boy your age needs to learn about things."

"Okay," I said, for lack of a better reply.

"Be seeing you then," Mr. Beresik said, cueing me to leave.

"Okay," I answered, echoing myself blankly. I stepped off the porch and headed down the path. The dogs watched me every inch of the way, never moving anything but their eyes. As I passed the pen, I could feel Sally looking at me, reading me, sizing me up. She blinked once, as if to say she knew me now and she would recognize me from then on. It was as though she could see beyond my boyish clothes and she'd figured out what no one else that day had—that I was, in fact, a girl. She knew.

As I walked down the hill, away from Mr. Beresik's house, I heard him cluck his tongue at the dogs. They obediently trotted off, returning to the barn where they'd come from. I wondered if they were aware of what awaited them, if they sensed that they would be fighting that night and that they would have to win if they wanted to eat and if they wanted to live. I also couldn't help but wonder what Mr. Beresik had meant when he said there were things a boy my age needed to learn. What things would a boy learn that I would never know? The question hung in my mind, taking shape in the form of my own shadow, which stood before me as I returned to town with the sun setting behind my back.

IT WAS ALMOST DUSK when I made it back to the butcher's shop. I clambered through the thicket of briars and into the field to retrieve the bicycle, which lay right where I had left it, then hoisted it onto its wheels and forced it toward the alley, thorny nettles scraping my skin and snaring my clothes as I went. I rolled the bicycle up to the rear door of Mr. Goceljak's shop, leaned it against the railing, and knocked on the door.

Mr. Goceljak's eyes went wide at the sight of me. "What happened?"

I thought I was in trouble. "Did I take too long?" I asked. "I'm sorry. I didn't mean to."

"No," he said. "Your face. What happened? Did you fall?"

I ran my fingers across my cheeks and the flesh stung. The briars had scratched me, yet in my haste, I hadn't felt the pain.

"No, I . . . I mean, yes, I tripped on Mr. Beresik's steps. But I'm okay. It's nothing."

Another lie. Though it tumbled out smoothly, it burned like scalding water in my throat. Mr. Goceljak believed me, though he still looked concerned. "I should've warned you about his dogs. Scary bunch, eh?"

I nodded emphatically.

"Walter Beresik's a good customer, though. Same order every day. He tell you what it's for?"

"Yes, sir. For the winners."

Mr. Goceljak was impressed. "Then I guess you must've fooled him. Walt never would've told a little girl what he does with those dogs. Means he believed you were a boy. You passed," Mr. Goceljak declared. "Now we better get you cleaned up. Turn you into a girl again."

The back room of the shop was cool and the air was stiff with the smell of bleach.

"The floors have to be done right or else they get to stinking," Mr. Goceljak explained as he pushed a mop and pail aside.

Two pigs' heads were resting on the block, eyes half closed as if they were dozing. Their downy cheeks and long eyelashes made them look almost angelic. Because meat was expensive, not an ounce of the animal was wasted. Ears were pickled. Any inedible fat was turned into tallow for candles. Even the skull bones were ground down to make a thickening agent for cheese. Not a scrap of flesh was squandered.

I took off the canvas cap and let my hair fall onto my shoulders. It felt light and silky on my neck, like a new sensation. Then I went to remove the trousers but stopped myself. Mr. Goceljak was standing right there and I was suddenly self-conscious.

"Oh, sorry," he said and quickly turned his back.

I untied the twine belt and the trousers dropped to the ground. I stepped out of them, folded them neatly, and held them out to Mr. Goceljak, saying, "Here. Thanks."

He turned to face me again and made a flourish with his

hands. "It's like you're Houdini, magically transforming from a boy to a girl in no time flat."

I liked that—that someone would think of me as a magician, a person with special powers. It seemed so far from the truth that it might be possible.

"All right then, s'pose I'll see you tomorrow," Mr. Goceljak said.

"Yes, sir. Don't forget to lock up the bicycle."

"Right. Good. Good thinking," he added.

"See you tomorrow," I said, though I was hesitant to leave. So much had happened that I wasn't sure I wanted it to end.

"Wait," Mr. Goceljak said, startling me. "There's blood all over your hands. It's on your skirt too. How'd that happen?"

Up until that point I hadn't looked at my hands. They were stained with dried blood, which had caked along the nail beds and seeped under my nails. The fabric of my skirt was matted with small bloodstains as well, tingeing the blue to brown.

"I wiped my hands on my skirt so I wouldn't get the pants dirty," I told Mr. Goceljak, hating the heat of the lie in my mouth.

"Don't trouble yourself about the trousers and don't worry about the blood. It'll come off with water. I should know."

Mr. Goceljak cranked on the sink's tap and handed me a cake of soap, which was tinted the same dull brown as my hands. Brown bubbles rested, unpopped, on top of the soap cake. The water was icy, so cold it almost burned. I washed the blood from my hands and dragged my nails over the soap trying to dislodge the remains. After a few minutes, my hands were clean. Mr. Goceljak soaped a rag for me and gave it to me to use on my skirt. The soap and water blurred the stains until they vanished.

Mr. Goceljak handed me a clean towel. "See. Good as new."

"All right then," I intoned, only to realize that it was the same phrase Mr. Goceljak kept using, though he didn't seem to notice how often he said it. "I guess I'll see you tomorrow." I took a step toward the front of the shop and Mr. Goceljak stopped me.

"Probably should go out the back way."

Instinctively, I dropped my eyes, hurt by his suggestion. Whenever my mother went to work at the church or at the rectory, she was not allowed to enter through the main doors. She was not a parishioner or a guest, but a servant. I'd come to believe that that was what back doors were for—servants.

"I'm only saying so because you told me you didn't want anybody to know you were working here. That's all." Mr. Goceljak's words were a relief, one we both felt. "I've got to lock the bike up. I'll walk you out."

THE SUN WAS HUNKERED LOW on the hills and the wind was picking up. Mr. Goceljak pulled the padlock from his back pocket, slung it between the bicycle's spokes and the railing, and snapped it shut. That was it. That was my first day as a delivery boy and it was over. I couldn't help but look at the bicycle with a bit of pride, as if it were an animal that had obeyed me, respecting my wish for it to stay hidden in the field while I made my deliveries. I wanted to pat it the way Mr. Beresik might have patted one of his dogs. Instead, I put my clean hands in my pockets to keep them warm and said, "Good night, sir."

"All right then," Mr. Goceljak replied. "Good night."

I began to stroll along the alley, thinking of all that had gone on, then I remembered something that made my heart seize—Martin.

I ran hard, harder than I had run that afternoon, tearing along the main streets until I could see the spire of Saint Ladislaus piercing the sky. I pumped my arms and my legs pounded against the ground. It was as if I didn't even need to breathe.

Soon I could see the figure of a small boy slumped on the bottom step of the school. It was Martin. He'd bundled himself in his coat and pulled it over his legs to keep warm. His schoolbooks were stacked neatly in a pile next to him. He didn't see me. He was staring at the ground and forlornly pushing up dirt with the tip of his boot. The street was empty and he was utterly alone. Then he heard my footfalls and turned.

My heart told me to sprint over to him, to grab him and hold him and tell him how sorry I was, but embarrassment kept me from him. I stopped and stood there in the road, panting. By the look on his face, I could tell Martin was fighting the same struggle. He wanted to come to me, to be happy I had finally arrived. But I had broken my promise and he was hurt. He had every right to be.

When I did approach him, Martin made no attempt to get up or even look me in the eye. He kept scrounging in the dirt with his boot, pretending to be busy. I was about to apologize, but the words were mired in my belly, stuck like pebbles in mud.

"You left me," Martin said.

"I know. And I'm sorry. Very sorry. I didn't mean to, but—"

"But you did."

"I know and I promise it won't happen again. Not ever."

"You know I was stuck with Sister Teresa for two hours

straight. Two hours. She fell asleep and she started to snore. Loud. Real loud. It was terrible."

A smile welled on my face, then Martin's, and I knew everything would be all right. I leaned over and picked up his books, then held out my hand to him. He took it gladly. His fingers were cold to the touch, so I rubbed them between mine, then put his hand in my pocket. Martin had his own pockets, but I knew he liked it when I put his hand in mine instead. It meant we would have to walk in the same rhythm and stay close to each other. We ambled home, conjoined, keeping in perfect step with each other.

As we neared Third, the distinct sound of Mrs. Koshchushko's voice rang in the air. She was shouting and moaning, slicing through the quiet of the evening. We were accustomed to the commotion because it occurred almost nightly. Mrs. Koshchushko would break into screaming fits during which she would beg one of her two children, a boy and a girl in their teens, Peter and Irene, to put her out of her misery. "Finish me. Finish me already," she would plead in Polish, turning it into a woeful chant. Like the rest of us, she was a Catholic, so suicide was an unutterable word, but I believe even Martin knew what she was asking.

Mrs. Koshchushko would smash dishes, throw chairs, anything that was loud enough to compete with the pitch of her wailing. Her children had no choice but to stay there and wait out the storm of her tirades. Sometimes it took hours, sometimes minutes. All anybody on Third could do was pretend to ignore the noise. That evening, however, Martin stopped outside their apartment, trying to sneak a glance in the window.

"We shouldn't stare," I scolded.

"How is it staring if they can't see me?"

Before I could stop him, Martin slipped his hand from my pocket and raced up to the Koshchushkos' front window.

"Martin. Get back here."

"I only want to see what it looks like when she does this."

By the time I caught up with him, he was standing on tiptoe, face pressed to the glass. There was one light on inside and the coal stove was burning. I could see Peter and Irene solemnly sitting in the corner, eyes riveted on their laps. In the middle of the floor lay Mrs. Koshchushko, her legs sprawled out as she wept into her own arms. She was clad in a green robe, which fanned out behind her, barely covering her pale legs. Each racking sob played itself out along her back. I tried to pry Martin away from the glass, but he held fast.

"Why is she crying so hard?" he asked.

"I don't know. Maybe she's sad."

"I know she's sad. You don't cry when you're *not* sad. But why?"

I could imagine a million things, a million reasons why she would be so rapt with pain, but none of them was worth conjuring in Martin's mind.

"Come on," I told him firmly and he finally heeded the order. He returned his hand to my pocket and sighed. "Okay, we can go now. I've seen enough."

It was true. He had seen enough, far more than he should have. It was as if each of the acute miseries of the world sprang from the dirt on Third and took root there. Living where we did, hearing what we heard, seeing what we saw, we were filled to the brim with the world and it seemed as though we would not be able to hold an ounce more of what life held in store for us. For a seven-year-old, Martin had seen enough for a lifetime.

When we turned away from the Koshchushkos' window, Swatka Pani was standing in the middle of the alley, watching us. Martin gasped aloud. I pinched his hand to silence him. She seemed to have appeared from nowhere, as though she had materialized out of the mud like all of the other miseries.

"I see you," she hissed in clotted Polish.

She waited for a response. Neither Martin nor I would dare speak.

"I see you," Swatka Pani repeated. "You were watching them. Wanted to see what happens in there, didn't you?"

She lifted her cane and started toward us in a slow, menacing crawl. My first instinct was to run, to flee, and Martin must have felt me restrain the reflex. His eyes flickered toward me, waiting for my signal. But I knew not to run away when Swatka Pani was addressing us directly. We were caught.

"You find what you were looking for, boy?"

As Swatka Pani drew closer, I stepped in front of Martin, shielding him from view.

"He was only curious. He heard noises and got curious. That's all," I explained in Polish, my voice shaking, then trailing off.

Swatka Pani switched her sights to me. She had a glint in her eyes like the kind of light that comes when a coal fire is burning so hot that the flame goes blue, then colorless, and the fire can't grow much hotter. The air seemed to change, to condense and solidify, as if Swatka Pani was pressing herself up to us without moving. Martin peered out from behind me, too afraid to look away.

"Mind your own business," Swatka Pani commanded. "Or you'll find someone else minding it for you."

I spun around and forcibly pushed Martin down Third, toward

our apartment and away from Swatka Pani. He kept glancing back at her, and I had to twist him on his heel to get him to run. I scrambled to retrieve the key to our apartment from inside my coat, then gratefully slid it in the lock. Before I could twist the handle, my mother flung open the door, a harsh expression stamped on her face.

"Where have you been?" she demanded, blocking our way. We could not enter the apartment before we answered her question.

My mother was never home that early, so I hadn't planned on concocting an alibi. I was at a loss and could do nothing but stare at her blankly.

"Well?"

Time came to a grinding halt. All I could hear was the absence of sound left in the wake of my mother's question. In that chasm, I swore I could feel Swatka Pani's eyes on my back. I swore I could feel her watching us from the end of the alley, waiting and listening to our every word. The urge to turn and look was irrepressible. When I did, she was gone. She had vanished completely. It was as if Swatka Pani had disappeared back into the mud she had come from.

I wanted to forget seeing her, speaking to her, what she had said, all of it. Better yet, I wanted to *unremember* the incident altogether. Forgetting something meant that some trace of thought must linger in the back of the mind, hiding in some secret corner. I didn't want the memory of Swatka Pani to occupy any space or make a home in my head. The worst part was that I knew it would.

"It's my fault," Martin blurted. "I was in the library at school. They got a new book and I wanted to read it. It's my fault we're late."

My mother eyed Martin, but his face was placid, certain. I knew he was lying and he knew he was lying.

"Fine then, get inside. Supper'll be on soon."

She made room for us to pass and closed the door behind us with an admonishing snap. The coal stove was burning low, but it was warm inside the apartment, a comfort from the cold and all that had happened. That comfort quickly burned off once I considered what Martin had done. I feared my own lies, but not the way I feared for Martin and what might happen to him for his. He didn't deserve to suffer for what I had started.

Since I could remember, the nuns had hammered the notion of sin into our skulls, pummeling us with threats of hell and damnation. The way they described it, each lie we told was like a straight pin thrust into God's heart. Martin had put his very soul in jeopardy without a second thought simply to protect me, and the gravity of his deed could have toppled me where I stood. Though I had begun in earnest and with the best of intentions, my lies had somehow become contagious and I believed I had infected my brother with them.

"Take off those boots," my mother said, returning to the stove, "or you'll track mud from the gutter all over."

Still shaken, Martin and I did as we were told. We removed our boots and lined them up near the door the way my mother liked, toes to the wall. She claimed that that was where all of the dirt went, though as far as I could tell it went everywhere, on the toe, the heel, the sole. Even the laces had to be washed regularly or they'd become caked in mud, ratty and untieable. My boots were filthy from all the running I'd done that day. The leather was dull with dust and clods of mud clung to the sides. Martin's shoes, on the other hand, were relatively clean except for a few blades of grass that had gotten caught in the treads. Martin's boots were another donation from the Benedictine nuns, also used and handed down from boy to boy in some other family. The boots were too big for Martin, so he often wore two pairs of socks to make them fit, yet they still seemed so small and delicate and precious. Seeing my brother's tiny boots sitting there next to mine made his gesture even more poignant, the guilt of what I had done to him even more fierce.

Martin was trying to act normal, but he was shaken. He took out his schoolbooks and prepared to do his homework, as he did each day when he returned from school. I always did the same, though it was only to keep him company. Schoolwork held little interest for me. I didn't like it, but I didn't dislike it either. I simply didn't care one way or the other. The work never seemed challenging. Worse yet, it didn't seem to matter. I imagined every twelve-year-old reading the same books, doing the same math equations, and printing the same grammar lessons all across the world and it depressed me. Nevertheless, I did my assignments, filled in all of the blanks and turned the work in on time, without fail. To do otherwise would bring consequences worse than any homework assignment—attention. If one of the children didn't turn in their homework, they were made an example of by the nuns, who forced them to stand in front of the classroom and explain themselves. Then they had to stay after school with the nuns and copy Bible verses. I would willingly copy a thousand verses rather than suffer under the eyes of my classmates for even a second, but the punishment came as a package, so I did everything to avoid it altogether.

While Martin and I began our homework, my mother started chopping a potato on a board at the sink. She cut it into slivers to make it seem as if there was more, though that only made things worse. The bits of potato would grow soft and mushy and, after a few days, they would disintegrate, turning the soup into a heavy, bland stew with the consistency of cream but none of the taste.

"Don't touch that shirt there on the table. I'm mending it," my mother instructed, never taking her eyes off the knife.

One of my father's shirts was on the table. The collar had been removed and my mother was in the process of turning it. The front of the collar had become too frayed to be presentable, but we didn't have the money for a new shirt, so my mother would cut off the collar, invert it, and reattach it so that the clean, unmarred underside was on top.

"Sorry," I said, inching my schoolbooks farther from the shirt.

The big stew pot my mother favored was already on the stove. We were low on coal, so it would take time to bring the pot to a boil. Once she'd minced the potato as finely as she could, she dumped it into the pot, then she took a parcel wrapped in butcher's paper from the icebox. My eyes locked on the package.

My mother unwrapped the paper as if she was unwrapping a present. Inside were the cleaved ends of six sausages. I was relieved when I realized what they were. The nubby scraps were the remnants of Father Svitek's supper. Early on, he had instructed my mother that he did not eat the ends of his sausages and that she was free to have them if she wanted. She took them without fail.

My mother retrieved the large iron skillet from inside the oven where she kept it, and carefully placed half of the sausage ends in the center. They were to be my father's breakfast. She dropped the remaining bits of sausage into the stew pot for us and gazed down at them like pennies she'd thrown into a wishing well, then she stirred them into the mix until they disappeared. She stood there at the stove staring into the pot for so long that even Martin ceased his studies to watch her. When my mother realized we were staring, she went to the sink to wash her hands.

"All right," she said, drying her hands on a rag. "I have to go out."

Martin and I shared a glance. My father spent his afternoons as well as evenings at the Silver Slipper and would come home only to shave, gobble down some food, and get his lunch. Even so, my mother made it a practice to be home when he arrived to eat and rarely left the apartment afterward. Her leaving before he came back was a bad sign.

"Where are you going?" Martin asked, genuinely perplexed by the sudden change in routine.

My mother's expression flashed with worry. It was the same look I imagined I must have worn minutes earlier when she'd asked me where we had been. She was deciding whether to lie or not.

"Just out," she stammered. "I expect your homework to be finished by the time I get back."

She went into the bedroom and when she came back out, she was pulling on her dress gloves. They were far from extravagant, merely a thin, brown kidskin, but they weren't nearly as beat up as her wool gloves, which bore holes from years of use. My mother was also carrying a small sack and trying to conceal it at her side.

"Don't touch the pot. It's hot," my mother said. Then she was gone.

THE APARTMENT WAS QUIET except for the sound of the stew pot beginning to boil. I pretended to read while Martin tried, unsuccessfully, to balance a pencil on its point. Finally, he faced me.

"I don't know," I said, preempting his question.

"But?"

"I don't know," I repeated. "I have no idea where she'd be going or why, so don't ask."

"She's got to be going somewhere. She can't be going *nowhere*. There is no *nowhere*. At least not around here."

"Then where do you think she's going?" I suspected he had his own guess and was trying to get me to ask him.

"I'll tell you where. She's going to the Silver Slipper to bring him home for his breakfast."

"Why would she do that?"

"Because she wants to. She doesn't want him to miss it or forget."

"When has he ever forgotten to eat?"

"He hasn't. But that doesn't mean she can't go there and remind him."

I wanted to drop the subject, so I picked up my pencil and resumed my reading. I wished Martin would do the same, but he wasn't giving up that easily.

"Why? Where do you think she went?"

"You already asked me that."

"You never answered."

"I said I didn't know. That was my answer. Now let's finish our schoolwork before she gets back or else we'll be in trouble."

Martin flopped back in his chair, defeated. He didn't like my responses, though thankfully, he believed them. The truth was, I didn't know where my mother was going. I could imagine a few possibilities, and none was heartening. Maybe she was leaving so she wouldn't be home when my father got back, punishing him for his absence with her own. Or maybe she was going back to the rectory to do some work for Father Svitek, some overtime to make up for the money my father was wasting at the Silver Slipper. Or perhaps she was going to meet someone, a man even. Images of her in her kidskin gloves holding another man's hand began to bloom in my mind, the man's face hazy. I shuddered to shake the vision from my head.

The nagging feeling of not knowing what my mother was up to had gotten to Martin. I could see that he wouldn't be able to concentrate on his schoolwork. He began to fiddle with the shirt my mother had left on the table. He pulled it close and studied the way she was sewing the collar back on, examining the stitches and the pins that held the half-sewn collar to the shirt.

"Be careful," I warned. "Or you'll stick yourself."

"No, I won't," Martin protested, then he let out a hissing wince. He had nicked his finger on one of the pins.

"See," I said as he sucked the tip of his finger woefully. "Don't get any blood on the shirt or then we'll be in real trouble."

"I just wanted to see how it worked," Martin mumbled, his finger still stuck in his mouth.

"Then you should've asked."

I slid the shirt around and propped it up on our schoolbooks so he could see the way my mother had started to resew the collar. Martin needed something to occupy him, to take his mind off her hasty departure, and so did I. I took the needle out and used it as a pointer, showing him the little stitches that held the collar in place. I explained how to pierce the material with the needle and how to make a single stitch. To my brother, it was as if I was creating magic.

"How does that little piece of string hold this big thing together? It's not strong. It's tiny."

"Alone it's tiny. But together with more stitches, the thread becomes strong. Strong enough to hold the collar on for good."

This was miraculous to Martin, inexplicable. "Can I try?" he asked, excited but hesitant, as if he might not be able to control such magic on his own.

I passed him the needle, smoothed out the fabric and pointed to the spot where he should start the next stitch. Martin took a deep breath and pressed the needle through the underside of the collar. When it surfaced, he seemed almost surprised.

"Not too far," I instructed. "You want the stitches to be small and strong."

"Small and strong," Martin repeated. He scrutinized his stitch, making sure it matched my mother's. While he forced the needle back through the fabric, creating a single stitch, I tried to recall how I had learned the technique myself. I sorted back through my memory, digging for a moment when I had sat with my mother like this and she had shown me how to draw a needle through cloth and line up each stitch. Then I realized that that moment had never happened. I had learned by peering over her shoulder while she sewed and stationing myself next to her at the table when she would hem my father's pants. My mother had never tried to teach me. Instead, I'd learned by watching her when she didn't know I was looking, or didn't care. Part of me believed she was aware of what I'd done, that she had agreed to our silent tutorial simply by staying put and letting me look on. I could never be sure and preferred to hope.

"Is that it? Did I do it?" Martin asked, showing me his completed stitches.

"Yes," I reassured him. "That's it. You did it."

A knock sounded at the front door, startling both of us. We rarely got visitors, and my mother's mysterious departure had set a foreboding tone.

As I got up to answer the door, Martin put his hand on my arm, cautioning, as if anyone or *anything* might be waiting on the other side. The incident with Swatka Pani had unnerved both of us. My lies had become a blight, contaminating Martin too, and Swatka Pani's words came as confirmation of my sins. The devil knew my heart as well as God, and he had sent a messenger to say as much.

"Don't get it," Martin whispered.

"I have to."

"No, you don't."

I put my hand on the doorknob lightly, testing its temperature. If it was indeed the devil, I thought I might feel the heat of him through the door. Yet the knob was as cold as always.

Another knock came. The noise made me jump.

"Don't," Martin pleaded.

I opened the door and braced myself for what I was about to behold. Standing before me was a boy of fourteen, a bucket in his hand.

"Here," he said peevishly, holding up the bucket. I struggled to place the boy's face. Alarm was overriding all memory. "It's the catfish," the boy added, already growing impatient. "Your father said you wanted one."

It was one of Stash Nowczyk's sons. He had come to drop off the catfish as my father had said he would. Stash Nowczyk had six children, all boys, and few people, including Stash, could tell them apart. Each one looked like the other, flat faced, with wet, blue eyes and a tuft of blond hair. I waved him inside.

"Where do you want it?" he asked, then his gaze snagged on something.

I followed his line of sight with a swelling dread. It was Martin who had caught his attention. He still had the shirt on his lap and the needle in hand.

"What are you doing?" the boy asked in disgust.

Martin floundered for an answer. This boy had only brothers, so seeing Martin sewing was as bad as seeing him playing with dolls.

Martin's silence was enough of a reply. The boy shoved the bucket at me, sending water sloshing over the sides. "Leave it outside when you're done with it. I'll come back for it later."

The boy slammed the door behind him, then Martin threw the shirt across the table.

"Forget about him," I said, trying to console him. "Come see the fish."

"I don't want to see the dumb fish."

The catfish thumped its fins against the bucket, splashing water onto my legs.

"Okay," I said to the fish. "Just a minute. Just a minute."

"Are you talking to the fish?" Martin asked indignantly, taking his frustration out on me.

I didn't bother responding. I went into the washroom, put the stopper in the tub, then turned the faucet on full blast. The pipes groaned to life and water came pouring from the spout. I tested it with my finger and it was icy cold. The catfish flapped its fins again anxiously, as if it knew what was coming.

"Okay, okay," I cooed softly. "One more minute."

"I hear you," Martin called from the other room. "You *are* talking to the fish."

"What does it matter? It's a fish. I can talk to it if I like."

Martin had no retort, so he huffed loudly enough for me to hear.

Once the tub was half full, I lowered the bucket and the catfish darted out into the water. It swam the length of the tub eagerly, fluttering its fins. The catfish was long and meaty, at least the length of my forearm, and it was mottled with orange and brown scales that glimmered with its every move. Whiskers hung from its face, longer than a cat's, making it seem more like a creature from a storybook than a real animal. I found myself entranced by the catfish, tracing its every turn. After a few minutes, it settled down and stopped swimming and began to hover in the water, gently swishing its tail from time to time.

"Maybe he's hungry," Martin said. He was standing in the doorway, waiting for another invitation to look at the fish.

"Maybe. I didn't think of that."

"We're supposed to feed him cornmeal. To clean out his guts. That's what he said."

"You're right," I answered, acting as though I'd forgotten. Martin was sorry for snapping at me, I could tell. Now he just wanted to get in on the fun. "You want to help me feed the fish?" I asked.

"I s'pose," he said sheepishly. "If you're feeding him."

I found a container of cornmeal on top of the icebox, though it was almost empty. Even though my mother had promised to pick up a new box, she must have forgotten. I hoped that that was where she had gone, but I doubted it.

"How much do you think we should give him?" Martin asked.

"How do you know it's a him?"

"Because he has a mustache. Girl fishes don't have mustaches."

"But all catfishes have mustaches. That's why they're called that."

Martin considered this thoroughly and finally conceded. "Maybe. But he looks like a boy fish to me."

"Why's that?"

"I don't know. He swims like a boy is all."

"Okay," I relented. "The catfish can be a boy."

"Can we name him?"

"Sure."

"Good. Then I think his name should be Joe."

"Joe?"

"He looks like a Joe. Joes have mustaches like that and stuff."

"All right, Joe it is."

Martin beamed, then as if on cue, the catfish made a loop around the tub. "See. He likes his name."

"Yeah, and it looks like Joe's hungry too."

As the newly named Joe swam another lazy lap around the bathtub, I sprinkled some of the cornmeal into the water and he started nipping the bits of meal off the surface in dainty gulps. Once the cornmeal was gone, Joe stopped swimming and positioned himself beneath me, waiting for his next helping.

"He must still be hungry," Martin said. "Maybe you should give him some more."

Before I could reply, the front door was hurled open. It was my father. He took two unsteady steps into the house and slammed the door hard enough to rattle the cross on the wall. He was drunk, and a lit cigarette was pinched between his teeth. His eyes drooped for an instant, then he blinked himself awake. He scanned the room, searching, then he spotted Martin and me, framed in the doorway to the washroom. His gaze swung to the bedroom door, which was wide open. He was about to ask where my mother was, but stopped himself, clenching the cigarette tighter to keep the question from escaping. Her absence said everything.

Martin and I held our positions. Even he knew better than to test my father with one of his usual inquiries. The silence that inflated in the room resonated like a roar. My father barreled over to the icebox and took out two eggs. He recklessly cracked them into the skillet with the sausage rinds my mother had left, hurled the shells into the sink, then prodded the coal in the stove. My father kept his back to us and seemed to be staring at the eggs, smoking steadily all the while. Every few seconds he would sway slightly, enough for us to see. The sizzle of the frying eggs was the only sound. When he could wait no longer, my father slopped the eggs onto a dish, plunked himself down at the table, and devoured the meal without a word.

Martin looked up at me questioningly. I shook my head, telling him we had to stay put. My father seemed to have forgotten we were there. He was eating his food in a measured way, concentrating on each spoonful diligently, as if testing it for poison. Martin and I had become part of the background, mute and motionless, and I couldn't be sure what my father would do if we suddenly sprang to life.

Once his plate was empty, my father pushed it away, dropping the spoon onto the dish hard enough to make it ring. He stubbed out his cigarette in the ashtray that was the constant centerpiece on the table and stood up, then almost lost his balance and had to steady himself against a chair. He hitched up his pants, covering for his misstep, then he did the one thing I'd feared since he had walked in the door—he looked at us.

"Get out of there," he mumbled. "I have to shave."

Martin and I broke away from the door, clearing room for my father as ordered. He charged past us and I could feel a gust of air in his wake. He shut the door behind him, then Martin let out a long breath.

While my father shaved, Martin and I waited on the edge of our bed, backs straight, fingers pressed into the mattress so we could be ready to hop back up if necessary. The faucet was running and I could hear my father tapping his razor against the basin, knocking it clean. I thought I could even hear the low fizzle of his dragging the razor across the stubble on his face and the rhythm of his breathing. I strained to make out every sound, waiting for the signal that he was done and would soon be opening the door. I was listening so hard that I ceased to see anything in front of me. Though my eyes were open, it was as if I'd gone blind from concentrating so intently.

Martin pressed the side of his hand next to mine. I nudged

back, reassuring him. We were both too scared to tear our eyes away from the door to look at each other. I had grown superstitious about things like that. If I didn't look away, everything would be okay. If I did, that meant something worse would happen. So I never looked away. Never.

The faucet cut off, and Martin and I readied ourselves for my father to reemerge. As we held our breath, I pictured myself underwater, floating calmly, like the catfish. As soon as the door to the washroom swung wide, I felt as though I'd inhaled water. Earlier, when he had first come in, his cheeks were slack, his eyes hazy. Shaving seemed to have filed down his features. Now his face was as sharp as a hatchet. He cleaved the room with his very presence.

As he strode into the bedroom, Martin and I tracked him with our eyes, then we were forced to wait again as he changed his clothes for work. The muffled sounds of cloth rubbing against cloth and a faint hiss of zipper drifted out of the bedroom, followed by footsteps. Martin and I re-braced ourselves.

My father stalked out into the main room, put on his coat, and grabbed his lunch pail from the icebox without even a glance. When he reached the door, he wheeled around to face us. He stared at Martin and me for an endless moment. Then he turned and left. Once the door was shut, Martin dropped his head onto my shoulder, exhausted.

IT WAS A FULL HOUR before my mother returned. Martin and I were sitting at the table, homework long finished, too drained to do anything but stare at our closed books. When the door opened, we both jumped.

My mother entered and glanced at us furtively. It must have appeared as if we hadn't moved since she'd left. Her eyes darted to the coal stove where the empty skillet lay, proof that my father had already come and gone. The stew pot had been boiling, but neither Martin nor I had noticed.

"I'll set out supper," she said as she removed her coat, guilt softening her tone.

By then, the coal was running low in the stove. The room had to have been cold, but Martin and I hadn't felt it. We were too numb to be cold.

My mother shoveled what was left of the coal into the base of the stove, stoking the fire so it would be high and hot, something she normally wouldn't do. She usually saved some coal for when my father got back from work, enough that the apartment would be warm for him. I couldn't tell if she was stoking the stove to spite him or to apologize to us.

An hour of sitting in the cold apartment had stiffened my muscles, and when I stood to set the table, my limbs burned.

Another reminder, I thought. *No sin goes unpunished.*

Like the run-in with Swatka Pani, I took the stinging in my muscles as a sign. The fire of each of my lies was coursing through my veins. In desperation, I turned to the wall where the Black Madonna had been. The empty wall shouted back at me as if to say, *You are alone in this.*

I laid out three plates for supper and Martin followed behind me, setting out the spoons. My mother ladled some stew into each of our dishes, purposefully putting the sausage rinds onto our plates instead of hers. I wasn't sure if this was another apology or if she felt like she didn't deserve them.

We ate our dinners sluggishly. Each mouthful was a struggle to chew. Staying awake took a sheer force of will. I could have fallen asleep there at the table, yet I kept my guard up, anticipating an attempt from Martin. He wanted to ask my mother where she had been, and though he was worn out, I guessed he still might try.

The soft chime of our spoons against the plates became a melody, one that lulled me off my watch.

"What's wrong with Mrs. Koshchushko?" Martin asked, eyes fixed on my mother. He was trying to draw information from her with a sidelong question.

"What do you mean?" She was either honestly confused or being cagey.

"Why does she act the way she does, always crying?"

My mother leveled her eyes on Martin, head tipped knowingly low. She had guessed his game. "I wouldn't know," she replied. Her voice was smooth and solid. She had put an end to the duel right there.

When Martin opened his mouth again, I pushed his knee with mine. It was over.

We finished our meals, and I cleared the dishes. My mother washed them and I took my position beside her to dry them while Martin prepared for bed. This was the one chore I looked forward to. It was always the same. My mother would scrub each dish, run it under the faucet, shake the water off and pass it to me, then I would pat it dry with a dishrag. There was a rhythm to the routine, a togetherness. For this and this alone, she seemed to need me.

Once we were finished, I stacked the dishes in the cupboard

while Martin finished brushing his teeth, then he stationed himself in the doorway to the washroom, biding his time until my
mother was unoccupied. She washed her hands, then began folding the drying rags into neat squares. Martin could wait no longer.

"We got the catfish today," he proclaimed.

"Oh?"

It was hardly the enthusiasm Martin had hoped for. He was
trying to cheer her up, to drag her out of her distant mood, but it
was like trying to shake somebody out of a deep sleep. My mother
was too far away to wake.

"We named him too," Martin explained. He waited for her to
ask him more but she didn't, answering only with a nod. "His
name's Joe," Martin went on. "Because he's a boy and all. So we
decided on Joe. Because it's a boy's name."

Another weak nod was all my mother could manage. Her
thoughts were elsewhere. Martin finally gave up.

We all went to bed early. My mother disappeared into her bedroom shortly after supper and never came out, leaving Martin and
me alone to listen to the dying embers crumbling in the coal stove.
Side by side in our single bed, we tossed and turned for a while,
neither able to get comfortable or find sleep despite our exhaustion. We were facing away from each other, me to the wall, Martin
to the room, when he whispered to me, "So what was it like?"

I rolled over, but still he kept his back to me. "What?"

"Working?"

"It wasn't so bad really," I said, unsure how to put the day into
words.

"What did you do?"

In his small, plaintive voice, Martin was really asking for a bedtime story, a tale he could fall asleep to. I snuggled up behind him and told him everything, each and every detail that I could remember, from the color of the bicycle to the size of Mr. Beresik's dogs. I narrated the story of that day until my brother drifted off to sleep.

A WEEK PASSED, but the warm tide of spring refused to arrive. Winter stubbornly held on, clenching Hyde Bend in its gray grip. We awoke each morning to find frost lingering on the windows. Every night was heralded by a fast-falling sunset, then trumpeted by blustering winds. There was neither the luxury of snow nor the relief of sunshine. It was a middling, bothersome sort of cold, the kind that kept the laundry from drying on the lines and that hardened only the top layer of mud on the alley. Though the weather was caught in a dreary limbo, my world had begun to fall into a rhythm.

Each day after school, I would take Martin to the library, where he would stay until I was finished with my route for Mr.

Goceljak, then I would sprint straight to the butcher's shop to pick up my deliveries. Mr. Goceljak would welcome me with a load of wrapped parcels and unlock the bicycle for me, usually remarking on the cold and cursing it for not having the good sense to know when enough was enough.

"All right then," he would say, then he would bid me a safe ride and return to his work. Once he'd gone, I would hide the bicycle in the field and run to each of my stops. I visited house after house in my boy's costume, and nobody ever questioned me or suspected I was anything other than what I seemed. Sometimes even I lost track of myself in the costume. The saggy pants hid my knobby legs and the cap concealed all but my nose and lips. I could have been anybody. No one looked at me on the street, though I was used to that, only now it was as though I was fooling them, and it made me feel powerful.

Those days, I ran so much that I began to think I was faster than the bicycle could be, but I still dreamed of riding it. I attempted to shave more and more time off my routes in the hope of having an opportunity to practice with the bicycle. However, there was one thing that held me back. Since Mr. Beresik lived the farthest away, I left his delivery for last, and I often found myself lingering at his house longer than I should have. Every visit started out the same way. As I approached the hill to his house, the dogs would begin to bark in the distance, announcing my arrival. The whole pack would be waiting along the pen's perimeter when I got there, barking and leaping against the fence in a frenzy. Then Mr. Beresik would appear on the porch to greet me and the barking would break off instantly.

Mr. Beresik always seemed pleased to see me. He would walk

me around the fence, pointing out each dog and describing its various weaknesses and attributes, listing its lineage and rattling off its wins. There were more than thirty dogs in the pen, but he could nevertheless recite with encyclopedic clarity the details of every match each dog had fought. He spun the fights into epic sagas, complete with the drama of defeat and the shining glory of victory. He could gesture to a certain dog, then snap his fingers and that dog would trot over obediently. The dog would sit perfectly still while Mr. Beresik pored over its pelt, pointing out each battle scar and explaining how the dog had gotten it. He would lift their collars and run his finger along the healed bite marks, regaling me with the traits of the dog that had inflicted the wound. Some were scrappy and fast, others oxlike and brutish. The scars were hard fought, and Mr. Beresik took honor in each and every wound.

On occasion, his tales would grow graphic and gruesome, like the time he told me about Flint, who had ripped another dog's throat out and had to be pulled off the body. Mr. Beresik recounted the bloody pit and the limp body of the fallen dog and the blood on Flint's teeth. Because he believed I was a boy, Mr. Beresik seemed to be trying to thrill me with the account, but he had the opposite effect. I pretended to yawn, yet in truth, I was stifling a gag. Mr. Beresik must have picked up on my discomfort because afterward, he never went beyond the most general of details. He didn't want to scare me off. He wanted me to come back. So instead, he began to explain to me how he trained the dogs. His voice would grow calm and measured. "Training is everything," he would remind me. "If you don't do it right when they're pups, you'll never break 'em in. Then that dog's a loss."

Mr. Beresik described how he would take each pup from its

mother one at a time and train them privately, rewarding the pup with a scrap of food when it heeded his whistle or sat when he snapped. He explained how he would wean them off the food reward and how they still did as he commanded. "That's the trick of it," he attested. "They're always hoping they'll get that scrap of food, so they obey even when they don't. They're still hoping."

As soon as the sun would start to dip in the sky, that was my signal to head back to town. "Better be getting on," Mr. Beresik would say. I always had the urge to thank him for talking to me, for spending time with me and telling me about the dogs, but I didn't think that was what a boy would do. Instead, I would simply wave, wish him good luck with the fights, and be on my way. Once I was far enough from the pen, Mr. Beresik would let out one short whistle, a cue to the dogs that they were free to move around as they pleased, and I always checked over my shoulder to see what they would do. Some would return to the barn or run the length of the pen, but there was one dog who always stayed near the fence, standing watch until I was out of sight—Sally. She had scared me at first, but after a few visits, I began to wonder what it was she saw when she looked at me. A liar or a friend?

WHEN THAT FIRST WEEK CAME TO A CLOSE, Mr. Gocel-jak gave me my pay. He placed two dull quarters in my palm and said, "It's a start, right?"

"It's a start," I agreed. The number fourteen still hovered over my head, circling at a dizzying height, still such a long way off.

"Just so you know, I delivered the kielbasa to Father Svitek myself. Figured it wouldn't be a good idea for you to do it."

I had totally forgotten about Father Svitek. Nothing I could have said to Mr. Goceljak would have conveyed how grateful I was. "Thank you," I told him, though the words were meager in comparison to what I felt.

As I walked to school to pick Martin up from the library that day, I would have sworn I could feel the weight of those two quarters in my pocket, light but perceptible. I kept my hand in the pocket for fear of their falling out. But I wouldn't hold them. I envisioned them snapping like wafers, too thin to stand even the gentle pressure of my palm. I showed the quarters to Martin and he begged to touch them.

"They're nice," he said. "Not very shiny, though."

"I don't care if they're shiny. I only care that they're mine."

"Where are you going to put them?"

"I don't know."

"You should hide them."

"Hide them?"

"You said that you being a delivery boy was supposed to be a secret. Remember?"

Martin was right. I needed to hide the quarters. If my mother found them, she would demand to know where I'd gotten them. I didn't want to consider what my father might do if he found them.

"Where do you think I should put them?" I asked.

Martin grinned. "I have the perfect place."

My mother was still at work when we got back to the apartment and my father wasn't home. Since that evening when she had left the house unexpectedly, they'd been avoiding each other, sidestepping each other in a clumsy, stilted dance. During those few days, a new routine had formed. My mother would hurry in from the rectory and fix my father's breakfast. He would roll in before his shift, light a cigarette, and eat his food in silence. The cigarette would only be half finished by the time he was through. Afterward, my father would change into his coveralls, then my mother would pass him his lunch pail as he walked out the door. Martin and I would pretend to do our homework while we surreptitiously studied the new dance, learning the moves and waiting for the next misstep. Once my father was out the door, my mother would prepare our dinners and tell us to set the table, after which she would usually remark on the catfish, reminding herself that it had taken up space in our bathtub for too long.

"Why do we have to cook Joe?" Martin would whine. "He doesn't want to be cooked."

"One more day," my mother would say. "But that's it. I mean it."

The care of the fish had fallen on my shoulders, which entailed feeding him and moving him into the sink when one of us needed to take a bath. Joe was the closest thing to a pet we'd ever had, and, for a fish, he seemed smart. He responded only to me, even recognized me when I entered the washroom. I was the one who fed him, so it made sense. It also made me feel special. Even after I would let Martin feed him, Joe would swim over to me and await his next helping.

"I named you, Joe," Martin would say. "You could at least act happy to see me."

He didn't appreciate the fish's favoritism, yet he was so happy to have a pet that he let the allegiance slide.

That afternoon when we arrived home to the empty apartment, Martin kicked off his boots and bounded for the washroom.

"In here," he hollered. "The hiding place is in here."

As I set down my books, I saw that my hands were stained again from the meat I'd delivered. It struck me that the blood had ceased to bother me as it once had. Nonetheless, I had to get it off my hands before my mother noticed.

Martin was waiting in the washroom, chin resting on the lip of the tub as he peered down at Joe. While I washed my hands, Martin asked, "Why don't you wash the quarters? Maybe they'll look better."

I'd been given pennies in the past, nickels and dimes too, but I couldn't remember even having held a quarter. It was as if the sheer size of the coin put it out of my league, that I couldn't be responsible for such a sum of money. I dug the quarters from my pocket, lathered them with soap, rinsed them, then patted them dry between the pleats of my skirt.

"See. They do look better," Martin said.

As he spoke, the front door opened. It was my mother. I could tell by the way she shut the door. While my father would hurl it back behind him, leaving the door to rattle in its frame, my mother would close it in one steady sweep and hold the handle so the lock would engage the instant she let go of the knob.

I held the quarters out to Martin. "What do I do with them?"

"Give them to me," he said, crouching down under the sink.

My mother's footsteps emanated from the main room. It sounded as if she was putting something away in the icebox, then the footfalls led into her bedroom. Martin nimbly slid his arm between the exposed pipes under the sink.

"Won't they fall out from behind there?" I asked.

"No, there's a little ledge where they can sit. They won't fall." Martin was straining to secure the quarters in their hiding spot. "Almost got it."

My mother must have heard the murmur of our whispers through the wall. Her footsteps stopped. "What are you two doing in there?"

Before I could answer, the front door sounded again. This time it was a wall-shuddering slam. It was my father. His footfalls were equally as distinctive, an even, menacing lumber that made the dishes in the cupboard quiver.

"There. Got it," Martin said, then I quickly pulled him up from the floor and led him out of the washroom with me. Both my father and my mother converged on us at once.

My mother repeated her question. "I said, what are you two doing in there?"

"We were looking at the fish," I explained, the lie burbling from my throat.

"That damn fish," my father lamented. "I've had enough of it. Anyhow, it's Friday. We have to eat it. I'm draining the tub."

"No!" Martin took a step toward the washroom as if he could bar my father's way.

"Can't we keep him? Please? Joe doesn't want to be cooked."

"Don't be stupid. It's just a damned fish." My father strode past Martin, then came the unmistakable sound of water beginning to drain.

My mother was behind me. I would have had to turn around to see her face, to see if she was conflicted, unsure whether to stop my father, to intervene. But I was afraid to look. I feared that what I might find was an expression exactly like my father's, an expression that said she didn't care.

The water from the bathtub made a gulping noise as it plummeted down the drain. Martin was about to protest once more, so I clamped my hand around his mouth. We were both facing the washroom, our backs to my mother.

"Don't. Please," I whispered. "It'll make him angrier."

Martin couldn't help himself. I could feel his mouth working under my hand, silently saying the pleas he wanted to shout. Then a single tear rolled onto my finger and down over my knuckles.

"Please don't, Martin. Please."

With that, my brother's face went slack under my palm and not another tear was shed. I released my hand and we listened to the last of the water slide down into the drain, culminating in one loud, sucking noise that sounded like a gasp for air. Martin must have thought it was the fish gasping for breath because he took a step forward. I held him fast.

The door to the washroom was halfway closed, but we could hear the unmistakable sound of the fish hurling itself around the tub in the throes of death, its skin slapping against the porcelain. Soon the slapping slowed, then stopped altogether. I tensed, waiting for Martin to cry out. He didn't. He didn't even move until my father appeared at the door, then Martin recoiled, taking a full step back. It was either out of fear, or repulsion, at what my father had done.

My father moved by us, his arm hidden behind his back, and laid the fish in the sink. My mother joined him. I could see her only in profile, though that was enough. In her hand, she held a carving knife.

"Take your brother outside," my father directed. "Take him for a walk."

I hustled Martin to the door. He was like a zombie, eyes glazed, limbs loose as I guided them into his coat and boots. I had one arm in the sleeve of my coat and was already spurring Martin onward, outside. The urge to glance back at my parents flashed in my mind, then fizzled. I didn't want this to be the one thing they did together. I didn't want to witness them making short work of the fish. I didn't want to see another thing. I opened the door and pressed my eyes shut, praying that the image might dissolve or be blown from my mind by the cold, night wind that was already buffeting my face. It didn't work.

THIRD WAS DESERTED. Lights were on in the apartments, but no one was in the alley because it was suppertime. The tramping sound of our footfalls on the mud was accompanied by the lonely sobbing of Mrs. Koshchushko, which eventually blended in with the wind.

Martin was plodding along at my side, barely keeping up. I took his hand and held it as we walked. His small fingers curled limply in my palm. My grip was the only thing keeping us together.

I led Martin toward the river. Like the nuns, my mother had forbidden us from going there, but I thought Martin deserved to do something he might like. The wind was stronger along the water. I still had my skirt on, and the cold was seeping through my tights. My toes tingled and the skin on my legs felt like stone, yet I kept walking. We reached the river and I guided Martin to the top of the stairway overlooking the shoreline. Moonlight was glinting on the water below and reflecting the long, orange silhouette of the cross on the other side of the river. The cross wriggled over the ripples, wavering on the water's surface as though it was sinking.

"I hate him," Martin said.

"Don't say that."

"I can if I want. I hate him. And I want him to die just like Joe died."

I gripped Martin's hand hard enough that he tried to pull away. "Don't say that, Martin. Don't ever say that."

"That's what she would say," he countered.

"Pray with me, Marty. We have to pray quickly."

I dragged him down to his knees, and we knelt together on the top step of the stairs, facing the cross.

"Say a Hail Mary. Say it with me, Marty."

"I don't want to."

"Say it."

In unison, we began rattling off the prayer in Polish. Martin was mumbling and squirming. "This hurts my knees," he whined. "Can't we stand up?"

"No. Keep praying."

I was squeezing my eyes shut and wrapping my breath around each word. My knees were digging into the step, grinding the cold flesh against the wood. I could have moved, shifted my weight, but I thought I deserved to be in pain. I deserved to hurt for what my lies had done to Martin.

We finished the prayer, yet it didn't feel like enough. "Now tell God you're sorry for what you said and that you take it back."

"I will not."

"Just say it, Marty, please. You have to or else . . ." I couldn't finish the sentence.

"Or else what?" He pushed to hear me say it aloud.

"You know what."

"All right. I'm sorry, God," he huffed.

"Now say you didn't mean it."

"I didn't mean it." His words were hardly sincere, though all that mattered was that he had said them, that God had heard him.

The whistle for the steel mill wailed, signaling the shift change.

"Now can we go?" Martin asked.

"We can go."

I had to pry myself up from my knees. The cold had nearly frozen me in place. I envisioned myself being trapped there in prayer like a statue, an icy reminder to other children not to do what I had done. The reflection of the neon cross bobbed on the river's surface, bidding us farewell.

I TOOK MARTIN BACK HOME the short route, down River Road. Along the way, we passed the crumbling house where the old woman lived. At night, the decrepit facade was even more forbidding. No lights shone from inside. The house appeared empty.

"See that house," I said. "There's a lady who lives in there who I've never seen before."

"Uh-huh." Martin was uninterested and still mad at me for what I'd made him do.

"No, really. I've never seen her in town or at the market or at church or anywhere. It's strange, don't you think?"

"Maybe you didn't really see her."

"What do you mean?"

"I heard that house is empty. That nobody lives there. So maybe you saw a lady at the house, but she wasn't really *there*."

"She was too. I brought a delivery to her. She took it right out of my hand."

"Did she say anything to you?"

I tried to recall if she'd spoken, then remembered that the woman hadn't actually uttered a word to me. "No, she didn't."

"Then maybe it was a ghost."

"She's not a ghost," I protested. "She was real. I saw her."

Martin shrugged indifferently as we passed the house, leaving it alone in the night. He was trying to scare me the way I'd scared him by suggesting that he would go to hell for what he'd said about our father. The thought that what I saw wasn't real, that the woman I had encountered could be a ghost, perched in my mind until we reached the apartment.

Our plates were set out and the food was already on them. My mother had chopped the fish into small hunks, making it almost unrecognizable—*almost*.

"Go wash up," she said.

Martin paused briefly to regard the plates. Despite my mother's attempt to conceal the food, he saw it for exactly what it was.

"Go on now," she added. "It's already getting cold."

We did as we were told and joined her at the table. By then, the food was indeed cold, which made it even harder to stomach. My mother ate quickly and kept her eyes on her plate. Both Martin and I picked at our food, poking at it and moving it around on the plate rather than consuming it. I split each piece of fish into bits and tried to hide them under a crust of bread. Martin made no such effort. He corralled all of the fish into the center of his plate, then left it there, uneaten, in a display of protest.

"If you're done, put your dishes in the sink," my mother said.

Together, we all cleared and cleaned the dishes, then Martin took out the lamb book he'd borrowed from the library and began to read. My mother disappeared into her bedroom and shut the door, leaving me with nothing to do. I fiddled with a loose part of the hem on my skirt until I grew desperate enough to get out one of my textbooks and flip through it. I wasn't reading. I just needed some way to occupy myself.

The evening dragged on in maddening silence. The air was churning with the unsaid. I could feel it roiling against my skin and raising the hair on my arms. When I couldn't look at the textbook a second longer, I went and stood at the window. The cold pressed itself through the glass. Shadows floated in the windows across the alley. Silence could be worse than any slammed door or sudden outburst. Silence burned slowly, like the coal in the stove, and the longer it went on, the louder it got.

I sighed hard to break the quiet, to remind myself that silence wasn't all there was, and my breath steamed the window, creating a blank page of glass. As it faded, I raised my finger and prepared to write my name. Then came a hard pounding on the door. Martin snapped up from his book.

"Don't answer it," Martin implored. "Wait for her."

"But?"

He guessed what I was thinking, that my mother might be

sleeping and if there was another knock, she would blame us for letting it wake her.

"I'll get it," my mother said, appearing from the bedroom still fully dressed. She smoothed back her hair before she opened the door.

It was Leonard. He was sweaty and breathing hard, like he'd run to our apartment from someplace else. He blinked at my mother, fumbling for what to say. I wondered if he had expected me to answer the door and was thrown when he saw her instead.

He muttered something in Polish and glanced at me, almost apologetically, then dropped his eyes and waited for my mother to answer.

"Go home, Leonard," she instructed softly.

He shuffled in place, debating what he should do next. He looked at me again, woefully. Leonard was scared.

"Go on," my mother said.

Leonard took a step backward into the alley, eyes fixed on mine as the door swung closed, blotting him from view. My mother didn't turn around right away. She seemed to be staring at the spot in the doorway where Leonard had stood. When she finally swiveled around, her expression was intent, as if she was reining in her thoughts and collecting herself.

"It's time for bed. Go and change into your nightclothes."

"But—" Martin began.

My mother flashed him a look warning him to mind her. He folded his book closed as commanded and dug his nightclothes out from under our pillow.

I was still standing by the window and I could see Leonard

outside. He was lingering on our stoop, confused, his head hanging low. After a minute, he lumbered off.

"You too," my mother said. She ushered me away from the window with a flick of her head.

Martin and I brushed our teeth side by side at the sink in the washroom. Real toothpaste was expensive, so we used pure baking soda instead. The tart taste of the baking soda always lingered in our mouths no matter how much water we washed it down with.

"What's going on?" Martin whispered, his mouth full.

"I don't know. All I know is that I want this day to be over."

"Me too," he confessed with a glance back at the tub.

My mother was waiting for us when we got out of the washroom. "Now your prayers."

"I think I've prayed enough for today," Martin mumbled.

Each night we would kneel in front of the cot, hands together, and bow our heads in prayer. We rattled off our prayers in Polish. That was my mother's rule, as though saying them in English would have dampened the meaning. Normally, I would stare at the ceiling as I recited them. Looking up always seemed more appropriate than looking down or closing my eyes. As I said my prayers that evening, my gaze drifted over to my mother. She was sitting at the table and had taken out the shirt she was fixing for my father, but she wasn't sewing. The shirt lay in her lap, untouched, while her eyes remained locked on some unseen, skyward point. She appeared to be drinking in our prayers and letting them fill her.

Where are you? I wanted to ask her. *Why aren't you here?*

My voice momentarily trailed off and Martin elbowed me to

keep going. We finished with a feeble, "Amen." Martin waited for my mother to tell us to get up. When she didn't, he turned around to find out why and caught her staring at the wall.

"What are you looking at?" he asked.

"Nothing," she said, hastily lifting the shirt from her lap to make it look as if she was sewing.

Martin inspected the wall, searching for whatever had held her attention.

"Go to sleep," she told us. "It's time for bed."

She gave the coals in the stove a final poke, rousing what little heat she could, then shut off the lights and strode into the bedroom. The dying coals slumped and crackled in the stove as a dense darkness billowed in the room. I kept my eyes open until they could adjust. Soon the moonlight from the window was enough to see by. It cast a pale shaft of light into the room, showing me what I had not seen before. There was a mark on the wall, a faint yet perfectly square shadow where the painting of the Black Madonna had hung. With a jolt, I realized I had forgotten about the Black Madonna. How could I have, I wondered, given all I had already done to retrieve it? It was possible to forget things, no matter how necessary or important, even when they were right before your eyes. That was what had happened with the Black Madonna. And that was what had happened with my mother. We were her children, but we had faded into the far reaches of her peripheral vision, and nothing we did to clamor or claw our way back into her line of sight would work.

SOMETIME LATER, my mother padded out of her bedroom and into the washroom. She had sent us to bed so early that Martin and I were both still awake. We listened as she washed her face.

"Are you tired?" he whispered.

"Are you?"

"Kind of. But kind of not."

"Do you want me to tell you about the dogs some more?"

I had been passing along all of the details I'd learned about Mr. Beresik's dogs to Martin, weaving them into an ongoing tale. He liked to hear about their names and what color they were and how they were trained, although I spared him the stories of their fights. I never told him that was why Mr. Beresik kept them.

"Okay. I could hear about the dogs."

The faucet in the washroom squealed to a stop and we waited for my mother to reappear. Instead the water came back on, this time in the bathtub.

"Do you think she's taking a bath this late at night?"

"I guess so," I said, but I hoped my mother was running the water in the bath to clean it and wipe away the scales left by the fish so Martin wouldn't have to see them.

"That's an awful lot of water," Martin declared.

The minutes crept by and I began to get nervous. A horrible idea started slinking around my mind. A year earlier, the police had been called to Mrs. Koshchushko's apartment. She had run a bath, submerged herself in the balmy water, and slit one of her wrists with a shaving razor. Her son found her and dragged her out of the tub, naked, wet, and half conscious. He tied a dishrag around her wrist, then went for help. She did not die, of course, but she was left with the winding scar of the hasty stitches that a doctor had used to close her wrist. Martin did not know of the incident and I had only heard of it because I was in the bathroom at school when two girls were gossiping about it. I wasn't sure if my parents knew or if people in town were aware either. With so many secrets in such a small place, it was no wonder that some fell through the cracks.

"Do you think she fell asleep in there?" Martin asked.

I pictured Mrs. Koshchushko drifting off in a pool of pinkish water, her soul draining out of her. I vaulted out of bed, startling Martin and hurling the covers to our feet.

"What are you doing? Don't go in there," he urged. My hand flew for the knob. I was about to turn it. "Don't," Martin pleaded.

I stopped myself, held my breath and pressed my ear to the door. A steady drip from the faucet was all I could make out.

"But what if—"

"What if what?"

I couldn't tell him what I feared. Martin gathered up the blankets from where I had kicked them. "Come back to bed. She'll be out soon."

My feet carried me back to the cot and I climbed in over Martin.

"What's the matter with you?"

"I don't know. Nothing."

Martin snorted quickly, sensing the lie. "Let's just go to sleep. Tomorrow things will be better."

I wanted to believe him. However, I couldn't fall asleep that night for hours. I was waiting for a sound, even the faintest hint, to assure me that my mother was still in there and that she was still alive. The tension made me restless, though I wouldn't dare move, not a muscle. Martin was sleeping and I was afraid to wake him. I was also afraid that even a brief shift in weight might obscure the noise I awaited. My neck stiffened into a solid, unrelenting cramp and the muscles tingled with pinpricks of pain. It was a strange sensation, like a twinkling of lights under the flesh, and I pictured myself glowing in the dark apartment, as though my skin were made of stars. After hours of waiting, I must have plunged into sleep. I bolted awake in the dead of night and craned to see through the darkness.

The door to the washroom was open. The door to my parents' bedroom was closed. That meant that my mother had returned to bed. I sank back against the wall, relieved, then a feeling overtook me, one far worse than dread. The sudden pain in my bladder almost doubled me over. I had to brace myself against the bed frame to gather my strength so I could climb over Martin without waking him.

As I forced my feet into my boots, worry began its steady climb from my belly to my brain. I gulped it back down. I took the roll of toilet paper from the shelf by the door where we kept it and hurried out into the frigid night air without my coat. The cramping was so violent it made me forget my self-consciousness about being seen in my nightclothes.

The alley was dark. No light shone in any of the windows. The moon was obscured, bound in dense clouds. I dashed around the side of the apartment, the tips of my toes barely touching the ground, barely breaking the frosty outer crust of the mud.

The door to the outhouse was ajar. I gave it one hard, warning kick, and when there was no sign of fleeing rats, I flung open the door and slid inside without taking the time to shut it all the way behind me. The burning soreness in my bladder released and subsided. It was like waking from a bad dream. I felt conscious again. I wiped myself, pushed my nightdress down, and was about to run back out when I heard something, not the scurrying of feet but a thumping in a three-part beat. It was the unmistakable, plodding rhythm of Swatka Pani stalking across the mud with her cane.

She was wending her way along the back of the apartments, checking the outhouses, I guessed. It was then that I noticed I hadn't completely closed the door to the outhouse and had forgotten to lock it. I leaned close to the jamb, poised to run if I had to. Swatka Pani's pace slowed. She was mere yards away. Then came another set of footfalls. These were light and quick and coming off Third, right toward the row of outhouses. The wind was picking up, blurring the sounds from outside. The laundry on the lines was snapping. The walls of the outhouses trembled.

The wind slowed, but I could no longer hear the footsteps. Neither Swatka Pani nor the other person had gone away, but they weren't moving either. The muffled hiss of whispers rose out of the silence. Swatka Pani was talking to whomever she had encountered, though not in her normal, brittle tone. This was different.

As I strained to decipher the words as well as the voice of the other person, I let my gaze fall to the stone slab floor. Three rats had crept into the outhouse or had been inside all the while, hidden. I clamped my hand over my mouth to keep from crying out. One scurried along the wall while the others sniffed at shallow puddles on the ground. I was surrounded.

The voices outside stopped for a moment. I pinched my nostrils and held my breath, waiting, then the whispering resumed. I raised myself onto my toes and watched as one of the rats neared, boldly nosing my boot. Another rat followed, whiskers glinting. Tears boiled over onto my cheeks, each a burning bead on the chilly flesh.

The whispers grew into sharp, nasty rasps. They were speaking in Polish, but the words were running together. Then I heard one word chime over the rest.

Smierc.

It was the word for death.

My body began to quake. I was standing on my tiptoes in the freezing night air, clad only in my nightdress, and my legs were threatening to give out. The three rats had encircled me, tails snaking alongside my boots. Then, from under the wall, two more rats entered, hopping onto the stone slab and darting across the floor to join the others. A scream welled in my lungs, rising like a glass bubble. I gripped it in my throat, swallowing over and over again. I tried to stifle the chattering of my teeth, gritting them, but it was no use. I wedged the heel of my hand under my chin to drive my teeth together, but still my jaw continued to quiver. The cold had taken over.

The conversation outside ended abruptly. The voices dropped off. I held my breath again until I heard the footsteps of the other person. I leaned into the door, trying to see through the narrow crack between it and the jamb. I glimpsed a shifting shadow. The person was marching off, away, back toward Third. I could see a sliver of Swatka Pani in profile. She did not move, not for a few moments. She was watching the person leave, making sure they had gone for good. I suddenly felt a weight on my foot. Without looking, I knew what it was. One of the rats had climbed onto my boot.

The scream that had clogged my throat was replaced by the urge to retch. The rat was balancing itself on the toe of my boot and snuffling at the laces. My stomach heaved. I gritted my teeth harder and dug my icy fingers into my cheeks. Through the crack in the door, I watched the silhouette of Swatka Pani wavering, then turning. The shuffle of feet and the thud of her cane hitting the mud began again and slowly receded as she made her way back along the outhouses to her house at the end of the alley.

After that ominous cadence had died down to nothing, I jerked my nearly frozen leg with all my might and catapulted the rat into the air, hurling it against the outhouse wall. I threw myself against the door with both hands, sending it flying back on its hinges as the other rats scattered. I was running blind, my feet hitting the ground in time with the thrashing of my heart.

I ripped open the door to our apartment and the bottled-up scream bled out of my lips in a whimper. My knees buckled. I grabbed a chair to keep from falling to the floor. My body was so numb with cold, I imagined that if I fell, I would literally shatter. Soon the icy weight of my body was too much to bear. I sank to my knees and slumped on the floor.

The coal in the stove had long since burned out, yet a faint current of warmth was still drifting through the room. I lay there on the floor, letting the heat swim over my body. Even the floorboards were warm against my skin. I tried to get up, but every muscle had hardened. The only things I could move were my eyes, and the first thing I saw was the sleeping figure of my brother, his body curled tightly under the blanket, his cheek nestled deep in the pillow.

Silent sobs rippled inside my chest. Tears flowed down the

sides of my face, tracing paths along my ears and into my scalp, where I could feel them purling around each strand of hair. My flesh stung as it warmed, then I started to shiver uncontrollably. My bones were rattling inside me and my teeth were clattering. My body was no longer my own. It belonged to the cold.

As I lay there on the floor, I decided that hell was not the fiery inferno the nuns insisted it was. Hell was a frigid, desolate plain where there was no shelter, no rescue from the cold. Once the shaking let up, I crawled on my hands and knees across the floor to my bed. I didn't want to wake Martin, but the numbness left me clumsy and I ended up dragging my unwieldy legs over his. The motion shook him out of his sleep. Drowsy, he blinked at me, eyes heavy.

"Are you all right?" Martin asked.

I was too weak to answer, so I lay down beside him and huddled close.

"You're so cold," he said. "What happened?"

"Just stay next to me," I said. "That's all. Stay next to me."

I AWOKE THE NEXT MORNING to Martin tapping my shoulder, gentle yet persistent. "Please wake up," he was saying softly. "Please."

"What is it?" I asked, reluctant to open my eyes. It was as though I'd fallen asleep only seconds ago.

"Something's going on."

Sallow, watery light was draining in through the window. It must have been a little past dawn.

"Listen," Martin whispered.

From outside came the unmistakable murmur of voices, doors opening, footsteps. That would have been normal on any weekday, but it was Saturday. Martin waved me over to the window. "Come and look."

My body was still sore and stiff. When my feet touched the floor, each muscle ached with the renewed burden of carrying my own weight. I struggled to the window where Martin was waiting. He had pulled over a chair and was kneeling on top of it.

"See," he said. "Something must have happened."

Third was a flurry of activity. Women in their robes and night-dresses were standing in the alley or on each other's stoops, clutching their clothes tightly to keep warm while whispering to one another and pointing toward the far end of Third. A few children huddled close to their mothers, listening in and gawking at something down the alley that I couldn't see. Then a man in a police uniform strode by, his pace swift.

"I told you," Martin said. "The police are here."

Another policeman was at the door of one of the apartments across the alley. He was talking to a woman who had her coat on over her nightdress and rags knotted in her hair. Rollers were costly, so women used rags or even newspaper instead and slept with them on so their hair would be curly come morning. The woman shook her head at the policeman, jostling the rags, then gestured to the end of the road at the thing that we could not see.

"What are they all pointing at?"

"I don't know," Martin said.

I was going to the door to see for myself when Martin grabbed my sleeve. "What are you doing?"

"I want to see what they're all talking about."

Martin was about to warn me not to when the door to my parents' bedroom opened. "What's going on?" my mother asked, pulling her robe tightly around her waist. Her hair was tangled, her eyes dark. "What are you doing up?" Martin hurried off the chair, saying, "Something—"

The key slid in the front door and it swung open, cutting Martin off. My father charged inside. He had his coat over his arm, then hurled it aside, revealing a towel below. A bright red bloodstain was blossoming on the cloth.

"I fell. There was glass on the floor. I didn't think it was that deep at first, but . . ."

My father collapsed onto a chair and laid his bleeding arm on the table. His eyes drooped. I thought it was the pain that had weakened him, then I realized he was drunk. My mother rushed to him and realized the same.

My father's face was covered in a thin layer of soot, as it often was when he returned home from work, but there was also a long smudge of dirt running down his cheek, as if someone had taken a swing at him and grazed him. I couldn't ask him what had happened and my mother chose not to. She didn't seem to want to know.

She peeled back the towel, exposing a short but deep gash in the underside of my father's forearm. A steady stream of blood cascaded from the wound as soon as the towel was removed. Martin immediately began whimpering.

"Take your brother outside," my mother ordered.

"No, no, I won't leave," Martin protested, panic-stricken. He was gaping at my father's slashed arm, unable to move.

"Go outside," my mother shouted.

"No," Martin squalled, tears falling freely. "I don't want to go."

"Do as you're told," my father snapped.

Martin searched my father's face and found only hardness, then he turned to me. I couldn't say a word and simply implored him to go with my eyes. He burst into frantic tears as he struggled into his coat and boots, then bolted out the door, slamming it behind him.

"Get me another towel and the soap and the iodine," my mother commanded. "And that shirt I was mending. Get it and the scissors too."

I did as I was told without thinking. As soon as I set the shirt down on the table, it dawned on me what my mother was about to do. My father knew too.

"Put the kettle on," my mother instructed.

I filled the kettle and shoveled all the coal we had into the stove, stoking the fire as fast as I could while my mother pressed the clean towel firmly against my father's forearm. The force of her hand was enough to make him flinch.

"Hold it there," she told my father with reproach. She took the threaded needle from the collar of the shirt and pulled the thread even and taut.

"Is the water boiling?" she asked through clenched teeth as she bit the end off the thread and knotted it.

Slowly, the water began to bubble. I was willing the kettle to sing. Minutes passed in silence as my mother waited for my answer. Finally, the kettle wailed a single high note. "Get a pot and pour it in."

I grabbed a pot and the steaming kettle in one swift motion and delivered them to her. My mother soaped the towel and cleaned my father's wound, then used another corner of the towel to swab iodine onto the gash. My father chewed the inside of his cheek, anticipating what was to come.

"You're going to have to help me," my mother told me.

All I could do was nod and stare at the opening in my father's flesh. I moved in close to him and he turned his head to look the other way, ashamed.

My mother held out her hand to him. "Give me your matches."

He dug in his pocket and dropped the pack into her palm. She struck one and carefully ran the needle through the flame.

"You're going to have to hold each end tight so the cut stays closed," she explained without looking at me. "And keep your fingers away."

My mother didn't wait for an answer from me. She slid the needle into my father's skin, and he gnashed his teeth to keep himself from jerking his arm back. She threaded the needle through the other side of the cut, drawing the skin together and tugging it up. "Keep it tight," she reminded me.

Eyes closed, jaw clenched, my father sat as still as he could. Though he was drunk, he appeared to feel everything, from the jab of the needle to the unnatural wrenching of thread through skin.

With swift precision, my mother wove six minute stitches. She didn't glance up once to check on my father, merely kept to the task. As she tied off the last stitch, my father began to squirm. The raw pain of the procedure was making him nauseous. My mother made a triple knot, snipped the thread with the scissors, and was about to wipe the closed wound down with iodine when my father jumped up, gagging, and dashed for the sink. He coughed and spat, but did not vomit.

"I'll clean it," he mumbled over his shoulder.

My mother laid the towel next to the pot full of water and stood up. There was no thank you, no hug, no kiss, no moment between them. She removed the remaining thread from the needle, then drove it back into the collar of my father's shirt and strode into the bedroom.

The needle was still bloody and it left flecks of red on the pale blue fabric of the collar. I couldn't be sure if my mother had forgotten about the blood or if she had made the stain on purpose, a reminder to my father of what he had done and what she had done for him.

My father waited until the door to their bedroom shut to turn around. He surveyed the table, the evidence of the impromptu surgery. The towel he had come in with was laying in a lump, the blood still bright, and steam was rising off the pot of water as it cooled. He seemed unable to approach the table, almost afraid, so I took the other towel and rung it out in the water, then soaped one corner and offered it to him. He hesitantly took the towel and blotted the wound clean, putting his back to me again. That way I wouldn't see him grimacing at the pain.

"I'll get the tape," I said and my father gave a little nod. Real bandages were expensive, so my mother bought lengths of what was used as surgical tape at the time. It was white and gluey, and each time Martin or I got a cut, we dreaded the tape. Pulling it off meant practically ripping the wound back open or at least taking some skin off with the tape.

I retrieved the roll of bandaging tape and brought it to my father. He moved to take the tape from me but paused. He couldn't wrap his arm himself. He never met my gaze, only offered his forearm to me by moving it ever so slightly in my direction.

I was more afraid of bandaging my father's arm than having to hold his skin closed for my mother to sew shut. That was an urgent cause, beyond necessary, but this was more like a favor, a plea. My father needed me.

I gingerly wound the tape around his arm, careful not to wrap it too tightly. The tape made a ripping sound as it spooled off the roll, and my mother would undoubtedly have heard the noise from the other room and known what was going on. Out of the corner of my eye, I kept watch to see if she would appear at the door.

After I finished, I tried to tear off the end of the tape, but it wouldn't budge. The tape was stubbornly sticky and bent in on itself as I tugged at it. I was embarrassed that I was making a mess of such a small duty. I picked at the tape, which only made it worse, clumping the length together in a matted ball.

"Get a knife," my father said solemnly.

The phrase rattled me, yet I did as he said, choosing the smallest knife we had. He took the roll and held it out, away from his arm, leaving me room to cut.

"Go on," he told me.

I sawed at the tape, not wanting to press too hard, but it just buckled in on itself again, forcing me to work the knife faster, ashamed that I still couldn't get this right. My father was starting to lose his patience. I had to do something. In one brisk stroke, I brought the knife down on the edge of the tape, severing it instantly.

Freed from the tape, my father leaped up. The front door opened and Martin peeked in. He was about to speak, then he saw me holding the knife and our father hovering over me. Nobody said anything. Martin stared.

"Swatka Pani is dead," he announced.

"What?" My father's arm fell to his side.

I reeled at the news. Snippets of the previous night streaked through my mind—Swatka Pani's cane thumping in the mud, her foreboding silhouette, her frenzied whispers.

"Did you hear that?" Martin said, looking past me. "She's—"

"I heard you," my mother replied. She was standing in the doorway to the bedroom, only half visible behind the partly open door.

My father snatched his coat and marched outside yanking down his sleeve to cover the bandaged wound. Martin followed on his heels. I was about to join them, but turned back. My mother was staring right at me, as if she knew that was exactly what I would do, like she had made me do it. She was still hidden halfway behind the door, keeping it in front of her, and she was holding me with her eyes, refusing to let go.

It was the chance I had pined for, for her to want to see me, to look at me as though I was there. An unnameable joy crested in my heart, a feeling so fragile I was afraid to believe it.

Then it was gone as quickly as it had come. I watched my mother grip the side of the door and shut it. That was how she slipped away from me. I must have stood in that spot for minutes without moving. I wasn't sure what had happened, what I had done to get her to see me, then to lose her. I felt as if I was crying, wailing and screaming with every fiber of my being, but I wasn't even blinking.

———

I DO NOT REMEMBER LEAVING the house. The next thing I knew I had my coat on over my nightdress and was walking over to join Martin and my father, who were gathered at the end of Third with a growing crowd. Other people were rushing past me, racing to see what all the commotion was about. Third was jangling with noise and movement. The alley most people feared to traverse was now nearly packed.

"What's going on?" one man asked.

"Somebody killed her," a woman answered.

"Good riddance," another woman snorted. "I hope they find the man who did it so I can kiss him." A few other women laughed.

"Killed her down at the river," a man announced as he passed me.

"Pushed her down the stairs," someone else offered.

The crowd was pooled around the front of Swatka Pani's clapboard house, huddled close to her stub of a porch. One policeman was guarding the open front door. Two others could be seen through the windows, searching the house. I wove my way into the crowd next to Martin. He was sticking close to my father's side and was almost on top of him. I could tell that Martin wanted to hold his hand but knew better than to reach for it.

"The police are inside. Everybody says they're looking for clues," Martin pronounced, pleased to have something to report.

"Clues to what?"

"To who killed Swatka Pani."

"But I thought someone said she was killed at the river."

Martin shrugged. He was too intent on enjoying the excitement to bother with an answer.

When I'd first heard Martin say the words *Swatka Pani is dead*, they had melted into the air, into nothing. It wasn't real. However, once I saw the people and heard them talking, alarm wound its way into my brain and knotted itself there.

"What if she just fell down the stairs?" I asked. "Maybe nobody killed her."

Martin rolled his eyes, exasperated. "Swatka Pani doesn't go to the river. Everybody knows that."

It was true. Nothing could get her to go to the river. At least, nothing in the past.

"Then why was she there?" I asked.

Martin preferred asking questions, not answering them, and he was getting tired of having his attention pulled away from watching the policeman on the porch, who was simply standing there with his hands on his hips, trying to look important.

"I don't know," Martin snorted.

"Quiet," my father ordered. "Somebody's coming out."

Two police officers exited Swatka Pani's house empty-handed. The crowd surged forward, bombarding the officers with questions.

"Who did it?" one man shouted.

"How'd she die?" another yelled.

"You gonna catch the guy?" someone else demanded.

"Yeah, what about us?" a woman sang out. "There's a killer out there. What are you going to do about it?"

Nods and murmurs rippled through the crowd, yet the policemen said nothing. The one who was standing on the porch led the others down the steps and pushed his way through the onlookers, saying, "Make way. Make way," in Polish.

The crowd pressed farther in. More questions flared and went unanswered. The police officers climbed into the police car that was waiting at the end of the alley. It was almost silly that they had driven. The police station was a minute's walk from the alley. The only thing closer was the Silver Slipper. The police car just added to the show.

As the policemen took off, the people booed them. Some muttered curses. Yet, we all remained there, watching them drive away.

After the police were out of sight, nobody knew what to do with themselves. People milled around outside Swatka Pani's house, whispering speculation, then the group began to disperse. Women hustled their children back to their apartments while most of the men headed off to the Slipper, eager to break the news to their friends and trump up the tale of what little they had seen.

"Go on back to the house," my father told us, wanting to join the other men.

"Don't leave now," Martin pleaded.

My father couldn't stand it when Martin begged. Martin's plaintive whine would always set him off, as if that wasn't what boys were supposed to do.

"You heard me," my father said, raising his voice.

"What about your dinner?" Martin was grasping at anything to change his mind.

"I'm not hungry." He was already walking away in the direction the other men had gone.

"But?"

"It's okay," I offered. "He's got to get hungry sometime."

Martin rolled his eyes, disappointed. We both knew my father wouldn't be back for hours, if at all.

"All right," Martin sighed. "We can go back now."

"You sure? We can stay if you want."

"No, there's nothing to see."

And there wasn't. All that was there was the same house we had seen every day of our lives, the house we never dared play near, the house we ran past if it was getting dark. Swatka Pani was dead. It was a concept I couldn't grasp. The fact that she had been killed, that someone had murdered her only hours after I had seen her, defied my comprehension. The long shadow of the stranger was all I could think of.

A few men were still loitering outside Swatka Pani's porch. I overheard one say that they were going to the river to see where it had happened.

"Let's follow them," I whispered to Martin.

"Why?" he protested. "I heard the policeman say they took her away to the big hospital in Pittsburgh. Anyway, we're not supposed to go to the river."

"Don't you just want to see?"

Curiosity made him relent. "I guess."

We trailed behind the men, staying far enough back that they wouldn't notice us.

"What if they get mad that we followed them?" Martin asked.

"What can they be mad about? You said she's not there any-more. So really, we're only going to look at the river. What harm can that do?"

Martin frowned but came along anyway.

At the river, the men studied the stairway, shaking the railing to test it and trying to gauge the distance down to the water. Beyond them, the cross stood on the mountaintop, a bright form against the dawn sky. The men were huddled in a tight circle, their backs to us. I edged nearer, trying to hear what they were saying.

"Too close," Martin whispered, pulling me back. Still, I pushed in closer, drawing him along with me against his will.

"Forty feet, easy," one man said.

"Maybe even fifty," another corrected.

"She could've slipped. The steps might have iced over in the night."

"Railing's rickety as hell too."

"Nasty way to go. A fall down these steps would have broken every bone she had."

"Mean old bitch probably did slip."

"Just proves that God'll get you if the devil doesn't first."

The conversation was upsetting Martin. He tried dragging me away. As he did, he slid on some gravel. One of the men spun around, then the rest.

"What are you doing here?" one demanded.

Neither Martin nor I replied.

"This isn't no place for you. Go on home," another told us.

"It's just the river," I said.

One man was about to argue but stopped himself. We were all thinking the same thing. This wasn't just the river anymore. It never would be again. People died in those waters all the time. It was a given that the river would claim the victims it wanted and ignore the others. Yet, we all flocked to it, offering ourselves up like sacrifices. Swatka Pani's death was different. She hadn't drowned. The river hadn't chosen her at random like it had the rest.

"Something's gone on here and it's nothing that kids should be seeing," one man declared.

"What's there to see?" I asked, knowing as well as he did that nothing tangible had changed. The stairs would still creak when you stepped on them. The railing would still shift under your weight. And the river would roll by indifferently, as always.

"There could be blood down there or something," a different man insisted. "It's not for children's eyes."

I wanted to laugh out loud. *If you only knew what my eyes have seen*, I thought.

Whatever awaited on those stairs didn't frighten me. It would be nothing compared to what I had already witnessed even in the last hour. I stood my ground, unmoving, and the men stared at me.

Martin tugged my sleeve. "Come on," he said out of the side of his mouth.

This time, I let him pull me away. Once we were halfway down River Road and far enough away, Martin laid into me. "Are you crazy? What were you thinking?"

"We had as much right to be there as they did."

"But they're grown-ups and we're not, so if they say go home, we go home."

I knew there wasn't anything down on the river's edge, but I wanted to see for myself. I wanted to see the spot where Swatka Pani had died. I wanted to be convinced that she was dead.

Martin took the lead, setting a brisk pace. He was anxious to get home. I was lagging behind, straining to remember every shred of sound I had overheard the night before. All that came to me was *smierc*.

Death.

"Hurry up," Martin called. "It's cold."

A flicker of movement caught my eye as I glanced up to answer him. The curtain in the front window of the decrepit house where the old woman lived was being drawn aside. A corner of the woman's face came into view. She was watching the men at the river.

"Look, Marty," I said, wheeling him around by the arm.

"What?"

When I spun back, the window was empty. The curtain had returned to its place.

"Did you see her? She was there. In the window."

"Who? What window?"

"The woman I told you about."

"So?" Martin said, shaking his arm free and marching on.

"Don't you want to see her? Don't you want to see that she's real?"

"No, I want to go home."

He went on ahead, leaving me alone outside the woman's house. I waited, hoping for some other sign of movement. But the house stood there as still and blank as before.

My mother was busy with the wash when we returned. She cleaned each garment by hand in the sink. The process usually took hours because she scrubbed every piece so ardently, almost unforgivingly. From that morning and on into the afternoon, my mother kept to her work, soaping and rinsing the clothes with an all-consuming fervor. She was rubbing the cake of soap into the clothes, driving it into every fiber of the cloth, then she thrust each garment underwater, rinsing it of soap, then wrung it dry, squeezing out each drop of water. She seemed to have forgotten we were there with her in the apartment. She simply continued washing.

The rest of the day inched by, one long hour after another. Our only distraction was the radio. My mother hadn't let us play it in weeks, so the music was a balm against the quiet. I don't remember what Martin and I did. All I remember was the heavy, leaden feel of exhaustion and the fact that my father didn't return until it was nearly time for us to go to bed. We heard him on the front step, talking to someone in the alley, then at last, my mother pulled the stopper from the sink and the water began to drain. A heaping basketful of wet clothes sat at her feet.

"Hang these while I fix supper," she told me.

I was hungry and tired and tempted to refuse, though I didn't dare. The weight of the overloaded basket was almost too much for me. I heaved it into my arms and struggled to open the door. Neither Martin nor my mother noticed, so neither came to help. I didn't want to put the basket back down for fear of not being able to pick it up again.

Gravity was taking over and the basket was slowly inching its way down my stomach and over my knees. My fingers slid frantically over the knob. Without warning, the door opened, bumping the basket and jarring me backward. It was my father, stunned to find me there, blocking his way. I rushed past him and into the alley, lugging the basket.

It was practically dark by then, too late to be hanging wash. The wet clothes would probably freeze, then we would have to leave them there for an extra day to let the hardened fabric thaw. Afterward, the clothes wouldn't feel the same. All of the softness would have been beaten out of them by wind and frost.

Night was gusting in, rattling the clothesline and making it difficult for me to get the clothes to stay on it. One clothespin popped off and dropped into the mud, and another, then I would have to wipe them clean on the side of the basket. With every fallen clothespin, my frustration mounted and I had to fight to keep from crying. The outhouse was entering my peripheral vision as I worked my way down the clothesline. Once I reached the outhouse, the first tear fell. I cried until I'd finished hanging every piece of clothing my mother had washed. I wasn't sure why I was crying. I would not miss Swatka Pani. I didn't mourn her death. Then I realized that that was the very reason for my tears. She was dead and I didn't care.

I didn't want to go back inside, yet I couldn't bear to stay out there either. I blotted my cheeks on the sleeve of my sweater and stared into the wind to dry my eyes, then returned to the apartment.

"Wash up. Supper's on," my mother said as I entered.

I ducked into the washroom and Martin followed. "Were you crying?" he asked.

"It was just cold out."

"You were crying. I can tell."

"So what if I was," I answered, splashing water on my face.

"Were you crying because of Swatka Pani?"

"No," I scoffed, though it was another lie.

Swatka Pani had embodied every fear I'd ever known. Each time she skulked down Third, her cane piercing the mud, I knew what was coming. Her presence would sound a warning in my mind. With her gone, there would no longer be a sign, no signal. All things frightful could now roam freely on the alley. I cried because I would no longer be able to see them coming.

"I'm not going to cry about Swatka Pani," Martin declared. "I'm glad she's gone."

"Don't say that," I scolded with a glance upward. "He can hear you. God can always hear you."

"Yeah, and I bet He knew Swatka Pani was going to hell, so he let the devil take her. That's who killed her, you know. The devil. He came to collect her the way she comes to collect our rent money."

"Martin, stop it. Stop saying things like that. It's not true. That's not how it works."

"How do you know?"

I stormed out of the washroom to avoid answering. Both of my parents looked up from the table. "What's going on in there?" my father asked.

"Nothing. It was nothing."

I took my seat at the table and Martin followed. We dropped our heads to pray over the meal of chicken, onions, and potatoes. My father lowered his head and mouthed the words as usual, like a song he was singing only to himself. My mother was always the loudest, enunciating each syllable crisply, her voice overriding ours. That day she was murmuring the prayer. Even Martin's small voice boomed over hers.

My father lit a cigarette, as he did before each meal, then we all began to eat. The radio was still playing and a news program was on. Two men were discussing the German army and their steady spread across Europe.

"Filthy Germans," my father muttered, responding to a comment one of the newscasters had made.

"Why are they filthy?" Martin asked.

"They're greedy. They want everything they can put their hands on."

Martin still didn't understand. "Does that make their hands dirty?"

That was one question too many for my father. "No, damn it, I don't mean dirty. Filthy's just an expression. It doesn't mean that they're really filthy." He took an irritated drag on his cigarette and exhaled a wrathful stream of smoke across the table.

"Well, I didn't know," Martin pouted.

"Well, now you do."

My father pushed aside his plate and mechanically finished his cigarette while he listened to the newscasters bicker over where the German army would head next, south to France or east and deeper into Europe. He nodded his head when he agreed with what the men were saying or clucked his disagreement with his tongue.

The radio program came to an end and music returned. An upbeat tune wafted through the apartment, then was interrupted by a knock on the door. My father grudgingly got up to answer it, as though he'd been in the middle of something.

A policeman was on the other side of the door. "Evening," he said in Polish. "Come by to ask about . . ." He gestured toward the end of the alley and Swatka Pani's house. "You mind if I come in?"

The policeman wore a long, heavy overcoat and stood almost a head taller than my father, who backed away to let him enter. The officer's presence threw the rest of the apartment out of scale. He seemed enormous in the small room.

"All of you here this morning?" he asked.

Martin and I looked to my mother, who deferred to my father.

He nodded, fast and silent, then touched his shirtsleeve to make sure it was down, covering his bound wound.

"What about last night?"

"I work the fourth shift at the mill," my father explained.

"So you weren't home until this morning?"

All my father gave him was another nod, then the policeman swiveled on his heel. "What about you?" he asked, addressing my mother, Martin, and me. "You were home, weren't you?"

Martin and I waited for my mother to reply. She merely nodded, though that appeared to be a feat on her part. She sat motionless in her chair, barely blinking.

"Hear or see anything out of the ordinary?"

Martin piped in. "What's out of the ordinary?"

The policeman warmed a bit and took a step closer to Martin. "It means something different, like you haven't seen or heard before."

Martin considered the definition, then shook his head.

"What about you?" the officer asked me. I glanced at my mother. Her body was there, but she had vanished. I shook my head as well.

"And you?" he said, addressing her again.

"No," she answered, her voice thin. "I didn't see anything."

"I'll leave you to your supper then."

The policeman closed the door behind him, then Martin hopped up from his chair to watch him from the window.

"Sit down," my father told him.

"But—"

"I said to sit down."

Martin returned to the table while my father hastened into his overcoat.

"Where are you going?" Martin asked.

"I've got something I've got to see about."

"What *something*?" Martin pressed.

"Something, is all. I'll be back."

Once my father was gone, Martin folded his arms heavily. "He's always going *somewhere*. Why can't *somewhere* be here?"

My mother glanced up from her plate. "I don't know," she said. We waited for her to go on, but that short phrase seemed to have drained everything from her. She set down her fork, as though even that small weight was too much for her to handle.

"I've got to lie down for a bit," she said, then she drifted into her room.

"I don't like this," Martin fretted. "She always helps us with the dishes."

"Maybe she's tired," I offered, though her sudden departure alarmed me too.

"Or maybe she's scared."

"Scared of what?"

"Scared of the man who killed Swatka Pani. Maybe she thinks he's going to come after us."

"That's not going to happen," I said, grabbing my plate.

Martin trailed after me with his plate in hand. "How do you know?"

"It just isn't. Now help me with the dishes."

"You always say things like that. You act like you know the answer for sure but you never explain it." Martin put his plate down hard, causing a resounding ping. "You're just like he is. Always saying things that you won't explain."

The insult stung, so much so that I couldn't reply. It was true. I was constantly asserting truths for which I had no backing, no real facts, more to protect Martin than anything else, but he'd seen through me. My intentions were good. Yet that wasn't enough.

Together, Martin and I washed the dishes without speaking. I was scraping and rinsing them while he dried. We finished quickly, and for once, part of me wished there were more dishes to clean, wished we could keep washing until things had gotten comfortable again and no one's feelings were hurt.

WE WENT TO BED, lying back to back in an uneasy silence. My mother never left the bedroom and I didn't hear my father come in, though he was the first one up the following morning. I awoke to his rustling in the washroom and his muffled cursing. When he stalked out of the washroom, cigarette bobbing at the corner of his mouth, the noise woke Martin as well. The bandages were hanging from my father's arm and he was trying to rewrap them, but the tape had tangled into a snarled mess.

"I can help you," Martin said, scampering out of bed.

"No, your sister'll do it," my father ordered, brushing Martin off. "Come round here and get this on straight for me." The command was directed at me.

Martin climbed back into bed to sulk while I pried the mangled tape from my father's arm and rebandaged the wound. Dried blood was crusted along the ridge of the cut and had stained the white thread of the stitches a blackish brown. The cut had become more gruesome than it was when it was fresh.

"Maybe we should wash it again," I suggested.

"No, not now. After church," my father said. "Go on and finish."

I took care to rewrap the tape and was about to set the roll down so I could cut it when my father waved Martin over, saying, "Get your sister the knife."

"She can get it."

"What did I tell you?" My father's tone was enough to send Martin trotting to the cupboard to get the knife.

"Here." Martin laid the knife on the table loudly.

"Get over here," my father snapped, putting down his cigarette. Martin remained where he was, clutching the side of the table. "I said come over here."

Martin reluctantly approached. Once he was within arm's reach, my father snatched him by the shoulder with his good hand, yanking Martin in close. Both Martin and I were then the same distance from my father, yet there was a world of difference in our positions.

"I won't have any of that back talk," my father said fiercely. "Now put your Sunday clothes on and get ready for church."

Martin squirmed out of my father's grip and went and hid in the washroom.

"Finish this up," my father instructed. I listened for some trace of guilt in his voice, but heard none. Martin's comment from the night before burned even hotter. I didn't want to be compared to my father or be like him. At that moment, I didn't want to share a single trait with him.

I picked up the knife, grasping it firmly. Temptation welled up and possibility pooled in my mind. The previous night I had held the knife with delicate purpose. That morning, I was gripping it.

My father took a long drag off his cigarette as I ran the blade over the bandage. With each stroke, the knife edged closer to his arm. He was oblivious, staring down at the floor. All thoughts ceased as I watched the progress of the blunt blade. The tape was giving way. The cut was arcing downward, closer to the exposed underside of my father's forearm. He flinched when he saw how close it was and the tip of the blade nearly nicked him just as it cut through the tape.

"Jesus!" he shouted, standing abruptly. "Weren't you watching? You could've cut me."

My mother threw open the bedroom door. "What happened?"

My father jabbed out his cigarette. "Nothing."

Martin was watching from the washroom. I could tell from his face that he'd seen everything. He didn't know that I had done it for him.

But had I? I wondered.

I tried to trace the origin of the urge that had been flowing through me, but like a breeze, it was gone as quickly as it had come.

It was the lies. They were changing me. By lying, I believed I had opened some sort of floodgate. Every fear imaginable suddenly became possible. Was it my fault my father had gotten cut the day before? Was it me who had made my mother recede from us even further? Was it my hatred for Swatka Pani that had killed her?

I started praying in my mind, hoping God would hear me.

Our Father, who art in heaven.

My mother came out of the bedroom. "What's the matter with you?" she asked, more out of habit than suspicion.

Hallowed be thy name.

"Get dressed for church," she said. She put the kettle on the stove for coffee and began to prepare breakfast. "And help your brother with his clothes."

The prayer continued in my head, drowning out my mother's voice.

Thy kingdom come. Thy will be done.

My father went into the bedroom to change. Martin was still standing in the doorway of the washroom in his pajamas. He took a step back when I approached.

On earth as it is in heaven.

I took his Sunday clothes from the closet, a white button-down shirt, a pair of gray trousers, and an ill-fitting blue blazer. The elbows on the blazer had thinned from wear and the cuffs had been shortened and re-hemmed so many times that the fabric buckled from the uneven underpinnings. Most young boys' church clothes weren't much different, though that didn't make Martin look any less pitiful in the outfit.

Martin hesitantly took the garments from me and closed the door partway to undress. I waited outside as he climbed into his clothes and struggled into the blazer. Through the crack in the doorway, I saw my brother as I had never seen him before, as a little boy wearing a grown man's outfit. Those clothes said more about the way he lived, the way we both lived, than I could ever bring myself to speak aloud.

Martin stepped out of the washroom, already itching to remove the blazer.

"I hate wearing this."

"I know. But you have to. You don't have any choice."

For once, Martin did not question my tone of voice or press me for the deeper truth of what I'd said. He did not see beyond the plain meaning of those words.

WE WALKED TOGETHER, as a family, to church. My father was in his one good jacket, and under her coat, my mother was wearing her church dress, a maroon wool ensemble that had a matching sash. Though simple in cut, it was a beautiful dress that appeared as if it had been tailor-made to fit my mother when, in fact, she had purchased it secondhand. She wore her good gloves, the kidskin ones that made her fingers seem long and slender. With her elegant dress and gloves and her hair pinned up in a sleek bun, my mother looked completely out of place strolling next to the rest of us, and even more out of place on Third.

With each step, my guilty conscience weighed on me more heavily. As my boots broke through the top of the thawing mud, I thought I might get sucked down into it and drown right then and there. God could see me and He could see into the farthest reaches of my heart, always. He knew what I had done. I was terrified that I would be struck down the instant I stepped through the church doors. The fear gripped me tighter and tighter as we joined the procession of other families making their way to Saint Ladislaus for Mass.

My father stopped outside on the church steps to finish his cigarette.

"I'll be inside in a minute."

My mother ushered Martin and me through the door, and I clenched my eyes shut in anticipation as I crossed the threshold. But there was no lightning, no pain, no thunderous voice condemning me for what I had done. I wasn't sure whether to be relieved or even more frightened.

My mother guided us to our usual spot in the far-right-hand side of the church, halfway from the front. We always sat in the same place. We often arrived early enough that we could have taken seats in the very first pew, but my mother never let us. She claimed that from that one particular vantage point where we sat, we had the best view of Father Svitek as well as the rest of the church, including the statue of the patron saint. Sometimes Martin would put up an argument, suggesting we try sitting somewhere else to show that this one spot wasn't the best after all. He would go from pew to pew, sliding along the seats, testing each position out while my mother remained, steadfast, in her favorite place. Eventually, he would give up and return, unwilling to concede that she was right, yet too afraid to sit by himself to prove his point.

That day as we took our seats, Martin offered no resistance. He plunked down on the pew and resigned himself to the service. I sat beside him, then my mother filed in after me, leaving room for my father at the end. This was the way it went every weekend.

The habit of coming to worship was so deeply ingrained in all of us that we could have been blindfolded and we still would have ended up in those same positions.

The church slowly filled. The musty-sweet smell of incense wafted through the air in waves, churned up by the people entering and taking their seats. The hum of moving feet and hushed voices was resonating off the stone walls, making it feel as if the pews were vibrating. The whispers mixed together, though there was no doubt what everyone was talking about. The hiss of Swatka Pani's name punctuated the din.

Father Svitek mounted the pulpit, draped in his vestments, missal in hand, and the church quieted. My heartbeat began to bellow in my ears as I prepared to bear the consequence of my lies. Perhaps Father Svitek would call me out by name and unveil my sins to everyone. Perhaps he would make me stand at the front of the church, an example for all to see. Instead, Father Svitek simply began the service in his usual monotone. He went on to deliver a bland sermon on the virtue of being humble and the danger of pride. Everyone in the church appeared to be expecting Father Svitek to mention Swatka Pani's murder, to rail against the evil deed, but he did not.

The priest brought his sermon to a close and the organist played as the altar boys, bearing the host, made their way down the main aisle. People turned to one another in the pews, wondering why Father Svitek had not spoken about Swatka Pani's death. They got in line to receive communion, whispering all the while. It was clear that Father Svitek had not been told.

My father rose to get in line for communion while my mother

lagged behind, letting me get in front of her. Martin was too young to receive the host. He grumbled something about being left out, then slumped back in the pew and swung his legs killing time.

The line for communion crawled forward. I couldn't see over my father's shoulder to tell how far back we were. I didn't want to know.

Soon we were at the front of the line and my father was receiving the host. I was trembling as Father Svitek took the wafer from a plate and held it up to me.

"The body of Christ."

I was terrified of opening my mouth. The instant I parted my lips, Father Svitek forced the wafer between them. The wafer lay on my tongue like a coin, refusing to dissolve. I thought I might choke on it.

The body of Christ.

I almost started to cry as I made my way back to my seat. I was too afraid to close my jaws and force the wafer against my tongue. I thought it might splinter into shards and cut my throat. However much I believed I deserved it, I was still scared. I passed the statue of Saint Ladislaus and, for an instant, he appeared to be looking me in the eye, his gaze unrelenting.

As I sat down, the pipe organ in the rafters groaned to life. The choir started to sing. The voices rang out in dense, indecipherable Latin, raining down on us as the melody of the music drifted up into the domed ceiling. My jaw ached from holding it open. I couldn't fight the reflex to swallow any longer. I inhaled hard and tried to gulp down the wafer, only to have it melt like candle wax and coat my tongue. I swallowed over and over again, desperate to rid myself of its papery taste, but it persisted, like a poison.

The choir's song came to a close, then people began to gather their coats and shuffle toward the door. Others stayed on, talking among themselves and nodding in Father Svitek's direction. Martin jumped up, eager to leave.

"Can we go now?" he asked.

"Put your coat on," my father told him, scanning the crowd, preoccupied.

Everybody was waiting to see if someone would go up to Father Svitek and tell him about Swatka Pani, though nobody approached him. We had all put our coats on except for my mother. She hadn't moved, hadn't taken her eyes off the tall cross staked high at the front of the church.

"Aren't you going to put your coat on?" Martin asked her. The question roused her. "Here, I'll help you," he offered, taking hold of one of her coat sleeves.

My mother stood up, drawing the coat along with her and out of Martin's grasp. "I've got it," she said.

My father leaned over and whispered something in her ear. Martin zeroed in on the exchange.

"Father Svitek doesn't know. That's what you think, right?" Martin was proud of his deduction.

My father hesitated before he answered. "No, seems nobody's told him."

Martin faced my mother. "Maybe you should tell him."

She blinked and didn't respond.

"He'll find out," my father said. "It's not our business."

"But—" Martin began.

"Put your coat on, I said," my father ordered.

"It *is* on," Martin replied.

My father headed for the door and Martin skirted past my mother to catch up with him. I stood alone with my mother as she cast her eyes around the church. Though it was a place she saw every day of her life, it was as if she was trying to soak up every inch of it and memorize it, as though she would never see it again.

THAT MONDAY MORNING, my mother took Martin and me to school on her way to work, as always. She was attempting to act normal, but her pace was faster, her step out of sync with ours. Her hair was unkempt under her kerchief and her clothes hung off her differently, more loosely. Her mind was elsewhere.

"Seems like it won't be so cloudy today," she remarked as she hastened us down Third. Her attempt at cheerfulness evaporated as we neared Swatka Pani's house.

"Look," Martin cried, darting ahead of us.

He stood at the fence to Swatka Pani's garden, peeping through the slats. Someone had come in the night and pulled up all of her rosebushes. Only the thorny legs of the flowers remained, lying limply with clods of dirt still clinging to their roots.

"Somebody broke all her flowers," Martin said. "Do you see?"

My mother didn't answer right away. She was transfixed by the overturned garden. "Yes, I see."

Martin leaned into the fence. "I wonder who did it."

"Could've been anyone," my mother replied.

"Who do you think did it?" he asked me.

My mother was right. It could have been anyone. My guess was that someone from Third was responsible, maybe a teenager or a child who had been afraid of her and had come to reap one final revenge. This was a desecration.

Then I wondered, *Had I done it?*

I skimmed back through my memory, sincerely asking myself if I was the one who had destroyed Swatka Pani's garden. Though I knew full well I hadn't, I was still unsure.

"Maybe it was crazy Mrs. Koshchushko," Martin suggested since I hadn't answered his question. "Maybe she snuck over here and ripped out all of the flowers."

"That's enough," my mother said, urging us onward.

Even at school, the air crackled with whispers about Swatka Pani. The nuns were on guard, vigilantly silencing any talk about her. There were no prayers as there had been for the girl who had drowned in the river, no moment of reverence. The nuns only offered a warning, the same warning we had heard time and time again: the river was off-limits, a place of danger. It had never seemed more true.

When classes let out, I took Martin to the library as I had done each day the week before.

"I don't want to stay here," he griped.

"You know I can't take you with me."

"But I'm all alone here. And what if the man who got Swatka Pani comes to get me?"

"At the library?"

"You never know."

"First of all, you're not alone here. You have Sister Teresa. You'll be fine."

"No, I won't be. I won't be fine. I'll be alone."

"I'll try to hurry. I'll be early this time. I promise."

"Oh, all right. I'll stay here. But I won't like it."

Mr. Goceljak was talking to a man in the front of the store when I arrived at the shop that afternoon. Their discussion sounded grave. I stayed in the back room until the front bell chimed the man's departure, then Mr. Goceljak came to greet me.

"I s'pose you've heard."

I nodded that I had, then he took up a carving knife and sliced a few ribs off a small rack of meat. It must have been a calf.

"Well, you know what they say," Mr. Goceljak sighed. "God'll get you."

It was similar to what one of the men had said by the river: *God'll get you if the devil doesn't first.*

The phrase struck a hopeful chord in me. Maybe I hadn't been responsible for what had happened to Swatka Pani. Maybe God had killed her.

"Did you know her?" Mr. Goceljak asked.

"I live on Third."

"Then you must've known her all right." He wrapped the ribs

in paper, careful to tuck down the bones, and taped the package shut. "She scare you?"

"I guess."

"No shame in it. She scared most people. Not everyone, I s'pose."

I liked the idea that God might have done it and I didn't want Mr. Goceljak suggesting otherwise.

"But maybe it was God."

"Could've been. Doubt it, though. There's been talk that it was that slow boy she had working for her. You know, what's his name."

"Leonard?"

"That's him."

"It wasn't him. It couldn't have been."

"And how would you know?" Mr. Goceljak teased, sensing my distress.

I remembered Leonard's face as he stood outside the door to our apartment, so nervous and upset.

"It just wasn't."

"I'd take your word for it, only problem is, the boy hasn't been seen since it happened. People been looking and he ain't turned up." Mr. Goceljak raised his brow and tapped the carving knife in the air to make his point. "He don't have any place to go besides the Silver Slipper, and he hasn't been back."

I refused to believe that Leonard had killed Swatka Pani. I had no proof, only instinct. Both my head and my heart told me it wasn't so.

"Don't worry yourself about it," Mr. Goceljak said, stacking the pile of deliveries before me. "Just go on and get these done. Ain't many of 'em, so you'll be done early today."

The first two stops were nearby. I dropped the deliveries off in a haze, then picked up the third to check the address. It was on River Road.

I cut across town past the steel mill, jogging rather than running. I didn't have the energy to run. Then I rounded the corner onto River Road and my feet slowed as a realization descended on me. The address belonged to the woman in the crumbling house and I would have to pass the stairway down to the river to get there.

I tried to run, to blow past the stairs, commanding my legs to move, but all I could force out were a few hesitant steps. My body stalled right at the head of the stairway. All of my bravery from the other day was gone. I was no longer sure I wanted to see what, if anything, was down there.

A breeze welled up off the water, pressing me backward, away from the river, then it curled around and blew against my neck, forcing me forward. Below lay the stairway. The wooden boards weaved down the steep slope to the shoreline, undamaged, unmarked, unchanged. Their plainness was shocking. The railing was not broken. The steps hadn't splintered. They were just as they had always been. The same was true of the river. The water was still an opaque gray, the color of the sky above, and it coursed by with unrelenting regularity.

I was ashamed of myself for being so afraid. What hurt more was the dull ache of reality, that nothing had changed. No trace of the murder remained. The ground was not harder. The wind was not colder. The sun was no less bright. The world had chugged on, ambivalent about what had happened, uninterested in any of us.

THE WIND OFF THE RIVER dwindled as I trudged up the rotting stoop of the old woman's house. The front door opened right as I was about to knock on it. Startled, I backed away. A wedge of the woman's face appeared behind the door.

"Here," I sputtered, holding the delivery out to her.

She raised her hand, then retracted it. I was too far back. She couldn't reach beyond the confines of the house to take the package from me. There was less than a foot of space between us, but for her, it was a vast chasm.

"Sorry," I said, inching in close enough to pass her the parcel. Then, in that instant when we were both holding the package at the same time, the woman looked me in the eye and whispered, "I know who did it."

"What?" I had heard her clearly, but didn't trust my ears.

"I know," the woman said, then she shut the door.

Her ominous sincerity sent me bolting off the steps and sprinting down River Road. I wanted to get as far away from there as possible. I ran all the way to the other end of town without stopping, then slowed to catch my breath once I got to the hill by Mr. Beresik's house. My face was numb and the cold flesh weighed on my cheeks as my blood beat hot. My head felt as if it was full of steam. As I came over the ridge, I sensed that something was different. It was completely quiet. The dogs were nowhere to be seen.

"Hello," I called.

There was no response. I knocked on Mr. Beresik's door, softly at first, then harder. I must have been knocking for a full five minutes. My knuckles ached from pounding. I tried the doorknob. It was unlocked.

"Hello," I called again. A lone light was bleeding in from the kitchen. The front room was practically empty, like it had been cleared out. Only a lopsided sofa and a steamer trunk remained.

"Mr. Beresik. It's me. I'm here with your delivery."

I took another step forward and felt something uneven underfoot, a worn rug caked with mud. The dirt had hardened into ridges. It was one enormous doormat that spanned the length of the room. I nudged at a clod of mud with my toe and up it came, along with a few matted blades of grass. I was about to call out for Mr. Beresik again when a low-pitched hum rose up from under the house, reverberating in the walls. I went into the kitchen, where the light was. Dozens of empty beer bottles were scattered on every available surface. The room was littered with them. Another rumble rolled through the kitchen like a wave, closer, more distinct, and peppered with voices.

There was a door at the rear of the kitchen. I thought it might have been a pantry, but as I neared, the voices got clearer. Cautiously, I opened the door and was met with a surge of noise, a jumbled gush of booing and cheering. A set of stairs led down to a basement, which ran the length of the house. At first, all I saw were men's backs, most clad in their winter coats or shirttails. They were hunched over a railing. Others were sitting on crates. They were all looking down, watching something beneath them. The room was cold, almost as cold as it was outside. When the men spoke to one another, clouds of breath steamed from their mouths. Soon I heard another sound under their voices and strained to make it out.

One man moved away from his position along the railing, and before the men on either side closed the space where he had been, I glimpsed what they were looking at. Beyond the makeshift rail was a dirt pit more than five feet deep. I couldn't see into it, but I didn't need to. An abrupt howl pierced the rumble of voices, followed by a smatter of cheers. It was a dogfight. I tore up the stairs and threw the package of meat on the kitchen table as I fled the house.

THE TRIP BACK TO TOWN was a blur. Mr. Goceljak was waiting for me in the back room. He was feeding meat into a grinder. With one hand, he spun the crank and with the other he forced the meat into the grinder's mouth. His was a steady, fluid motion, never pushing or prodding, graceful in its precision, as if he were dancing with a partner who was standing still.

"I know," Mr. Goceljak told me as he turned the grinder's crank.

Those two words bulged in my brain, an echo of what the woman on River Road had said earlier. He could have been talking about any number of things I had done, so many I had lost count.

"You didn't have to lie about it."

I struggled to come up with a reply, but wasn't sure what to apologize for.

The grinder chewed up the last of the meat and spit it into the shallow dish that lay waiting on the table. Mr. Goceljak sniffed loudly, annoyed by my silence. "Didn't you notice anything when you came in?"

I was dumbfounded and desperate to come up with whatever answer he wanted.

"The bicycle," he said finally. "It's still locked up."

I hadn't noticed, hadn't even thought about it. I'd totally forgotten to hide the bicycle in the field.

"So what have you been doing this whole time? Running around town on those two feet of yours?"

I nodded apologetically.

"I'm surprised your shoes ain't full of holes." A small yet forgiving smile formed on Mr. Goceljak's face. "Didn't think I'd give you the job if you said you didn't know how to ride the bicycle, did you?"

I shook my head.

"Smart girl. I probably wouldn't've. So what did you do with the damn thing when I thought you were riding it?"

"I hid it in the field, out behind the shed. I figured nobody would go looking back there."

"You're right. Nobody'd be fool enough to go tromping into that briar patch. They'd get cut to shreds. But you went back there, eh?"

"Yes, sir," I answered, modesty making me mumble.

"You must want this money pretty bad."

I didn't answer.

"I'm not angry," Mr. Goceljak explained. "Just remember one thing: the length between a lie and the truth is like the length between the thunder and the rain. One always comes after the other. Always."

His words struck me as the truest thing I'd ever heard, and possibly the most intimidating.

"It rains a lot here in Hyde Bend," I replied, not knowing what else to say.

"Yeah. Maybe not enough. Go on home then. I'll see you tomorrow."

I removed the canvas cap from my head, releasing my hair. "Sir?" I asked. "Who lives in the house on River Road?"

"Which house?"

"The one where the packages go and they have no name on them, just a number."

Mr. Goceljak shifted his jaw, mulling over how to answer me. He set down the dish of ground meat on the butcher block.

"There's a clean pail under the sink. Get it for me." I did as he asked and held it out to him. "You stand here," Mr. Goceljak instructed, positioning me on one side of the sink, then he got a sack from the icebox. Inside lay a heap of pig's entrails, glassy and opalescent, not yet frozen. They were casings for the kielbasa and kishke he made.

"Got to make sure there aren't any holes. Sometimes they get nicked with the knife. Hard to tell, though. So I'll run the water through and you watch for leaks."

He cut a few lengths of intestine, then put one end to the tap and handed me the other. It was silky and slick, like wet hair, which made it difficult to hold on to.

"You've got to get the right grip or it'll slip right out of your hands. That or you'll tear it with your fingers. Just hold it softly. Lay it in your palm and once the water gets going it'll be easier."

Mr. Goceljak turned on the tap, sending a stream of water coursing through the piece of intestine. The thin, filmy flesh inflated and now felt as strong as rubber. I watched carefully, waiting for any sign of a leak.

"This one's fine. Put it in that pail there."

I carefully placed the length of intestine at the bottom of the pail. Mr. Goceljak looked on approvingly. We did a few more lengths, working in tandem and in silence.

"I don't put her name on the packages because she asked me not to. Asked years ago, I can't even remember how long. But she asked, so I didn't."

Mr. Goceljak passed me another length of intestine and we went on working as he spoke.

"It was so long ago that sometimes it seems like it didn't happen. One of those things that your head doesn't want to keep inside, so it lets it slide away until you make it remember."

Unconsciously, he was shaking the piece of intestine, jostling it to force the water through faster.

"She had a son. He was a smart one, smarter than anybody else around here, that's for sure. Smarter even than those engineers they got working over at the salt plant or those who come to inspect the mill. That boy knew things. Could tell you anything you wanted to know about any subject. But he wasn't just smart and nothing else. He had this way about him that made everyone take to him, no matter who it was. Never made you feel dumber than him, never tried to show off. People started saying, 'See if the painting on the dome of Saint Laddy's is missing a saint because looks like we got us a real one.'"

The memory made Mr. Goceljak pause and smile.

"Wasn't no doubt he would be something someday, be somebody important. We were all surprised though when he decided what. One day, the boy packed up and went off to the seminary. Came back a few years later a full priest, youngest one we'd seen. And was he something in that pulpit. Looking so much like a king in his robes and speaking so strong you'd think he could turn a convict into a Catholic. Laddy's would be full up for every service. No one could get enough of him. That boy shined when he spoke, that's what they said. Shined like a song going in your ear and straight to your heart. Hell, that boy even made me want to do things better," Mr. Goceljak admitted. "And the way he talked when he talked about God, you saw how he loved Him. Almost doesn't sound right to say, but it was true. That boy loved God, saw God in everything, and made you see it too. That was why people loved him. He could make you think a heap of dirt was divine."

A few drops of water fell from a spot in the middle of the length of intestine we were holding.

"Look," I said, interrupting.

The droplets quickly turned into a threadlike stream and, within seconds, the intestine tore, causing a rush and splatter of water. Mr. Goceljak pulled the piece from the tap and shook out the remaining water.

"What do you do with it now?"

He took one of the smaller knives and cut out the center of intestine, excising the portion with the tear. "I'll use what's left. Can't throw the whole thing away because one part's bad."

He handed me the two halves of the remaining intestine, now as slack as string, and returned to the task as well as his story.

"Didn't seem like things had changed. But they had. Just that nobody had known it." Mr. Goceljak's voice sank lower, more rueful, as if recounting this part made his tongue hurt. "The boy sounded the same, looked the same as always, so when the day came that we heard, people were shocked. More than shocked. It was like a hole had been torn in 'em."

"What happened?"

"He killed himself. Someone from the church found him. Strung up a rope in the rectory and hanged himself."

Mr. Goceljak swallowed hard, as if he were trying to get the taste of what he'd said out of his mouth.

"It was too much. Too much to believe. Like stuffing a whole pillow into your ear and clear through to your brain. Everybody was thinking about it, but nobody dared talk. At least not right away."

Mr. Goceljak handed me the next piece of intestine and put it up to the faucet. The water from the tap seemed colder, hard and unforgiving, as it swept through the intestine.

"No one knew what to do about it, especially about burying the boy. They had to get a letter from the archbishop to figure out the rules, what could and couldn't be done. Turned out the boy couldn't be buried on church grounds, not in no sort of consecrated earth. Nobody liked the idea, but there was no choice about it. Couldn't put him on someone's property, someone's farmland or such, so they found a spot on a piece of land the town owned. Hadn't built anything there because of some problem with the soil. Unstable to build on for some reason or another. So they put him there."

The pail was nearly full, the intestines glistening cleanly. The story seemed to have tired Mr. Goceljak. He kneaded his temple with his knuckle.

"I s'pose I still haven't answered what you asked."

I shrugged slightly.

"After the boy died, folks were looking for someone to put the blame on. They seemed to need to have someone to blame. That person ended up being the boy's mother. Rumors spread that she'd pushed him to join the clergy, that he'd wanted to go off to college, be a doctor maybe or a lawyer. Something big. Something that would've meant he didn't have to stay here in Hyde Bend. The family had enough money for it. Father had passed long before and left the mother and son with more than most of us will ever see. Don't know if there was any truth to it, but by then, it didn't seem to matter." Mr. Goceljak dipped his head a little. "People turned on her. Wouldn't speak to her. Made her unwelcome every-where. Even at the church, the church where her boy had preached. There was nothing right about it, nothing decent, but it was done anyhow. People stopped seeing her around town and the house on River Road looked like it had been closed up. After a time, people thought she'd left Hyde Bend, moved away. But she hadn't."

Mr. Goceljak heaved the pail up from the sink and onto the counter, setting it down with a resounding thump. "Some people around town know. Not many, but some. Josef Buza at the market, he knows. Been bringing her milk and such to the house for years. Same as me. She puts the money she owes in the mail. Never pays in person, but always pays. When children got to talking, saying the house was haunted, I thought, fine. Let them stay away from the place and think it's haunted. Give the woman her peace."

"She doesn't leave her house? Not ever?"

He shook his head solemnly. "Afraid to. Especially now, after so many years."

"And no one talks to her?"

"More like she doesn't talk to them. She only sends me notes about her orders. Mails them with no name or return address. I just know it's her by the handwriting."

Mr. Goceljak went to put the pail in the cooler.

"She said something to me."

He stopped short. Over his shoulder, he asked, "She did?"

"Yes, sir."

"What'd she say?" Astonishment and curiosity were coloring his voice, though he wouldn't face me.

"She said she knows."

"Knows what?"

"Who killed Swatka Pani."

Even in profile, I could see Mr. Goceljak's expression change, his brow furrow. "Is that all she said?"

"Yes."

His shoulders dropped slightly, relieved, then he hoisted the pail into the cooler.

"If she doesn't ever talk to anybody, why did she talk to me?"

Mr. Goceljak shut the cooler door. "Don't know."

"Did she talk to Donny or any of your other delivery boys?"

"Never."

"Then why me?"

He shrugged. "Maybe you're different."

I didn't care for the sound of *different*. It rang of indictment. "Different how?"

"Just different," Mr. Goceljak replied, then he added, "I want you to do something for me. Promise me you won't tell anyone what I told you. And promise me you won't tell anyone she talked to you. Nobody."

"I promise."

Mr. Goceljak locked eyes with me briefly, as if to seal the deal we had made. "You better get changed and get home. It's getting late."

He pushed through the curtain and into the front of the store, leaving me the privacy of the back room. I hung the clothes on a peg next to where Mr. Goceljak hung his overcoat. They were merely a pair of pants and a cap then, hanging there next to a real man's clothes, no longer a disguise. I considered thanking Mr. Goceljak for his kindness, for not firing me for lying about the bicycle and for telling me about the woman on River Road, but I simply slipped out the back door without realizing I still hadn't gotten her name.

THE BELLS OF SAINT LADISLAUS sang out sonorously, cleaving the cold air and sounding the time. It was four o'clock. I arrived at the school earlier than usual, as promised, and went to the library to get Martin. Sister Teresa was in there alone, eyes shut. There was no sign of Martin's things. My stomach cinched, registering his absence.

"Sister Teresa?" I said loudly. "Sister Teresa?"

The sister's eyes fluttered open. She clutched her heart. "My word, girl. You nearly scared me to death."

"Sister, where's Martin?"

"Who?"

"Martin. My brother. I left him here with you right after school."

"I don't know. He must have left."

"Left?"

"Yes."

"Where'd he go?"

"I don't know. Perhaps the boy went home. Did you check there?"

I raced out of the library and went running down through the corridors, calling his name. My voice was bouncing off the hallway walls and being pelted back at me. Martin wouldn't have gone home. He was too scared to walk back on his own. All of the doors to the classrooms were closed, the lights off. I went to the front office to see if he was waiting there, but the room was empty except for one of the nuns, who was busy filing.

I combed through the building, shouting, "Martin, it's me. Where are you? If you're hiding, please come out."

I got to the end of the second-floor corridor and listened, hoping I would hear him, hear something. All was quiet. It was one of the worst sounds I'd ever heard.

I pictured every room in the building, trying to imagine where he'd be, then I took off toward the other end of the building, to the bathrooms. I was about to throw open the door to the boys' room and go charging in, but thought better of it. I made sure I was alone in the hallway, then inched open the door. The handle was low, built at a height for young children, and the sign on the door was in both Polish and English.

"Hello?" I called. "Martin? Are you in there?"

I heard a sniffle.

"Martin?"

Another sniffle sounded, timed like a reply. I rushed inside. Stalls lined one wall, urinals the other. I'd never seen a urinal and the curious shape had me staring. This was nothing like the girls' room. With its blue tile and gray paint, it was a foreign realm made solely for boys.

"Martin, where are you?"

"In here."

I could see the shadow of his feet in the last stall. The door was closed.

"Can I come in?"

"Uh-huh," he whimpered.

Martin was standing in the corner of the stall and had wedged himself behind the toilet. His face was tear streaked. His clothes and hair were a mess.

"What happened?"

"I . . ." he began, then his chin started to quiver.

I pushed myself back into the corner with him and held him.

"I was in the library," he said, talking into my shoulder. "But you said you'd be early, so I went outside to wait. I was sitting there, just waiting, not doing anything wrong, and some older boys came up to me. They took my books and threw them in the grass. Then I saw that one of them was that boy, the one who came to our house with the catfish. He pulled me up by my coat and said that I was a sissy and called me a little girl. When I said I wasn't a little girl, that I was a boy, he pushed me and I fell into the road."

Martin wiped his face with the back of his hand. "I didn't

mean to start crying when I fell. It didn't even hurt. I didn't mean to cry, but they saw me start and then they were laughing and I couldn't stop."

I pulled Martin to me, into my arms.

"Do you believe me? That I didn't mean to cry?"

"I know you didn't mean to."

"I don't think that Nowczyk boy would believe it. He thought it was funny."

"Well, he's stupid."

"You think so?"

"I know so. He's stupid and ugly and nobody likes him."

"Really? Nobody likes him?"

"Sure. Plenty of people hate him."

Martin was eager to believe that his hatred was confirmed by others. I wasn't sure that what I was saying was true, nor did I care. All I knew was that I now hated the nameless Nowczyk boy.

"I want to go home," Martin said.

"Okay."

"You have to promise not to tell anybody I cried."

"I promise," I replied, thinking of the promise I'd already made to Mr. Goceljak. All of those promises, I wondered if I was the person to be making them.

"We'd better get home before anyone sees you looking like this."

"Why? What do I look like?"

Martin slid past me out of the stall and gawked at himself in the mirror. Dirt clung to his sweater and darkened the bottom half of his pants. His hair was matted on one side and his eyes were puffy and bloodshot from crying.

"I look terrible," he said in genuine amazement.

"You'll be fine once you take a bath and get out of those dirty clothes."

Martin prodded his swollen cheeks and rubbed his eyelids, studying his reflection. "I don't even look like me. I didn't know I could look so different." He admired his face as though it were a surprise gift and his anger and distress faded. "Will it go away?" he asked.

"Eventually you'll go back to normal."

"Oh," he said, regretfully. "I guess that's okay. I don't know if I'd want to look like this all the time."

For all we had suffered through, it was a wonder my brother could be charmed by the change his own tears created. We should have looked like that every day, teary, red eyed, beaten. Perhaps those were our true faces, we just didn't know it.

I RAN A BATH FOR MARTIN and helped him change out of his soiled clothes. "She's going to notice," he said, wriggling out of his sweater. "She'll ask why I got so dirty."

"I'll shake the clothes out while you take your bath."

"So you're going to leave? While I'm in the tub?"

"I'm only going to go out the door."

"But what if I sink?"

"You've never sunk before."

"But you never know. I was never in a fight before either."

"Do you want me to clean your clothes or not?"

"Yes, but couldn't you do it now, while the tub is filling, and then, I thought, maybe, you could stay in here. Just in case."

"All right. I'll shake the clothes out now. But first I have to put the water on to heat."

We had no hot water. We always had to boil some on the stove and add it to the tub to keep the temperature right. Each bath was a trial to see how long we could stand the changes in temperature. Initially, the water was scalding hot, then it cooled rapidly, dipping down below tepid. In total, the bathwater was bearable for about ten minutes.

I stoked the coal stove, put the big stew pot on to warm and went to shake Martin's clothes out on the front stoop. Before I opened the door, I thought I felt something, an undercurrent of noise roiling up and coursing down Third. I stuck my head out the door tentatively.

Two or three children flew past the apartment, racing for the end of the alley. Then the sound hit me. It was the angry cawing of women's and children's voices, all shouting out of time.

A cart stood at the end of the alley. Though it was mostly obscured by the crowd, I could tell that it was the rag cart, Ragsoline's cart. The women were screaming at him in Polish and he was shaking his head, confused, unable to understand them or what he had done. Slurs burst out over the din and jammed against one another.

Get out of here. You killed her. The nigger killed Swatka Pani. Leave, nigger. Leave.

With the front door open, Martin heard the shouting. He came out of the washroom dressed only in his long underwear.

"What's happening?"

Ragsoline was backing away from the growing crowd and wrenching his mare's reins in an attempt to flee. A few children were tugging at the rags hanging from his cart. Then others started throwing pebbles at him.

"No!" Martin shouted. He burst past me and set off running toward the crowd.

"Martin. Wait."

I ran after him. Martin's tiny, shoeless feet hit the ground and came up black. Mud spattered onto his white long underwear. He dove between the legs of the women, pushing them to stop and flailing at them with his small fists. His shouts melted into the churning crowd. I tried to reach him, but he was enmeshed in the tangle of limbs.

Soon the women were picking up stones too, bigger than the pebbles the children had been throwing. They hurled them at Ragsoline and his cart. One hit the horse and sent it bucking. Another caught Ragsoline on the cheek. The impact sent his head snapping back.

Martin's cry rang out over the tumult. "No!"

Ragsoline stumbled and covered his head with his arms, still furiously yanking at his horse's reins. Spooked, the old mare began to trot and Ragsoline took off running. Blood streamed from the cut on his cheek.

"Stop!" Martin shouted, swatting at the women and older boys. I saw his hands and head bobbing between people's waists. Then someone pushed Martin backward, sending him to the ground.

"Martin!"

He was pinned down under the crowd, trapped in the mud. All my anger at the Nowczyk boy boiled over and I slammed my body forward, knocking into anyone in my path. I jammed my elbow into the ribs of a young girl who stood in my way. One woman squawked as I pushed her aside.

"Little bitch," the woman hissed.

I grabbed Martin's arm, which was slick with mud, and wrenched him to his feet, my grip sliding up his forearm. The crowd was turning on us. One boy my age pushed me in the back. While still holding Martin, I whipped around and smacked the boy with a muddy hand, connecting with his nose. Stunned, the boy reeled and stumbled onto one knee.

"Run," I told Martin.

We took off for our house, the shouts of the women at our backs, some of the children on our heels. I shoved Martin inside and slammed the door behind us, quickly bolting it with muddy fingers. The angry jeers of the kids rumbled outside as they pounded on the door and beat on the window.

"What do we do?" Martin's whole body was streaked with mud, his chest and face spattered. His long underwear was hanging off him, sopping with muck. He was shivering so hard his body quaked.

"Nothing," I said, pressing all my weight against the door. "The door's locked. We stay here." Through the door, I could feel the pummeling of the hands and fists against my back.

"Are we safe here?" Martin asked.

Were we? Were we ever?

For once in our lives, this was the one place where we were safe.

"Yes," I said, unsure if this was another lie to add to the list. "We're safe here."

After a few minutes, the yelling died down and the pounding ceased. I eased back from the door. The onslaught was over.

Martin's teeth were chattering loudly, the clatter falling in with the gurgle of the water boiling on the stove.

"Go. I'll get the water."

Martin scurried into the washroom while I went for the stew pot. Without thinking, I grabbed each of the metal handles. I heard the hiss of my palms being scalded before I felt anything, then came agony. I jerked my hands away, but it was too late. A pink line rose in the center of each hand.

"Hurry," Martin pleaded from the washroom.

I took two dish towels to grasp the handles with and tried to ignore the pain. Filled high with water, the stew pot was nearly too heavy for me to carry. I hauled the sloshing pot off the stove, holding it out in front of me so I wouldn't get burned again.

Martin shivered in his mud-caked underwear as I dumped the boiling water into the bath. Steam rose, sizzling as the hot water hit the cold water that was already in the tub.

"I can't feel my feet," Martin said through chattering teeth.

"Get in. The bath will warm you up."

He was about to strip off his pants, then he said, "Don't look."

"Sorry." I faced the door and heard him dip his foot in the water.

"It's too hot."

Careful not to turn my head, I leaned over to run more water and winced as pain shot up from my palms when I touched the faucet, but Martin couldn't see my face. "Try it now," I told him.

Martin tested the water with his finger and swirled it around to mix the cold in with the hot. "Better."

He climbed in, and seconds later, the water darkened to a pale brown. "Uh-oh," Martin intoned.

"It'll have to do. She'll be home soon."

"What about my hair?"

"You'll have to wash that too."

"By myself?"

My mother usually helped Martin with his hair because he didn't like dunking his head underwater. She would hold his hand while he held his nose.

"Well, if you don't want me to turn around, how am I supposed to help wash your hair?"

Martin weighed his options. "Okay, I guess you can turn around. But don't look."

I swiveled around slowly, and the sight before me was almost amusing. Martin was hunkered down in the dirty water with his chin above the waterline. I tried to contain a giggle.

"What?"

"I'm not sure how we're going to get your hair clean if the water's already turned back to mud."

"That's not funny. And you can't dunk me," he added. "Not in this stuff."

"I won't. I've got an idea. Hand me the soap." We'd used up all of the hot water, so I refilled the stew pot in the sink, gripping it with my fingers instead of the palms of my hands.

"This is going to be cold," I warned.

"I'm already cold."

"Then you shouldn't feel the difference."

"All right," he said, squeezing his eyes shut in preparation. "I'm ready."

Though it hurt to grasp the pot, I poured it over Martin's head, drenching him. Clumps of dirt sluiced out of his hair and down into the murky bathwater.

"Is it over?" he groaned, eyes still clenched.

"Halfway done."

"Do you think Ragsoline's okay?" Martin asked as I worked the soap into his hair with the tips of my fingers.

I hoped so, though I knew better than to say as much to Martin.

"He got away. I'm sure he's all right."

The soap built into a thick lather as I scrubbed Martin's head and neck and ears. My palms were pulsing with pain as I ran the water to refill the stew pot but I didn't want to tell Martin what I'd done to myself. In my mind, it was another punishment for my lies.

"It's going to be cold again," I explained.

"Okay."

"Don't open your eyes."

Martin trembled as I spilled the icy water over his head. The water gushed down over his shoulders, washing away all of the dirt and the soap at once. He was finally clean.

With a shiver, he asked, "Now is it over?"

"It's over."

I opened a towel wide, held it up, and closed my eyes. Martin hopped out of the tub and into my arms, wrapping himself in the towel. I got him fresh pajamas while he dried off, then left him alone to change.

He came out of the washroom holding up the towel. "Look," he said. The pale, worn towel was a grimy mess.

"Well, there's nothing we can do about that, not now."

"Come look at the tub."

The brown, brackish water sat in the bathtub like a murky soup.

"She can't see this," I said. "I have to clean it."

"I can help," Martin offered.

"No, you're already clean. You can't get dirty all over again."

He gave me no argument, just lent his support by keeping me company while I drained the tub and sopped up the muck with the towel he'd dirtied. In spite of the pain in my hands, I refilled the stew pot over and over, rinsing the tub with fresh water to force the mud down the drain.

"You're good at this," Martin said. "You're like her. You're both good at cleaning."

He meant to be helpful, to rally me along, yet the compliment stung worse than my hands. It was difficult for me to believe that my mother and I had anything in common. To think that, of all things, cleaning was all that we shared.

The tub was finished, back to its normal state of spotlessness. The towel, however, was an oozy brown. Martin grimaced. "What are you going to do with it?"

"I guess I could wash it too."

"Where? In the bathtub?"

"I guess not. What do you think I should do with it?"

"Throw it away."

"No, she'll know it's missing."

"If she asks us, we'll say we don't know anything about it."

"Martin!"

Before, my brother would never have tempted fate by uttering such an idea. I reminded myself that I had changed us.

"Well," I relented. "Where are we going to put it?"

Martin thought for a second. "Throw it out back. By the laundry lines. Then she'll think it got blown down and got dirty that way. I can do it."

"No," I insisted. I had dragged him too far along with me already. "You'll get dirty out there. Stay here. I'll do it."

I BUNDLED MY COAT over my clothes only to discover that they were also splattered with mud. My boots were caked to the ankles. My tights were streaked as well. My mother would undoubtedly notice.

"Maybe you should bury it a little," Martin suggested. "You know, push it down in the mud back there."

"All right," I answered, too busy checking to see if the coast was clear outside our door.

"Are they still out there?" he asked.

"I don't think so. But lock the door behind me. I'll take the key. And don't open the door if anyone knocks. And don't go near the window."

Martin took my instructions seriously. "What if they're hiding? Hiding and waiting for you around the corner?"

"I'll find out, I guess." I inched open the front door cautiously, preparing to run. Third was clear. "Lock the door behind me. Do it now."

Martin slammed the door and swiftly locked it, sending a gust of air rushing against my back. As I neared the corner of the apartment, I steeled myself for someone to jump out at me. There was no one, no waiting ambush, nothing except the rutted, narrow path.

The sight of the outhouse up ahead made the memory of that

night with Swatka Pani rear in my mind. The wind mimicked the hissing of her voice, beckoning me back into what seemed like a nightmare, something apart from reality.

This is all your fault. You did this. I shook my head to dislodge the thought from my ears.

You hated her. You're happy she's dead.

I tried to cut between the laundry lines, but the wind started kicking up the clothes, sending them flapping and twisting, keeping me back. The sleeves on the shirts and the legs of the pants swelled high, waving, lifelike and warding me off.

You hated her so much that your hate killed her.

I felt as though I was sinking, being sucked down into the mud, into the depths that I imagined Swatka Pani had inhabited. I dropped the towel right where I stood and pried my boots from the mire, backpedaling from the groping limbs of the empty clothes, then I slipped on a stone and my feet skidded out from under me. Arms flailing, I collided with the ground with a sickening thud. Mud oozed through my fingers and sucked at my legs.

I've got you now.

I scrambled to get up, but slid down onto my knees. I clawed at the mud and my fingers caught on the very rock I had tripped on. Using it as an anchor, I pushed myself to my feet and took off running.

With trembling, mud-slick hands, I fished the key from my pocket to unlock the door, but it was already open.

"Martin, I told you to—"

My mother was standing at the stove, taking off her coat. Martin was at the table, warning me with his eyes.

"What happened to you?" she demanded.

The front of my clothes were spattered with mud while the back of me was black with it.

"You're filthy."

"No she's not," Martin protested. "The Germans are filthy. That's what—"

A fierce glare from my mother stopped Martin in midsentence.

"I fell," I said. "I tripped and I fell."

"I told you she went to the outhouse," Martin said. He blinked purposefully, signaling me to play along.

"Start running the bath," my mother said, barely concealing her irritation. "And get those dirty clothes off. You can hand them out to me and I'll wash them in the sink."

Wearily, I went into the washroom, turned on the tap to fill the tub, then slunk out of my grungy skirt and sweater. Flecks of dried mud skittered to the floor as I peeled off my stockings. My hands were throbbing from the burns. Tiny blisters had bubbled the skin. I caught my reflection in the mirror. Droplets of mud were sprayed across my face, and one solid slash of mud was streaked under my eye like war paint. Through the door, I heard my mother asking, "Where's the stew pot?"

It was in the washroom with me, sitting beneath the sink. I rushed to put my clothes back on.

"It's in the washroom," I heard Martin say. "I took it."

"What for?" my mother demanded.

I was yanking on my skirt, willing Martin not to say any more, not to lie for me again. I burst out of the washroom with the stew pot in my arms because I couldn't bear to hold it in my hands.

"What are you still doing in those clothes?" my mother admonished. "Go back in there and take them off. You're making a mess of everything."

She's right, I thought. I had made a mess of everything, in more ways than I could count.

My mother plucked the pot from my arms and began filling it. Martin nodded to me to get into the washroom before she could say any more. I re-stripped the clothes from my body, each piece heavy from the cold muck that clung to it. Naked, I eased the door open a crack, slid my arm through, and held the clothes out for collection.

"Here," I said. There was no reply. "Here," I repeated, more loudly. The water from the sink was muffling my voice. I pressed my body to the door while pulling it to me to keep it from opening all the way and exposing me. "Here," I shouted.

Footsteps followed. My mother flashed by outside the door and the clothes were snatched from my arm. I remained there at the door until she set the stew pot down outside. Two dishrags hung from the pot's handles, a cruel reminder. I crouched down to cover myself and edged the door open enough to drag the pot into the washroom. I dreaded picking it up, but it was that or bathe in the freezing water.

With the tips of my fingers, I lifted the heavy stew pot to the lip of the tub and spilled it over the side. The pot wobbled along the rim, threatening to overturn, and I had to resist the impulse to brace it with my leg. The metal would have burned me yet again. I tested the water with my pinkie. It was lukewarm, though that would have to do.

Climbing into the tub was the next hurdle. I couldn't hold on to the edge because of my hands, so I balanced myself on my muddy knuckles and forearms, then threw my legs into the water. I tumbled into the tub, sending up a splash that caught me in the face. Once my body settled to the bottom, the waterline pushed up over my lips and under my nose, leaving me just enough space to breathe. Wisps of dirt curled into the clear water while the larger clods of mud from my hair and arms sank. Exhausted, I wallowed there, feeling the water's temperature already dropping.

See what you've done. You've made a mess of everything.

I rubbed the soap cake over my head and scrubbed my hair. Soap bubbles drifted over the top of the water, eventually covering the surface and turning it opaque.

You know what they say. God'll get you.

I hunkered down in the tub, lower still, holding my breath as my nose slid underwater. Fiercely, I continued to lather. My lungs began to burn from the lack of air.

God will get you.

My eyes and the tops of my ears were the only things left above the water. With a bobbing jerk, I dunked down below the surface, hoping to drown out my thoughts altogether. Feet braced against the tub to keep me under, I gazed up from beneath the water. Bubbles filled the space where my head had been, sealing the surface in a soapy film. It was as if I hadn't been there at all.

The world went mute, the thoughts hushed. Lungs throbbing, eyes stinging, I lay there. Perhaps if I punished myself, God wouldn't have to. If I made myself suffer, He wouldn't. Light-headedness set in and I lost the strength to keep pressing my feet against the tub to hold myself down. My head burst through the water's surface and I let out an enormous gasp.

I was back in the world and it was no different from before. Tiny streams of water trickled across my face, trailing from strands of hair. I looked myself over. I was clean, at least on the outside.

I toweled off, then realized I had no clothes to change into. I cracked the door partway. My wet hair was dripping down my shoulders. Water was pooling on the floorboards. My mother was busy ringing out my skirt in the sink. Martin was at the table with one of his schoolbooks.

"Martin," I whispered. He didn't hear me. "Martin."

My mother turned. The one time I didn't want her to hear me, she did.

"What is it?" she asked.

"I don't have anything to put on."

"Get your sister her nightdress."

Martin sprang from his seat and rushed the dress to me. He clamped his eyes shut and pushed the nightdress at me through the slit in the door.

"Don't come out if you don't have to," he whispered. "Stay in there as long as you can. Something's wrong," he said, then hurried back to his seat.

Through the crack in the door, all I could see was my mother's back. Then I heard it, a noise mingling with the water running in the sink. My mother was humming. The sound was high-pitched and glassy, so sweet it seemed unreal. Martin nodded at me from his chair, urging me to return to the washroom. I tried to pull myself away, but it was as if the tune she was humming was warming the air and wicking the chill from my skin.

I shut the door and the spell was broken. I could no longer

hear her. A shiver rattled through my body, shaking me back to reality. I pulled on my nightdress and patted my hair dry, wondering what to do with myself. There was nowhere to sit except the edge of the bathtub, which was dirty again. I filled a few minutes by cleaning it for the second time that day, Martin's comment clinking in my ears all the while.

"You're good at cleaning. Like her."

How could you be good at cleaning and at making a mess of everything at the same time?

After I finished the bathtub, I had nothing to do, then I remembered the quarters. I squatted under the sink and slid them out from the ledge where Martin had hidden them. I couldn't cup them in my palms because of the blisters, which had formed a line of fierce red bumps across the inside of my hands. Instead, I held the quarters lightly between my fingers, tipping them so they would catch the light and glint at me, a secret wink.

The slamming of the front door signaled my father's arrival. I returned the quarters to their spot and went for the door, knowing my father would want to get into the washroom to shave before his shift. We both grabbed for the handle at the same time. My father got to it first. Discovering me in the doorway gave him a start and he snorted angrily.

"Sorry," I mumbled, scooting past him. My time for hiding was over.

DURING SUPPER, my father seemed to be in an unusually good mood. That meant he actually spoke at the table. He was describing what he'd heard people saying about Swatka Pani.

"Seems no one cares much that she's dead. But they do care about knowing who done it to her." He exhaled a spurt of smoke, punctuating his statement. "Word is, that retard she kept around for handy work's gone missing. People are saying it must've been him. Police've been looking for him high and low, and ain't nobody seen him for days. Hasn't been back to the Slipper neither. And that's the only place he's got to sleep. I say, could've been him. Strong as an ox. Dumb as one too. I seen him carry beer barrels half his weight like they were sacks of sawdust. He could've pushed the old bitch down those stairs as easy as breathin'."

Martin wanted to interject and was pursing his lips to keep the words from springing out.

"Swatka Pani wasn't no saint," my father said, stuffing a few forkfuls of food into his mouth. "But that don't give that retard the right or reason to kill her."

Martin finally let loose. "Leonard was here that night."

My mother's eyes darted toward Martin, then I heard myself screaming inside my head, *Don't tell him that*. It was too late.

My father's head snapped up from his plate. "What?"

"He came over, knocked on the door, then left," Martin recounted. "I forgot about it. I forgot to tell that to the policeman."

"Leonard was here? That night Swatka Pani died? Damn it, why didn't you tell me that?" He threw a ferocious glance at my mother. "What else did he do?"

"Nothing," Martin said, sad that he didn't have more to offer. "That's it."

My mind was sputtering. "He only came by looking for food," I said.

"Food? Why the hell would he do that?" my father demanded.

"Because sometimes, sometimes I'd give him one of our apples. Just the littlest one. He never has any food, so I thought . . ."

I was afraid of what my father would say, but was even more afraid to look at my mother, to read the reproach in her eyes.

"Don't give that retard our food," my father ordered. "Don't ever do that again. Do you hear me?"

As I lowered my head to hide from my father's glare, I caught a glimpse of my mother's expression. Instead of drilling me with angry eyes, she was searching my face.

She sees me.

My father shoved away his plate and stabbed out his cigarette. "You thank God your brother said something," my father told me, already halfway out the door.

"What about your lunch?" Martin called, running to retrieve his lunch tin from the icebox for him. The door was closed by the time Martin had it in his hand.

Martin returned to the table and slumped down on his elbows. "I didn't think it was so important. If I knew it was, I would have told him sooner, I swear," he said. "Did you know that Leonard coming here was important?" he asked my mother.

"No," she answered hollowly.

"It's not important," I found myself shouting. "It doesn't matter. Leonard didn't do it. So it doesn't matter."

"How do you know?" Martin asked.

I had to stop myself from saying what I always did, that I just knew. But that was truer than ever before. I felt it. I felt it the same way I could feel the floor under my feet. The feeling was so strong it had to be fact.

"Enough," my mother said. "The dishes need doing."

"But I'm not done with—"

My mother and I simultaneously shot him a glance, then Martin set to gobbling down what was left on his plate before I whisked it out from under him and took it to the sink.

Our bed felt especially cold that night, as though the blankets had gotten thinner during the day. Martin shivered and snuggled close to me. I pulled the blankets up over our heads so our breath could warm us. We would stay under until the air ran out, then I'd lift the edge of the blanket enough for us to breathe.

"I saw your hands," Martin said. "You burned them on the pot, right?" I nodded. "Do they hurt bad?"

I nodded again. I didn't want him to feel guilty. The mistake was mine and I was paying for it. Worse yet, I couldn't bandage my hands for fear of my mother noticing. Every movement pulled at the blisters. I laid my hands out along my sides, palms sideways to keep the skin from coming into contact with anything.

Martin fidgeted with the tip of the sheet. "I have to ask you a question, but I don't want you to get mad."

"Ask."

"How did you know?"

"About Leonard?"

He nodded and dug his hands under his armpits to warm them.

"Does it matter? You know what I'm going to say."

"Yeah, I know what you're going to say. *You just do.* But how? I never just know. Never."

"I'm not sure. It's like a feeling. But it feels real. And I believe it."

"That's all?"

"That's all."

"You don't get scared that your feelings aren't telling you the truth? What if they're lying?"

The awful possibility that I was deceiving myself terrified me. If I'd let myself believe that could be, I would have been inconsolable.

"You can lie to other people, but you can't lie to yourself," I replied, hoping to convince both of us.

"Why?"

"We're just made that way."

That was enough to satisfy Martin. He blew on his hands one last time, huddled next to me, and closed his eyes.

"I'm sorry I told about Leonard."

"You don't have to be."

"But I am. I want God to know I'm sorry. And you."

"He knows."

Sleep came quickly, then I awoke in the night to a shuffling sound. At first, I thought it was the wind against the rear wall of the apartment, though that was such a familiar noise it shouldn't have woken me. A new thought arose, replacing reason. I pictured the laundry on the lines out back scraping at the wall, trying to get in and clawing to get at me as it had done before. I clenched my eyes to cast off the image.

The blanket was still covering my head, creating a tent and muffling the sound. The air inside was congested, nearly unbreathable. I tipped up the blanket's edge to vent it and discovered that the sound that had woken me was coming from inside the apartment.

I didn't dare move. I balanced the blanket on the tips of my fingers and peeked through a gap in the covers where Martin's shoulder had raised them. The room was too dark to discern anything other than sound, the noise of cloth sliding over cloth, the thump of treading feet, then the crisp click of the front door unlocking.

The door opened little more than a sliver, but in the half-light I could make out a figure, shoulders hunched, head wrapped in a scarf. It was the unmistakable silhouette of my mother. She slipped into the night and disappeared.

My father was at the mill finishing his shift, so she wasn't going to the Slipper in search of him. Then where? To find Leonard? I wondered. She had kept his visit a secret, just as I had. Would she know where to find him if no one else did? What if she was going to see another man, the lover I had imagined before?

The idea of that didn't ring true, but it clanged in my head nonetheless. Faces of men I had seen in the street or at church or coming out of the salt plant swam before me, features blending. If she had taken a lover, that would mean she'd found someone to show love to, a person rather than her lost painting. That would also mean there was hope, a hope of that love spreading. That possibility could have kept me warm all night. I would have torn off the blankets, even my nightdress, if I thought the chance existed, and let it wrap me in its heat.

I MUST HAVE LAIN THERE for hours that night, waiting up, trying to talk myself into believing that my mother was with a lover. Sleep overtook me and I woke with a start the next morning to the same shuffling sound. It was my mother, fully dressed, busy at the sink, sunlight streaming in from the window beyond her.

I grabbed the blanket to push it aside, forgetting the blisters, and the pain in my palms made me cringe. My mother turned. I feigned a yawn as cover, stretching out my arms, hands down to hide the burns.

"Wake your brother. I need to be at the church early today."

Her coat and scarf were hung in their usual place, her shoes right where they always were.

I wasn't sure if I had dreamed her late-night departure.

"Wake up, Marty," I said, prodding him with my elbow.

Martin sat up and let out an exaggerated yawn as fake as mine. He'd only been pretending to be asleep and had heard what my mother said.

"All right, I'm awake," he said, affecting a groggy voice.

"You can have the washroom first," I told him. I always let him go ahead of me, that way he could get into his clothes and stand by the stove to warm himself while we waited for breakfast.

"No, you go first," Martin said. "I'll wait."

My mother, who usually noticed everything, seemed oblivious to the change. She was at the table making sandwiches for our lunch.

"All right," I agreed, unsure as to what Martin was up to. He got out of bed so I wouldn't have to crawl over him and I went to the closet for my clothes, then recalled that my mother had washed them the night before to rid them of the mud.

"They're outside on the line," she said without looking up from the sandwiches. "I'll go and get them."

She headed out the door and it dawned on me that she hadn't put my clothes outside the night before. She'd only left them hanging on the edge of the sink.

Was that where she went? Was that all?

With my mother outside, Martin and I were alone in the apartment. "What are you up to?" I demanded.

"What do you mean?"

"I know you were awake." Martin's face revealed his disappointment. He thought he'd fooled us. "Why were you pretending?"

"I wanted to hear what she would say if she thought I was sleeping," he confessed. "I wanted to see if she'd say she was mad at me for telling about Leonard. I thought maybe she would tell you."

Such a confidence was beyond my mother. Martin was paying me an undue compliment to suggest that was possible.

"She wouldn't say anything, least of all to me," I told him, as I began to make our bed.

"It's like she's always thinking about something, but she won't say what. It kind of scares me," Martin admitted, standing close. "Does it scare you?"

I shook the blanket out and let it drift down to the mattress to lay flat, erasing any trace that we had slept there and that I had spent most of the night wondering where my mother had gone. "Yes," I told Martin. "It scares me too."

"What do you think it is, the thing she's thinking about?"

"I wouldn't know." It was the truth, so my voice did not betray me enough to make Martin doubt me.

"Do you think she's thinking about Swatka Pani?"

I shrugged. "Help me tuck in the blanket."

"Maybe she feels bad about her being dead."

The door opened and my mother entered, my school clothes folded neatly over her arm. "You're not dressed yet," she said to Martin.

"He was helping me with the bed."

"Well, you're finished now. Go on and change. Both of you."

I nodded for Martin to go into the washroom first, then I was left alone with my mother. She set my clothes on the table in a tidy stack. She must have stood out in the cold folding them as she took them off the laundry line. Such patience, such care, but for what? For me to unfold them and put them on. Her neatness always seemed like such a waste to me, a useless attempt to make what we had appear better than it was. Hand-me-down clothes were still hand-me-downs no matter how clean they were.

"I got most of the stains out," my mother said after I picked up the clothes. A night in the cold air left the wool of my sweater brittle. The pleats of the skirt were stiff. "But there was something on your skirt. It looks like dried blood." She was setting out the bowls for breakfast. Then she looked straight at me and asked, "Where did it come from?"

Until that moment, I'd never noticed how much I had to tilt my head upward to meet her gaze. I had to lift my chin in such a way that it made me aware of just how much taller she was, how small I was compared with her.

"School," I lied. Even eye to eye with her, the lie was easy, supple on the tongue. The act no longer scared me as it once had. "I cut myself on a desk at school."

My mother brushed a stray hair out of her eyes as though she wanted to get a full look at me or, perhaps, wanted me to get a full look at her. Then Martin came out of the washroom, dressed and patting down his hair instead of brushing it. "You can go in now."

I scooped up my clothes, anxious to get away from my mother and from what she'd said. Through my nightdress I could feel frost lingering on the skirt. Had she really taken my clothes out in the night and that was all? The question squirmed in my mind for the rest of the day as I sat through school barely paying attention to my classes.

After lunch, Sister Bernadette was giving a lecture on church history. Under the fractured sound of her uneven English came a whisper.

"Psst."

The noise was directed at me. A boy two rows behind me was trying to get my attention. I ignored him and faced front, afraid the sister would notice.

"Psst," he hissed again. "I heard your brother's a sissy."

The insult shot through the air at me like an arrow. All of the children nearby heard it. I folded my arms and clenched my teeth, silently seething. Sister Bernadette prattled on, unable to detect the whispers over the clacking of her chalk against the board.

"I heard he plays with dolls and sews like a little girl."

My fists curled into balls in spite of the pain in my palms.

"Your brother's a girl. He's a girl just like you."

"Go to hell," I shouted, whipping around to face the boy head-on.

The words had exploded from my mouth with enough force to send the boy back in his chair and leave him blinking. I should have been shocked too, I thought fleetingly. I should have been stunned at myself. I wasn't. It was as if those words had been curled up and waiting for their chance to escape.

In the wake of my outburst, the classroom went quiet. It felt as if all of the air had been sucked out of the room, my lungs, everything. Sister Bernadette's face stiffened, framed in the white wimple of her habit.

"*Chodz tutaj!*" she commanded.

With a black-winged flourish of her robe, she was ordering me to the front of the room. It was an ominous sign that she had switched to Polish, and it left the other children murmuring.

"*Cicho.*"

Sister Bernadette demanded silence and the whispering stopped at once.

I walked to the front of the room on unsteady legs and stood next to the sister's desk as she opened her top drawer, the creak of the wood saying everything. From the drawer, she retrieved a pair of rulers.

Unconsciously, I had slipped my hands from my sides to my back.

"Darzyc mi twoja reka."

She was ordering me to put out my hands. I raised my arms slightly, then the sister grabbed them, digging her thumbs into the blistered flesh of my palms. I grimaced, stifling a moan.

"Ja jeszcze nie byc w kontakcie z."

I haven't even touched you yet.

The admonishment was as embarrassing as the punishment that followed, though hardly as painful. Sister Bernadette took up the rulers back to back and brought them down on the top of my left hand, then my right. The harsh thwacking of wood against skin made a sickening sound. My knuckles bore the brunt of the beating, the bones quivering below the thin layer of flesh. Each hand received three blows.

"Jeden za kazdy slowo."

One time for every word.

Sister Bernadette dropped my hands as if I were the one hurting her, then quietly, so none of the other children could hear, the sister whispered to me in stunted English, "With a mouth like that, you're the one who'll be going to hell, girl."

The sister put down the rulers and began the lesson right where she had left off, as though nothing had happened. I returned to my seat, blind to the stares from my classmates, deaf to the sister's voice, numb to everything but the relentless stinging of my hands, top and bottom.

I did not want to cry, not from the pain or the humiliation. I believed I deserved it, that I ought to suffer. I hoped that God had seen this and taken it as a penance for what I had done.

THE REST OF THE AFTERNOON went by without event. The other children in class were on their best behavior, careful not to re-spark Sister Bernadette's temper. I kept my eyes on the blackboard and my hands hidden in my lap. The tops were covered in welts and the skin on my knuckles was broken. I caught my classmates sneaking glances at me, all curious to see how bad my wounds were.

Once the school bell rang, no one moved for a few seconds. They were all waiting to see what I would do. Sister Bernadette finally had to urge the other children out of their seats, saying, "That was the bell, you know."

While the others packed their books and got their coats from the cloakroom, I had to figure out how I was going to gather my things. My fingers had grown so stiff they refused to work. Lifting my notebook took maneuvering. I had to pinch the book's spine between my fingertips like I was holding a grain of sand, then nudge it along with my other books into a pile. The rest of the children scurried out of the classroom, eager to get away from Sister Bernadette, then I was left alone with her while she sorted through her papers, as she did at the end of each day. I couldn't carry my books with me to the cloakroom, so I had to come back for them. It took me a full minute just to get my coat on, clumsily tugging the sleeves up with my thumbs. When I came back to retrieve my books, Sister Bernadette was at her desk, acting as if I wasn't there. I slid the books to the edge of my desk so I could push them into my arms and hastened for the door.

"Just because your mother works in the church doesn't mean God likes you any better than the rest," Sister Bernadette intoned.

No, I thought. *He likes me less.*

Martin was nervously pacing outside my classroom door. "When you didn't come for me, I came to find you." His eyes went wide when he saw my hands. "What did you do?"

"Nothing." I headed toward the library, forcing Martin to trail behind me. "Hurry or I'll be late."

"You had to have done something or else—"

"It was nothing," I interrupted, raising my voice. I couldn't tell him what I had said or why I'd said it. It would have hurt him far more than my hands hurt me.

Martin ran ahead of me and stood in my path, blocking my way. "You're not telling me something. I know you're not."

"Then you know enough."

"Fine," he sighed. "Give me your books. I'll carry them."

Gratefully, I lumped the books into his arms. The overflowing weight was almost too much for Martin, yet he held fast, juggling the books into balance.

"How are you going to make deliveries if your hands are hurt?"

"I just will. Now don't leave the library this time," I instructed, changing the subject. "Stay in there and don't leave."

"I won't, believe me. I don't even know if I'll go to the bathroom."

A different nun was at the desk in the library that day. It was Sister Anne. She wore thick glasses and normally worked in the front office. I'd have to tell her the story I'd made up about helping my mother at the rectory in order for her to let Martin stay late. I would have to lie again.

"Excuse me, Sister Anne," I began, and the lie flowed from there. Martin was unfazed. He'd become accustomed to my lying and I hated myself for that. While I recounted the fictitious tale of working with my mother, my hands seemed to hurt more than before.

"That's fine," Sister Anne replied. "I've got plenty of shelving to—"

She cut herself off, squinting at my hands. Even the thick lenses of her glasses couldn't soften her scrutiny. I put my hands behind my back.

"The boy can stay," Sister Anne added, her tone clipped.

I went to say good-bye to Martin. "She saw," he whispered, and I nodded. "Too bad she had her glasses on. If she hadn't, she probably wouldn't even have seen that you were a girl."

"Martin."

He shrugged in his defense. "It's not a lie."

It was a distinction Martin made often. Now it seemed like the only distinction there could be. Something was either a lie or it wasn't. Like Mr. Beresik's dog pen, either you were on the outside or you were on the inside with the pit bulls. There were no two ways about it.

MR. GOCELJAK WAS in the curing shed when I arrived. The door was propped open with a brick. He came out holding two buckets, each filled with kishke, and the heavy load was testing his arms to their limit.

"Get the door, would you?"

I darted ahead of him and grabbed the doorknob, momentarily forgetting about my hands. A lash of agony leaped up each arm and left me dizzy. Still, I managed to open the door for Mr. Goceljak, who set down the buckets with a groan. "I would've made you carry one of these, but I bet it weighs more than you do."

When I didn't answer, Mr. Goceljak looked at me curiously. "What's the matter with you?"

That question was all I ever got from my mother and father and now Mr. Goceljak. I was too exhausted to come up with an excuse. I showed him my hands to avoid explaining, then he let out an impressed whistle. "You must've done something real good to get ones like 'at."

I dropped my head, unwilling to disclose what I had done to earn them. Mr. Goceljak guessed as much and didn't wait for an answer.

"I remember getting the ruler," he recalled with a chuckle. "So many times I lost count. Nothing to be ashamed of. Some say it builds character."

"I'm not sure about that."

"Me neither. Sounds good, though. I got a few deliveries that need making, but I'll understand if you can't."

"No, I can do it."

"You sure?" I nodded. "Then that'd make you tougher than most of the boys that came before you. Once one of 'em came to work with just his left hand beat and claimed he needed two days off for it to heal up."

Mr. Goceljak patted my shoulder, then left me to change into my outfit in private. Because of my hands, I couldn't tie the rope belt, so the pants kept dropping to the floor.

"You all right?" Mr. Goceljak called, poking his head through the curtain.

My faced bloomed red. "I can't tie the belt."

Mr. Goceljak wiped his hands on his apron, more out of courtesy than necessity, then stood in front of me and looped the rope into a knot. "Too tight?"

I shook my head. He was standing so close to me that I instinctively lowered my gaze. My father wouldn't even come that close, yet Mr. Goceljak thought nothing of it.

"There you go," he said. "You still want to do this?"

"I've got the pants on. Might as well."

"True enough."

Mr. Goceljak stacked the packages on the counter. "Not too many today. God must be smiling on you."

The comment singed. I tried, with difficulty, to collect the packages and Mr. Goceljak stopped me. "Hold on. I've got an idea." He went to the front of the store and came back with a used paper bag. "We'll put 'em in here, then you can carry the bag in your arms."

"Would that be all right with you?"

"Why not? How were you carrying 'em before?"

"In the pants," I confessed, pointing to the waistband.

"Then this'll be a definite improvement." He shook his head, amused. "Let me pack 'em for you."

Mr. Goceljak loaded up the paper bag and gently set it in my arms.

"There's one in there for her today," he added. He meant the woman in the house on River Road. "Figured I'd better tell you beforehand," Mr. Goceljak said, lowering his gaze just as I had when he was tying the belt for me. "She's not due, but I thought it might, well, I thought she might try talking again if it was you who came round."

THERE WERE ONLY FIVE deliveries that day, and though it was hard to run with the bag in my arms, I ran nonetheless. I wasn't willing to leave Martin at the library any longer than necessary.

The first delivery was to a woman whose house I'd been to before. She'd been smoking when she'd answered the door the first time and she was smoking when she answered it this time, as if it were the very same cigarette. The only difference was that she was dressed in a housecoat rather than day clothes. She coughed hoarsely as she opened the door. Her hair hung in droopy pin curls that bobbed with each cough.

"Thanks," she said hoarsely, then another fit erupted from her throat. I could still hear her choking even after the door was closed.

I made the next two deliveries, then hurried to Mr. Beresik's house. I was relieved to hear the dogs barking as I came up the hill. Before I got to the porch, I ditched the paper bag under a bush and put the last delivery into my coat pocket. The bag didn't seem boyish enough and might have raised questions from Mr. Beresik, who was opening his front door as I reached the porch steps.

"Afternoon," he said. He had a knife in one hand and a stick in the other. I was so taken aback by the knife that it took me a moment to realize Mr. Beresik was only whittling, killing time until my visit.

"Afternoon, sir."

"About yesterday. It was an unplanned thing. Some of the guys came round and we put a game together at the last minute. I would've asked you, but like I said, it was last minute." He seemed to think he'd hurt my feelings by not inviting me.

"It's okay. I mean, I'm sorry too," I stammered. "I should've put the delivery in your icebox."

Mr. Beresik waved me off. "It's not like you're the maid," he chuckled. "Anyway, I used those shanks up right away. My dog took this other one down in under eight minutes. That's a good time. Good thing too 'cause there was a lot of money riding on mine. It was a tough match, but my dog took the bites, biding his time and tiring the other one down. It was smart like, real smart. Like a person smart. It was a good match. You should've seen it."

"Sounds good," I said, for lack of a better answer.

"There's another one tomorrow. You should come. It'll be a good time."

"I don't know."

"Come on, boy. Must've made some money off of old Goceljak by now. A little money can turn into a lot if you play it right."

The thought of the money and my mother's painting waiting in the pawnshop swirled together in my mind.

"Here," I said, handing Mr. Beresik his delivery and changing the subject.

"Well, I'll be damned."

He was marveling at the welts on my hands. "Give 'em here," he said. "Let's have a look." I reluctantly offered them for inspection.

"Both of 'em, eh? You must've been something other than quiet for the nuns today." Mr. Beresik surveyed the wounds, examining them closely, then he turned my palms up, revealing the blisters from the burns. His expression darkened. "Nuns do this to you too?"

"No, sir. It was just an accident."

"Accident?" He wasn't convinced.

"Yes, sir," I said and began to unspool another lie. "I was helping my mother and I picked up the pot for her, but it was hot and I didn't know to use a rag. That's girl stuff," I added for good measure.

"Girl stuff or not, we got to bind these up or you'll get an infection faster than you can blink."

"Oh, no, it's all right. I—"

Mr. Beresik was already ushering me inside. "Seen it happen in the dogs plenty of times. A tiny scratch'll turn ugly if it don't get washed up properly. Dogs don't like 'em bandages much. Try to lick 'em off even. But I can't have no sick dog going in the ring."

He led me to the kitchen, which was spotless compared to the previous day. All of the beer bottles were placed neatly in a box on the floor. A pile of empty tin ashtrays was stacked on the icebox. The muddy footprints had been mopped away.

"Got to wash 'em hands up first," Mr. Beresik said, wringing a rag out in the sink. He brought the wet rag to the table along with a basin of water and a cigar box, then he laid another cloth on the table in front of me and smoothed it out. "Okay, put your hands on this." I did as he told me. "Now this is just soap and water for cleaning, but it's going to sting some."

I fought the instinct to pull away, reminding myself that, to Mr. Beresik, I was a boy, and a boy wouldn't do that. He lightly dabbed the wet cloth across the tops of my hands, then flipped them and did the same to the blisters.

"You said it was an accident?" he said, mulling it over. "You know, you can say if it was otherwise. Like if it was your father, say, thinking this was the way to give you a licking for something you done."

There was no doubt I was afraid of my father, but he had never spanked me or backhanded me the way I'd seen other children get beaten. He had never raised his hand to me or touched me, never in anger, but never in love either.

"It was an accident," I attested. "Really, it was. I did it myself."

"Good then," Mr. Beresik said, taking me at my word. "A beatin' is one thing, but these," he sighed, gazing at my palms, then he let the subject drop. "Well, I'll see what I can do."

He opened the cigar box, displaying its contents—bandages and wraps and jars of ointments. He dug through and picked out one small tin in particular as well as a roll of soft bandaging cloth. "You should see the way I got to wrap 'em dogs sometimes," Mr. Beresik began in a lighter tone. "Looks so funny with all of 'at tape on 'em. They hang their heads, even walk different. It's like they know they look silly."

Mr. Beresik dipped the tip of the wet cloth into the tin, which held a yellowish salve. "Top first," he said, then he dotted the ointment into the skin. "Am I pushing too hard?"

I shook my head, unable to answer because of the pain, and Mr. Beresik could tell. He turned my hands over and began to dab the ointment onto the blisters. The coolness was a relief, but even the slightest pressure on the burns brought tears to my eyes. Though Mr. Beresik's hands were massive compared to mine, he moved them gracefully and with a surprisingly gentle touch. He finished with the salve and capped the tin. "Now comes the hard part."

"I thought that was the hard part."

"Wish it was. Wrapping hurts worse. But it's got to be done."

I knew I would have to remove the bandages later so my mother wouldn't see them, but I didn't stop Mr. Beresik from putting them on. I didn't stop him from taking care of me.

"If you were older, I'd give you a drink. Dull the pain."

"Then I wish I was older."

"Try to think about something else," he suggested. "Think about something good."

Mr. Beresik wound the bandage around my right hand and the pressure of the thin gauze was excruciating. My breath came faster, chugging audibly through my nose. I raked my mind in search of something to think of, something good, but all that materialized was the Black Madonna. I could envision it hanging on our wall, the Holy Mother gazing down at me, the baby Jesus looking off into the distance, not at me, not at anyone.

Once Mr. Beresik had finished both hands, he secured each bandage with a safety pin. "You're a pretty good patient," he said. "With the dogs, I got to worry about them biting me while I wrap 'em."

"At least I didn't bite you."

Mr. Beresik laughed as he closed up the cigar box. "Nope, you didn't."

"Well," I began, unsure of what to say next. Part of me didn't want to leave. "Thanks. I mean, thank you, sir."

"Just don't go doing it again. That'll be thanks enough."

"I should get going. I've got another delivery left to make." I stood and tried to push in my chair, but recoiled before my fingers met the wood. Mr. Beresik pushed the chair in for me.

"Boy with manners. That's something you don't see much. Least of all around here." Mr. Beresik nodded approvingly. "You should come tomorrow. It'll be a good match. A good time. I always save the best matches for Saturday. There's real money to be made at a dogfight," he added. "Money to be lost too. But you put down a one-dollar bet and you could make double your money back. Never hurts to try."

Mr. Beresik wanted me to come to the match, wanted it enough to tempt me with the promise of winning, winning money I desperately needed, and it was working. He wanted me to see what he did, to see what he'd spent all his life training his dogs to do. He wanted to show off to me and I was genuinely flattered.

"All right."

A broad grin flourished on his face. "You'll see. You won't be sorry you came."

As he walked me out to the porch and down the path, the dogs barreled to the fence, bouncing against one another and jockeying for position. A few barked intermittently, then Mr. Beresik whistled and they fell silent. The dogs were so docile around him, so happy to see him, to please him. In the flurry of flopping ears and moving bodies were flashes of white, glimpses of the bandages on the dogs' pelts, their hind legs, their shoulders, everywhere.

"See, you're one of them now," Mr. Beresik joked.

"I guess I am." That meant I was on their side of the fence.

"So I'll see you tomorrow?" he asked.

Sally was standing in the corner of the pen where the ends of the fence met. She seemed to be waiting for me. She blinked a few times, nostrils puffing, though the rest of her body remained motionless.

"Yes," I replied, the words falling out automatically, without feeling. "I'll see you tomorrow."

Mr. Beresik patted my shoulder. "You won't be sorry."

Halfway down the road from his house, I glanced back. Most of the dogs had scattered, but Sally hadn't moved.

She knows. She knows what you've done.

I tore down the hill, letting the cold air swim through my lungs. I cut across town, passing the far end of Third along the way, the end where Swatka Pani's house was. The green limbs of the uprooted roses remained scattered in the garden, unwilling to turn brown or succumb to the cold. They were a reminder of all I had done, and the worst part was, they wouldn't die. They refused to.

RIVER ROAD WAS QUIET except for a faint radio melody from a radio floating out of one of the houses. I climbed the steps to the woman's front porch and took the parcel Mr. Goceljak had given me from the waistband of the trousers, then studied it as if the name should have been there. Of course, it wasn't. The woman must have heard the porch boards creaking because when I went to knock, the lock was already being turned.

"Today's not the day," she said through a sliver in the doorway.

All I could see was one of her eyes, hooded and anxious.

"I know, but Mr. Goceljak had some extra kielbasa. He wanted to give it to you."

It was another lie to add to my tally. There were so many, I'd lost count. The woman was still suspicious and wouldn't open the door any wider.

"You don't have to pay for it," I told her. "It's a gift."

Her face firmed into a confused expression, as though the word *gift* was unfamiliar to her.

"If you don't want it, it's all right. Or I can set it down here on the porch and go."

"No," the woman replied quietly. "I'll take it."

I held the package out to her on the flat of my hand, the bandages making the pain bearable. She hesitated, fingers dangling in midair, then she opened the door a few inches farther, offering me room to pass the package in to her. She took it from me, then her eyes landed on the bandages.

"What did you do?" she asked.

It was a weighty question, one I could have answered a thousand ways, a thousand times over. I had to consider how to reply.

"I fell."

I had said the line so many times it was starting to feel true. I showed her the other hand as well, the matching set of bandages.

"Does it hurt?" the woman asked, her concern sincere. I nodded that it did. "It'll heal up though," she consoled. "Children always heal so quickly." The phrase, once uttered, seemed to prick her like a thorn.

"Well," I said.

"Well."

"I can go."

The woman opened the door a hair's breadth more. "The butcher, he told you about me, didn't he?"

"A little," I admitted.

Even with her voice hovering at a whisper, the woman still sounded refined, dignified. She wasn't angry, yet she seemed to want to clear things up. She appeared to want me to know the truth and only that.

"A little can sometimes be a lot."

While she spoke, I glimpsed the person she must have been, with her hair done up, rouge on her cheeks, and wearing a clean dress. She had been a beautiful woman once.

"I don't leave this house. Not anymore. I'm sure he told you at least that much." The woman cast her eyes over my shoulder at the river beyond, taking in the view and savoring it. "But just because I don't leave doesn't mean I don't know what goes on out there." She gestured to the road as if pointing to a distant land.

"Is that how you know about Swatka Pani?" I ventured.

The name roused the blood in the woman's cheeks. "Nobody here in Hyde Bend forgets. Remembering's all they have. It's all any of us have. A gift from God, my son would always say." She swallowed hard. "Now I know he was wrong."

A silence followed, lingering until the woman began to turn the doorknob back and forth in her hand. It was squeaking with each twist as she worked up to what she wanted to say.

"There was one thing I thought nobody knew, that way nobody could remember. But I was mistaken." The woman eased the door open an inch more, drawing it to her, into the nook between her arm and her breast. "There are worse things than taking your own life. Even for a priest."

The peril in those words, the danger of speaking them aloud, rushed at me like a gust of heat coming from inside the dark house.

"To fall in love. That's far worse."

The woman seemed unable to keep herself from going on. She rested her head against the door, propping herself up to prevent the memory from toppling her as the story flooded out.

"I never knew her name. She was young. A girl, really. Perhaps seventeen. I never met her, never even saw her, but she must have worked at Saint Ladislaus. In the rectory, I believe, doing the cooking and the wash. She was poor. Her father had died early, the way my husband had, and her family had little money. Maybe that was why. Maybe he saw himself when he saw her. I don't know. I don't know if it was love. I believe it must have been. I tell myself it had to have been."

The woman paused, struggling to continue. "It was a secret. All a secret. But then the girl, she became pregnant. It was too much for him. That's what he wrote to me. He left a letter. He must have slipped it under the door in the night. I didn't see it for hours. When I finally found it, it was too late."

Tears welled in her eyes. "No one would have known. Not about the girl or the baby. Not ever. But it was my fault. I was stupid for believing, for trusting her. I should have never trusted that woman."

Her voice turned bitter but she gave no name. She was talking about a different woman than the girl she'd already mentioned.

"Her own husband had just died and her son had drowned and I felt for her. I did. She said we were alike, she and I. Alone. She pleaded with me. She said she had no money and no one to help her. So I gave her a job cleaning the house once a week so she could get by until her husband's will was settled."

The woman tugged the door tighter to her. "She found the letter my son had left. I believe she had been searching for it, searching for something to hold against me. She hadn't wanted the job, hadn't needed it. The money from her husband's will came quickly and she got his land, his entitlements. It was all a lie. Then she said I had to pay her not to tell anyone what my son had done, the girl, the baby, all of it," the woman said, stiffening with resolve. "But the money wasn't what she wanted, not truly. She wanted somebody to suffer as she had. She had no husband, no child, nothing but herself. She wanted someone to be as miserable as she was and as alone."

"I refused to pay her. I told her there was nothing more she could do to me. There was nothing anyone could do to me that would be worse than what had already happened. After that, she never came back. I waited, thinking she would return to hound me. How afraid I was waiting for that knock on the door. It never came. I realized she must have found someone else, someone to replace me. From the letter, I believe she figured out who the girl was, then tracked her down and demanded money from her instead. A young girl, unwed, with a child on the way, would've had nothing, not then, but they must have struck a deal, some way for the girl to pay her off. I never saw Katarina after that day."

"Who?"

"That was her name," the woman said, surprised that I hadn't known. "That was Swatka Pani's real name.

"I'm glad she's dead," the woman declared. "God will hate me for it, but it's true." She chuckled lightly. "Not that He doesn't hate me already."

I wanted to put my hand over the woman's mouth to stop her, as if she could get us both in trouble.

"I'm glad Swatka Pani's dead. I'm glad I wasn't the one she came after. And I'm glad that I'm not the one who had to do it, to kill her, but I'll tell you something, I would have. So help me God, I would have."

"Don't say that," I shouted, stunned by my own voice. The woman had spoken the words that had been rattling through my mind, and it was a horror to hear them aloud.

"There's nothing I could say that could make Him hate me more," the woman defended, opening the door wide, exposing the shambles of her home, her prison.

"Don't say that," I shouted again, backing away from her.

"God doesn't care. Not anymore."

I was panting and trying to pull myself away from the woman, to extricate myself from her, though she wasn't even touching me. Without warning, the top step gave way beneath me. The wood splintered, sending me tumbling backward over the porch steps to the ground.

The wind was knocked out of me. My lungs stung, waiting for air. I opened my eyes, but couldn't see. Seconds later, the world returned, blurry. I could make out the woman in her doorway, her face frightened and her body frozen, unable to cross the threshold. The woman's mouth was moving, but I heard no sound. Then came an echo of words I could recognize.

"Are you all right?"

She must have asked me a number of times, however I only heard the last. I sat up, ears ringing, breathing hard. The blood rushed to my head and the first thing I felt was the sensation of the canvas cap. It was sitting askew on my head, ready to fall off and expose me. I yanked the cap down over my hair and eyes and scrambled to my feet, but stumbled, still dizzy, and braced myself on the ground. The once-white bandages were dingy with dirt. My clothes were covered in a fine powdering of dust.

"I'm sorry," I said, staggering away.

There was no feeling in my legs as I bounded down River Road. My ears were buzzing, drowning out all other noise. I ran until I cleared the corner and careened over the cobblestone curb, then my knees gave out, pitching me to the ground again. I thrust my hands out to break my fall and a searing pain shot through my arms on impact. I remained crumpled there on the corner, desperate to catch my breath.

Smoke from the steel mill's stacks was pirouetting into the air in gray swirls until it blended in with the clouded sky. The full weight of what the woman had told me had not sunk in yet, nor would it for some time to come. As I lay there, I made no connections, drew no conclusions, had no idea of the gravity of what I had learned. Though I must have sensed it.

All of my bones felt as if they had been loosened and were now out of place. Each rib cried out with each breath, resenting the movement. My body was like a sack of nails, each threatening to poke through with the slightest shift. I could not get up. I didn't even try.

AFTER WHAT SEEMED LIKE HOURS but was merely minutes, I stood, using my forearms for leverage. Once I was up, momentum took over and I found myself wandering back to the butcher's shop. All I could do was walk. I didn't have it in me to run.

I could hear Mr. Goceljak speaking with a customer in the front of the store, then soon afterward he stormed into the back room, looking agitated. "It's been so busy today I haven't had time to think. That and I forgot to give you one of the deliveries," he began, then he stopped and gawked at me. "What happened? You look terrible."

Before I could answer, the bell over the shop door chimed. Another customer. Mr. Goceljak's eyes shifted to a package on the block. I could tell it was kishke by the way it was wrapped, how heavily the meat slumped inside the paper. "I would do it myself, but . . ."

Customer's voices sounded from the front of the store. "It's for the Pierwszas over at the Slipper."

"But that place is—"

"I know. But you're only dropping off the delivery. You're not staying around for a drink."

"But my outfit. Now I look—"

"Like a mess. I can see that much. Makes you look even more like a boy. Just tuck those stray hairs under the cap and nobody'll be any the wiser."

A woman called out in Polish to Mr. Goceljak, saying she was in a hurry. He pleaded with his eyes. "You can tell me about what happened when you get back," he offered, then he cut through the curtain into the front room.

Grudgingly, I forced my hair under the cap, pulled it low, and headed out the back door as always, passing the bicycle on the way. I paused to touch the handlebar and pet the seat. The bicycle seemed far less grand to me then, a flimsy jumble of rusted metal, yet it was everything I wanted and still couldn't have.

The Silver Slipper sat on the other side of Field Street. Decades earlier, it had been a house, and the clapboard remained, clinging to it for life. A few coats of navy paint were caked on the boards and wilting in long, jagged strips that flapped when the wind blew. What was once a porch had been boarded up to create a covered alcove, and an ill-fitting door made for a smaller opening was put out front. The sign above the door was as ravaged as the rest of the building. The lettering appeared to have bite marks in it, but it was actually buckshot from when a drunken patron tried to blow out the building's windows, but was too intoxicated to aim straight.

The front door to the Silver Slipper was always open. That was the saying, a familiar motto around Hyde Bend, and it was true. The door could not be locked because the bolt had been broken long ago and never fixed. I entered and found the porch unlit except for the dim light that was coming through the windows of the house's old facade. Empty kegs were piled high, leaving little room except for a path that led directly to the old front door. Burbling voices and music from a radio bled into the alcove. Then came shouting, not playful, but raucous and harsh, followed by the thud of chairs overturning. I took a deep breath and pushed the door with my knuckles, the package nestled in the crook of my arm.

It took a moment for my eyes to adjust to the darkened room, then I was greeted by an upturned table. Broken beer bottles were scattered on the floor. In the middle of the barroom a mass of men were struggling in a tangle of flailing arms and twisting legs. All the while a tinny trumpet tune was jingling from the radio.

Then one of the Pierwsza brothers appeared from another room. It was Clement, squat, with his shoulders up near his chin, his ruddy face seeming to cave in under the weight of his brow. He was wielding the infamous baseball bat. Four nails protruded from the end. Clement lumbered toward the swarming mass, footfalls thundering on the floorboards.

"Get up. Get off of him. Now," he shouted in Polish, charging at the heap.

A few men pulled away, then a pained, guttural moan seeped out from under the pile. Clement hoisted the bat high.

"Move!"

The rest of the men clambered to their feet, though one remained splayed on the floor. At first, all I could make out were his legs, one foot with a boot, one without.

"*Jezu Christe*," Clement uttered, then he dropped the bat to the floor where it embedded itself in the wooden planks. The men backed off farther still, revealing the man that lay before them. It was Leonard.

I clamped my bandaged hand to my mouth, stifling a scream. Blood streamed from Leonard's nose and mouth, ebbing over his teeth. He heaved once, then blood sprayed from his lips with a gurgle. The blood rained back down on him, spattering his face.

"Look what you've done," Clement shouted.

"That stupid bastard shouldn't've come back after what he did," one man yelled.

"He killed her," another called out. The other men sounded off in agreement.

"He's a murderer," another barked.

Clement cursed them and knelt next to Leonard. As he pulled him into his arms, Clement dislodged something from under Leonard's body, which skittered across the floor and came to a stop at my feet. It was the bottom half of a broken bottle, the rounded end still intact. The jagged, broken rim was slick with blood.

I was holding my breath to keep from sobbing as tears poured over my fingers, hidden in the shadow of the cap. I inhaled once, too loudly, and all the men in the room turned. Their faces were blank and unrecognizable, all except one. It was my father. He was looking straight at me. I drew in a sharp breath. He continued to stare, but he didn't recognize me.

Leonard let out another gasp and the men swiveled back to him. Clement was rocking him gently, smoothing Leonard's hair with a stubby hand. Leonard raised his arm to Clement, then it dropped limply. His gaze drifted and settled on me. A thin vein of blood rolled from Leonard's nose, over his lip, and into his mouth, then his eyes went dull.

"Leonard?" I whispered.

Some of the men spun toward me.

"Get the boy out of here," one of them said.

My father was staring down at Leonard's body, his jaw flexed, resisting an expression. If it was disgust or guilt or satisfaction, I would never know. Nobody moved.

I took a step forward, toward Leonard, then two men started in my direction. I dropped the package and took off running.

"Let him go," I heard one say as the door swung shut behind me. To them, I was a boy, but that was all and it wasn't enough to make a difference.

I ran hard, arms pumping, dashing across Field Street to the butcher's shop and flinging myself against the front door. Mr. Goceljak was with two women, customers, each in wool overcoats and clean shoes.

"They killed him," I shouted. "They killed him."

The women went wide-eyed and exchanged glances. I was raving, tears streaking my face, my clothes grubby.

"Go around back," Mr. Goceljak ordered.

"But—"

"Now," he commanded. The women watched me, waiting for me to obey. I tore outside, slamming the door hard enough to leave the bell jangling.

The alley behind the shop was empty. The door to the curing shed was closed and locked, the bicycle chained by the stoop. Everything was the same. I hated the sight of that alley, that sameness, more than I thought possible.

In a fit, I began to kick the bicycle. First with my toe, then I jabbed at it with my heels, ramming the delicate spokes with my boot. I kicked the wheels and the pedals and the basket until my limbs blurred with the motion.

I hate you. I hate you. I hate you.

I couldn't tell if I was shouting out loud or hearing the voice in my mind, yet I kept kicking. The bicycle slumped lower against the railing, hanging on by the chain.

Mr. Goceljak came flying out the back door and wrestled me away from the bicycle, pinning my arms behind me and forcing my head to his chest, the bloody apron pressing against my face.

"Stop. Stop it," he said. He pushed me up against the shed to restrain me. As soon as my body stopped moving, I started to sob. Mr. Goceljak loosened his grip on my arms and they dropped to my sides. The cap fell from my head as I wept, and my hair slid down onto my shoulders and stuck to my teary cheeks.

Mr. Goceljak kept his arms around me and let me cry. He held me lightly, as if he were holding a glass rather than a little girl. He was the only thing keeping me standing. If he had let go, I would've crumpled to the ground.

"Leonard came back, didn't he?"

I nodded, chin quivering, and Mr. Goceljak sighed.

"Would've been a full shift've men from the mill there this time a day," he said, calculating how bad it must have been. He shook his head dismally. "That boy never should've come back here. Something like this was bound to happen. But I s'pose he didn't have anywhere else to go. No family. No friends. Nothing for him to go back to 'cept what he knew."

"But I—"

"What? You thought you were going to fight off all of those men? You might've done some damage to that poor bicycle over there, but boy clothes or not, you wouldn't have had a chance against 'em." Mr. Goceljak tipped my face to meet his, to make sure I knew how serious he was. "You couldn't have helped Leonard. You understand?"

My head pounded from crying and my eyes ached. Even nodding hurt, but I did it anyway to prove to him that I'd understood. Mr. Goceljak let go of my arms and I wavered, then steadied myself against the smokehouse door.

"Easy there," he said, preparing to catch me if I fell. "Think you can walk?"

"I think so."

"All right then, we have to get you inside and cleaned up. You look worse than the bicycle."

The bicycle was listing against the steps. One of its wheels was turned up and spinning slowly.

"I'm sorry about the bicycle. I don't have enough money to pay you back for it."

"That's for sure considering what I pay you."

Mr. Goceljak led me inside, where a few pots were boiling on the stove, steam rattling the lids. The syrupy smell of the stewing meat made the room feel warmer than it was.

"Let's start with the pants," Mr. Goceljak said. "They even look dirty to me, and that's saying something."

I went to untie the rope belt he'd tied for me earlier, but it was no use. My fingers were numb.

"Let me," Mr. Goceljak said. I tried to step out of the pants and couldn't get my balance. "Lean on my shoulder," he told me, leaning over so I could reach him. I shook off the pants, legs stiff, and he pulled them from my boots, then put them aside along with the cap. "Now we've got to do something about those bandages."

Mr. Goceljak unpinned the wraps and removed the bandages as gently as he could. My palms were worse than before. Without the protection of the bandages, they quickly turned an angry red. The skin around the blisters was puckered and still slick with ointment. "These are pretty bad," Mr. Goceljak lamented. "You got more bandages at home?"

We did, but I couldn't use them, couldn't be seen with them on. Mr. Goceljak took my silence as his answer, then riffled through one of the drawers and came up with a roll of his own. "You put 'em on at night. Once you're in bed if you have to, then wake up early to take 'em off. But put 'em on, okay?" He held the roll out to me, but my fingers were too stiff to grasp it. "Here," he offered, slipping the bandages into my coat pocket.

"It's late," I said. "I have to go."

"Just one more thing."

Mr. Goceljak dug around in another drawer and came up with a little black comb. "Can't have you looking like you been in a fight. Well, not more than you already do." He held the comb out to me, then realized I wouldn't be able to hold it either. "Sorry. Forgot. You want me to do it?"

I was too tired to be embarrassed or to protest. Mr. Goceljak stepped around behind me and ran the comb over my head in tentative strokes. The tines of the comb slid through my hair and down my scalp. This wasn't how my mother brushed my hair. This felt different, gentle, soothing. Then Mr. Goceljak hit a knot and the comb came to a tugging halt.

"Sorry," he said and I actually felt him flinch. "Sorry."

"It doesn't hurt."

Mr. Goceljak began again, working his way around my head until he reached the front. "Now what do I do?"

"What do you mean?"

"Is it done?" he asked.

"I don't know. I can't see."

"Don't have a mirror here," he apologized. "No need for it."

"I'm sure it's all right."

Mr. Goceljak was worried about whether he'd done a good job. "Best I could do."

"It's fine, really. I'm sure it's fine."

"All right then, I guess you should be on your way."

I doubted that Mr. Goceljak was aware of it, but that was the same phrase he had spoken to me every single day since I'd met him. I liked that we had a routine, that that was the way things always ended.

"Should I come on Monday?" I asked, half-expecting him to fire me there and then.

"Wouldn't be Monday if you didn't." Mr. Goceljak offered me a smile. "Here," he added, taking two quarters from his pocket. "It's Friday, payday."

He held the quarters out to me. "Oh, sorry," he said, then he dropped the quarters in my coat pocket along with the roll of bandages. "You don't have a hole in that pocket, do you?"

"No, it's all sewn up." There had been holes in each of the pockets when I got the coat from the nuns. There were holes in everything we wore. That was a given.

"Good. We don't need you losin' the bandages or the money."

He opened the back door for me. The bicycle lay wounded against the steps.

"Sorry," I offered again.

Mr. Goceljak waved me off. "Hey, you didn't say if the woman—" he began. He was about to ask me what had happened when I went to the house on River Road. Instead, he looked me up and down, taking in the sum of what I'd been through, and simply said, "I'll see you Monday."

FIELD STREET WAS FULL OF PEOPLE, all gathering outside the Silver Slipper. The women kept their distance while packs of men pushed in close to the Slipper's front porch. Even some of the shopkeepers were leaning out of their stores. Though there was nothing to see, just people standing around as they had outside Swatka Pani's house, I couldn't bear to look.

Sister Anne was standing on the steps of the school holding Martin's hand in a rigid grip when I arrived. He was staring at his shoes, his books clutched in his free arm.

"What's going on?" I asked in English. The nuns refused to be addressed in Polish. To them, English was the formal language.

"Your brother has a discipline problem," the sister declared, her accent sharpening each word. Martin rolled his eyes furtively. "He tried to steal one of the books from the library."

"Martin?"

"I didn't. I—"

Sister Anne squeezed his hand between her bony fingers. "He had not checked out this book," she said, holding up the one with the lamb on the cover, "and he packed it up with his school textbooks and tried to walk out with it."

"But—" Martin tried again. The sister clasped his hand hard, choking off his excuses.

"There's got to be some mistake. This book is Martin's favorite. He checks it out all the time. Why would he try to steal it?"

"Like you said, it's his favorite. Maybe he didn't want to have to check it out anymore."

"That doesn't make any sense."

"Girl, are you telling me I'm mistaken? That I didn't see what I saw?"

I was standing on the step below Sister Anne and she was towering over me while clutching Martin, unwilling to let go.

"No, Sister," I apologized, trying to pacify her. "All I'm saying is that maybe he forgot. He's so used to having the book and checking it out that he probably thought he'd already signed for it."

Martin looked up at Sister Anne hopefully. "That's what happened. Really, Sister. I forgot."

I took the lamb book from him and flipped to the back cover, hands aching. "See," I said, offering the book to her. Martin's initials filled the check-out card.

"Fine. But don't let it happen again."

Sister Anne held out Martin's arm to me like a leash. I went to take his hand and she eyed mine, the top of which still bore the welts she'd seen earlier. Though I'd convinced her to let Martin go, the welts confirmed to Sister Anne that she was right about us, that we were bad children capable of back talk, stealing books, anything.

"Come on, Martin."

Martin scurried to my side and we hastened down the steps and away from the school. Out of the corner of his mouth, Martin whispered, "Do you think she's still watching us?"

"Yup."

"When we get around the corner, you think she'll go inside?"

"Yup."

"Then can I stick my tongue out at her?"

"Yup."

Once we'd turned onto the next street, Martin stuck his tongue out in the direction of the school.

"Feel better?"

"Much." He slid his hand into my coat pocket as we walked. "I did try to steal the book, you know."

I stopped midstride, forcing Martin to lurch forward to keep his hand in my pocket. "What?" I asked, assuming I'd misheard him.

"I wanted the book, so I took it. You saw for yourself. Nobody reads it but me, and nobody likes it the way I do, so I thought it should be mine."

I couldn't believe what I was hearing. My brother was so calm, his argument simple, collected.

"Martin, we're not supposed to steal. It's not right. I don't care if you take the book out every day for the rest of your life, that doesn't make it yours."

"Why not?"

"You didn't buy it. You didn't pay for it."

"But I'm the only one who uses it. I think that makes it mine."

This is all your fault. My thoughts resonated like strings being plucked. *This is all your fault.*

"Martin," I said, facing him sternly. "Don't take the book again. Please don't. What would God think?"

"I think God would want me to have the lamb book."

I strode off in frustration, moving fast enough to dislodge Martin's hand from my pocket. He ran to catch up. "It's about Him anyway," he defended.

"Martin, I don't ever want to see that book in the house again."

He was horrified at the thought. "What? Why?"

"I just don't."

"That's no answer."

"It's enough of one."

"What if I promise to check it out next time? You can make sure I haven't stolen it. Please. Don't say I can't read the lamb book."

"No, Martin."

He ran ahead and got right in front of me. "Your face is different. I saw it when you came to get me. You were crying."

"I wasn't crying."

"Liar."

I pushed Martin, nearly knocking him to the ground. "Don't call me that."

He scowled, shocked, and righted himself. "If you're lying, then that's what you are."

"I said don't call me that."

"Then say you were crying."

"Fine, I was crying," I shouted. "Does it make you happy?"

"No, but I don't want you to lie. You can lie to everyone else. But not to me."

I laughed aloud. By then, I didn't have a choice. I couldn't *not* lie anymore.

"Don't laugh."

"I can't laugh and I can't lie. That doesn't leave me much else to do, Martin."

"Yes it does. Tell me why you were crying."

"No," I yelled. Martin backed away, genuinely scared. I had to say something and I knew what it would be. Another lie.

"I fell when I was making my deliveries. I fell on my hands and hurt them even worse." I proffered my sticky, blistered palms as proof.

Martin examined my hands. "We could put bandages on them like you put on . . ." He kept himself from mentioning my father's accident.

"Mr. Goceljak gave me some. He told me to put them on at night, in secret, so no one sees."

"I can help you. We can do it under the covers. She won't find out if you take them off before she wakes up."

Martin was so glad to hear what he thought was the truth that it made my heart feel as blistered as my hands.

"WHAT TOOK YOU TWO SO LONG?" my mother asked as we entered the apartment. She was sitting at the table, her feet propped on a chair, massaging her calves.

"I was at the library," Martin told her. "I was reading this book and I forgot what time it was."

Hearing Martin lie again should have made me wince like before. That time, it was more like a pinprick, sharp and then gone.

"And where were you?" she asked me. I could see her flexing her toes beneath her stockings, spreading them wide, then curling them inward.

"I was there. I was doing my schoolwork. I didn't know how late it was."

"They don't have clocks at school anymore?"

Martin and I swapped glances in the uneasy silence.

"I made her stay. I wanted to finish the book before we left."

"That book you've got right there?" My mother nodded to the book he was carrying on top of his textbooks. There was a tautness to her question, like she was testing us.

"Yes," Martin replied.

"If you finished it, then why did you bring it home?"

"It's the one I like, the one I always bring home, the one about the lamb."

"You and that lamb book." My mother slumped deeper into the chair, as if she'd lost interest in the topic, and started kneading her right shoulder with her left hand. "Put some tea on, will you?" she asked.

While I filled the kettle, Martin unloaded his books on the table. I gestured for him to set out mine as well. It would be too difficult for me because of my hands.

"I thought you said you finished your homework," my mother said to me.

"No, I said I was working on it. But I didn't finish it. There was a lot today."

Carrying the kettle the short distance from the sink to the stove was a torture, punishment for the lies I'd just told my mother, I assumed. I switched on the burner, but there was no flame. "It won't light."

My mother sighed. "Try it again."

I did, but still nothing. "It still won't light."

"Get a match," she said. Normally, she kept a box of long matches on top of the coal stove to light the fire with; however, the carton was empty.

"There aren't any left."

"Try your father's cigarettes. There's a pack next to the bed."

I hadn't been in my parents' bedroom in a long time. We weren't forbidden to go in, not verbally, yet Martin and I rarely ventured beyond the doorway. Sometimes we would peer in, though we rarely crossed the threshold.

The bedroom seemed different, darker. There were more shadows. The bed was less kempt. The blanket was pulled up to cover the sheets below, but it was as if my mother was only making her side. My father's side was rumpled. The pillow seemed deflated and it hung out from under the blanket.

"Did you find them?" my mother called.

A pack of cigarettes sat on the chair next to my father's side of the bed. A shirt hung from the back of the chair, which filled out the shirt like a set of shoulders. Tucked in one side of the pack of cigarettes was a paper book of matches. Beneath it was a five-dollar bill.

There's real money to be made at a dogfight. You could double your money.

For us, five dollars was a vast sum. If my mother found out my father had been keeping the bill in a pack of cigarettes, and hiding it from her, she might not have forgiven him.

We're not supposed to steal. That's what you told Martin.

"Be quiet," I said, trying to douse the thoughts with my voice.

"What did you say?" my mother called out, growing impatient.

"Nothing," I answered, then I took both the book of matches and the five-dollar bill from the pack. I hid the money in the pocket of my skirt and rushed out of the room.

"I found them."

"Then put the kettle on."

"But the stove?"

My mother's face drew in, angry. "I've been on my feet all day. You can see that, can't you?"

"I'll do it," Martin offered. "I can light matches. I know how. I've seen—"

"Your sister'll do it."

My mother talked me through the process of relighting the pilot light without turning to watch me. She was too tired even to swivel her head. "Put on the burner," she directed. "Now strike the match."

I got the burner on, but fumbled with the match, my hands thrumming with pain. Once I had one match free, I struck it against the pack, but it wouldn't spark. I tried again and again with no luck. The match began to buckle.

"What are you doing?" my mother demanded. "Light the match."

"I'll do it," Martin repeated, restlessly moving in his chair.

"Sit down," my mother told him.

"I am sitting down."

"Then stay there."

"It won't light," I said, still desperately dragging the match over the pack.

My mother mumbled a few words. All I could make out was something that sounded like, *You will be the death of me.*

"Give it here," she ordered.

I was about to hold out the pack to her but she would have seen my hands.

"No, I can do it. Really, I promise I can." I pulled out another match, held my breath, and flicked the match head along the pack. It ignited with a tiny spark. "I got it."

"Hold it up to the burner."

I tilted the match to the stove and a lick of flame sprang into the air, sending me backpedaling.

"You left the burner on. That's why it caught so high," my mother stated flatly. "Won't make that mistake again."

I shook out the match and put the kettle on. "Anything else?" I asked.

"You sound like somebody's maid," she said.

Martin folded his lips in to keep from defending me. My mother was staring off at the other end of the apartment, as if her eyes were jammed, her neck stuck in place.

I stood at the stove, behind her and out of view, until the water in the kettle rattled, then I took the kettle off the burner before it could blow. I poured her a cup of water and dropped in a tea bag so I wouldn't have to do it at the table, then slid the cup toward her elbow so she wouldn't notice my hands.

"A spoon," she said, as she sifted in a tiny bit of sugar from the bowl on the table.

I did the same thing with the spoon, setting it down slightly behind her.

"And the milk."

She dunked the tea bag in and out of the cup, wound it around a spoon, then poured a few drops of milk into the tea, precise despite her exhaustion.

"Put the milk away or it'll get warm."

Hour after hour, Martin and I sat with her at the table as she drank the whole kettleful of tea, repeating the same process of preparation, time and time again, as though trying to hypnotize herself.

Night fell and we waited for my father to arrive. I was steeling myself for the moment when I would have to see him. He hadn't recognized me at the Silver Slipper, but I had seen him and I had seen what he was a part of. I reread the same sentence in my grammar text over and over, unable to understand it and unable to move on.

Footsteps sounded outside the door, then singing. It was my father. He was belting out a song and fumbling for his key.

"Mariska busia dac," he sang.

Mary give me a kiss!

He rattled the key in the lock clumsily, bolting it, then stumbled into the apartment.

"Momusha nie pytac."

Don't ask your darling mother.

He struggled to take off his coat, thrashing himself out of the sleeves and singing all the while. His work clothes were more soiled than usual. He hung his coat on the hook, but it fell and he left it where it lay. When he realized we were all staring, he ceased his song.

"What? What is it?"

"Your clothes are filthy," my mother said.

"No, the Germans—" Martin began and I elbowed him under the table.

"You're going to get yourself killed," my mother sneered.

The mill was an easy place to get hurt. Men had their fingers crushed and wrenched their backs regularly. Injuries were a daily occurrence. Going to work drunk only made the mill more dangerous.

My father bristled at the word *killed* and appeared to sober up momentarily. "Feet up. Must be nice," my father shot back at her. "I'm hungry," he said, slapping his stomach. "You hungry?" he asked Martin and me.

With a jerk, my mother pushed out the chair she had been resting her feet on, almost toppling it. The chair legs raked across the floor and came to a groaning stop right in front of my father. He grinned as if it were a magic trick and plunked down in the chair, far from the table or Martin and me, and I was grateful for that small distance.

My father tried kicking off his boots, but the laces were too tight. Each attempt sent sprays of dried dirt raining down on the floor. He tried shaking off the boots, yet they wouldn't budge. His frustration grew and he growled under his breath, furiously pulling at his boot. My mother refused to turn away from the sink to witness the commotion. To compete, she made a racket of taking out the stew and putting it on the stove. She knocked the pot heavily against the burner and clanked the dishes as she took them down from the shelves. The cacophony made the apartment quake.

"Damn it," my father snapped.

Martin hopped up before I could grab him, knelt at my father's feet, and picked the double-knotted laces loose. My mother glanced back to see what had quelled the noise, in time to watch my father patting Martin's head as he freed one boot, then the other.

"Wash your hands again before you come back to the table," my mother said, addressing Martin.

My father slid off his boots and left them where they lay. "You're a good boy," he slurred as Martin got up to go to the washroom.

"You too," my mother said, reminding me to wash my hands as well.

When Martin and I were safely inside the washroom, he whispered, "Close the door."

"I can't, not all the way. They'll think we're up to something." I left the door slightly ajar. "Why did you want me to close it?"

My father's voice sprang up. "You don't even know what you're talking about," he yelled, responding to something my mother must have said to him softly, so we wouldn't hear.

"That's why."

The hiss of my parents' hushed voices, barely restrained, seeped through the crack in the doorway. I turned the faucet on high to muffle the sound, then Martin lowered it, trying to listen in, but all we could make out were a few curses from my father. Martin and I took turns at the sink. At first, washing my hands made them feel a little better, yet the cold water soon hurt more than it helped.

"I don't think my hands can get much cleaner," Martin said.

"Mine neither."

"Do you think they're done? I can't hear them anymore."

Our parents' voices had blurred with the rushing water. Then came another staccato curse from my father.

"No, I don't think they're finished, but we can't stay in here forever."

"You want me to go first?" Martin asked.

"No, I'll go. Just sit down as quick as you can and don't say anything."

The second I opened the door, my parents halted their argument. My mother spun back to the stove and my father, who had stood up, sat back down. Martin and I pulled our chairs in close to the table and my father followed suit.

"Don't you think you should wash your hands too?" my mother sniped.

Fury flexed in my father's cheeks. In one swift motion, he stood up and pushed back his chair, nearly hurling it to the floor, then stomped to the washroom. He paused at the door.

"Leonard Olsheski is dead," my father announced, eyes tight on my mother. "Didn't know if you'd heard." Then he slammed the door to the washroom.

My mother blanched, her eyes glazed and she wavered on her feet. She was about to faint. Her knees buckled and both Martin and I jumped from our seats, but she caught herself on the icebox and went sliding down a few inches before the sleeve of her dress snagged on the handle, dragging her to a stop.

"Are you all right?" Martin asked, frightened by what he'd seen.

She steadied herself on the sink, putting her back to us, then nodded and straightened her dress.

Martin glowered at me. My lack of surprise at the news had given me away. He'd figured out that I'd lied to him earlier. Angry, he folded his arms and dropped into his seat, angling his chair away from me.

I mouthed the word *sorry* to him, but he wouldn't acknowledge me.

My mother set the dishes out with trembling hands. She kept her head low. "Put your school things away," she muttered.

Martin snapped his book closed and snatched up his pencils, making a show of how hurt he was. I nudged my books together with my knuckles, trying to keep my hands inconspicuous as my mother continued to lay out the knives and forks.

"I'll do it," Martin snorted, grabbing my books as a favor to me, but mad nonetheless.

My mother leaned over to put out a plate of bread, then paused. The tips of my fingers were resting on the table's edge, leaving the purplish mounds of bruised flesh in full view. She blinked at the welts, trying to comprehend them, then she must have realized how I'd gotten them.

I inhaled, anticipating her admonishments, but my mother continued to set the table, taking out the jug of milk, a coffee cup for my father. I waited, hands exposed. Though she'd seen the bruises, I was tempted to lift my hands into the air and present them to her again. I wanted to get whatever she was going to do over with. However, my mother went about preparing supper without comment. She seemed unwilling to look at me rather than unable.

Martin returned to the table and pulled his chair even farther from mine, closer to my father's.

"Did you wash your hands?" my mother asked him. She was frying two eggs for my father's breakfast.

"I already washed them."

"Oh. Right."

My father came out of the washroom shaking water from his hands. He hadn't shaved as usual. He was too drunk to remember to do so. He hauled his chair up next to Martin's, then fumbled at his shirt pockets in search of his cigarettes.

I jumped up from my seat, saying, "I'll get them."

I came back with three single cigarettes to keep him from noticing the missing money and quickly dropped them onto the center of his plate, then slipped my hands behind my back to keep him from seeing the welts as well. My father gazed at the plate full of cigarettes, bewildered.

"That's how many you usually have at dinner," I said.

He was puzzled but not sober enough to care. The matches remained on the table from when I'd used them to light the stove. They were closer to Martin, who handed them to my father.

He struck one of the matches with ease and lit his first cigarette. He took a hearty drag and patted Martin on the head again for getting him the matches. "You're a good boy."

———

SUPPER WAS A MUTE EVENT. While the rest of us poked at our food, my father ate fast and ravenously. In one hand he held his fork, in the other a slice of bread, which he used to sop up the eggs and shovel them into his mouth. When he'd finished each piece of bread, he'd pause to take a drag off his cigarette then resume eating. He was done in minutes. My father lit his last cigarette and headed for the outhouse. He tracked two muddy footprints on the floor on his way back in.

"I'll get your lunch," Martin offered, grabbing the tin from the icebox.

"'At's a good boy," my father said in a singsong as he pulled on his coat, still very drunk. "You sleep well," my father told Martin. "And say your prayers. Don't forget. You won't forget, will you?"

Martin eagerly shook his head.

"'At's a good boy. Never forgets to say his prayers."

My mother folded her arms, a sign for my father to leave. He took the hint and was gone. Afterward, Martin spotted the muddy footprints and put his feet next to them, happily comparing his small feet to my father's.

My mother got up from the table, went into her room, then came out in her nightdress and robe. She strode into the washroom, then the water began to run.

If she draws a bath, this time she'll do it.

I found myself being drawn to the door. I pressed my ear to the wood.

This time she'll do it.

"What are you doing?" Martin said, reprimanding me. "What if she opens the door?"

I hushed him with my finger, a gesture he took as an insult.

"Get away from there," he said, both warning and pleading at the same time. Martin came over and grabbed my hand to pull me away from the door and I hissed in pain.

"I'm sorry. I'm sorry. I forgot. I'm sorry."

I held my palm to my chest but kept my ear to the door. For a few seconds, the pain was deafening. I strained to hear if the water was still on, then came the distinctive creak of the faucet being shut off. I hurried away from the door just as my mother drifted out of the washroom. Her cheeks were dewy with water. Wet tendrils of hair clung to her forehead. She had merely been washing her face.

She slipped into her bedroom in a fog. After she closed the door, Martin called out, "We won't forget to say our prayers. Don't worry. We won't forget."

Before bed, we said our prayers sitting instead of on our knees. I held my hands together as close as I could without them touching while we perched on the edge of the cot, hastily humming the prayers in unison. Afterward, Martin pulled the blanket back so I could crawl in, more out of habit than courtesy.

"The bandages," I said, remembering. I retrieved the roll from my coat and checked on the money. When I'd changed into my nightdress, I slipped the five-dollar bill out of my skirt and into my coat pocket, hiding it with the quarters Mr. Goceljak had given me. Together the money remained safely hidden.

I held out the bandages to Martin. "Can you do it for me?"

"I said I would."

He took to the task with adult diligence. I explained to him how Mr. Beresik had wrapped my hands, and Martin followed my instructions, winding the bandage on in small passes, lining each layer up as closely as he could.

"Is it my fault?" he asked softly.

"What?"

"Leonard?"

"No," I told him, though I couldn't be sure. "It's not."

Martin was gauging my tone, hoping to believe me. "I don't know."

"There's nothing to know."

He started on my other hand, then the roll of bandages slipped and unfurled out along the floor in a white line, carving the apartment in two.

Martin leaped up from the bed to collect the bandages. "Did I ruin it? Is it ruined?"

"No, it's not ruined."

"But now it's dirty."

"It's just a little dust." I shook out the bandage. "See, it's all better."

Relieved, Martin set back to work, carefully tucking each of the ends in when he was finished. "Did I do it okay?"

The bandages looked as good as when Mr. Beresik had applied them, tight and precise, perhaps even better. I admired my hands, proud of what Martin had done.

"Better than okay."

"Really?" He was pleased.

"Maybe you could be a doctor someday," I said, then I recalled what Mr. Goceljak had told me about the priest, how he could have been a doctor, how he could have gotten himself out of Hyde Bend.

Martin warmed with the compliment. "Maybe."

He held the blanket open for me, then bundled it around us and tucked me in. "She's different still," he sighed.

"I know."

"Is it going to be like this from now on?"

"I don't know."

"I hope not. I don't like it like this."

I wanted to tell him that things would change, but my voice would betray me. Martin would hear my lack of conviction. At least, that was what I told myself.

MORNING CAME, ARRIVING with an impatient sun. Even with the blanket pulled up over my face, the sun streaming in the window was unrelenting.

"Are you awake?" Martin asked.

"Uh-huh."

"He should be home by now."

"Uh-huh."

He huddled closer and made a tent out of the blanket. We lay there with the sheet touching the tips of our noses and curving around our foreheads. "She's usually awake by now," he huffed, sending up a stream of air that fluttered the sheet.

"Uh-huh."

"Should we wake her?"

"No."

"What should we do?"

Mr. Beresik would be expecting me. I had to get ready. I had to leave. "I have somewhere I need to go today."

"Where? It's Saturday."

"I can't tell you."

"Why?"

"Because I can't take you."

Martin gave a little snort because it was another one of my vague excuses. "Then what are you going to do with me? Leave me here?"

"Why not?"

"Then I'll be alone."

"No, you won't. She'll be here. She doesn't have to work today."

He rolled his eyes. "You can't leave me here with her. What if she doesn't wake up?" He meant if she didn't wake up for a long time. Martin realized what he'd said. "You know what I mean."

"Martin, please. I can't take you."

"I won't have anyone to talk to or any food or anything. It'll be terrible."

"You have the lamb book to read and I'll make your breakfast."

He folded his arms sullenly. I didn't want to take him with me to Mr. Beresik's, but I didn't want to leave him with my mother either. I couldn't be sure which would be worse.

"All right, you can come." Martin clapped and I shushed him. "But you have to do exactly what I tell you. Understand?" He nodded emphatically.

We hurried into our clothes and I made us sandwiches and put them in one of our school tins.

"We're having lunch for breakfast?"

"Martin."

"I like lunch. Lunch is fine."

I retrieved the balance of the quarters from behind the sink. In total, I had one dollar in change, plus the five-dollar bill, which made six, six whole dollars. Holding the money in my hand felt dangerous, risky. The quarters slid over one another, clinking, sounding their presence. I put the coins in my pocket with the bill. That tiny weight seemed as if it could have thrown my whole body off balance.

We made the bed and were about to leave when Martin asked, "What's she going to think when she sees that we're gone? Isn't she going to get scared?"

"I didn't think about that."

"Let's leave her a note."

"A note? What's it going to say?" We'd never left a note before and, more important, we had no place to go—not school, not church, and certainly not the river. Martin was already getting a piece of paper from his school pad. He sat down and carefully printed out the note in perfect, block letters: *My od bawic sie.*

The note read: "We went out to play."

This lie was like a waft of air. It didn't sting or twinge. Lying had become like everything else, like blinking, like breathing.

We sneaked out of the house, then both of us started to run though there was no reason to. I was leading, running down Third, past Swatka Pani's house and beyond. Martin was keeping up, the lunch tin swinging back and forth in his hand, but he soon slowed.

"I'm hungry," he panted, lopping to a stop.

"We'll eat soon. I've got somewhere I have to go first."

"Where?"

"The butcher's shop. I need my clothes."

"But you're already wearing your clothes."

"You'll see."

Mr. Goceljak was carving down a pig's leg on the block when I tapped on the back door. He waved me in with his knife.

"I must be nicer than I thought if you want to come see me on your day off."

"I came by because . . . I mean, I wanted to know if it would be all right if I borrowed the clothes."

He was confused. "What do you need them for?" My reticence left him room to guess. "Going up to Walt's, eh?" Mr. Goceljak was working the knife's blade close to the bone and the flesh was slumping off in a thick sheet. "Well, just be careful with that money. You worked hard to earn it, but it'll only take you a split second to lose it."

I hadn't considered losing, only doubling my money like Mr. Beresik had described. The prospect of having all of the money taken away almost made me change my mind on the spot.

"I'll be careful."

"That your brother out there?" Mr. Goceljak asked.

Martin had his face pressed to the door, then he ducked down and scrambled away.

"Yes, sir."

"Don't look much alike."

"Everybody says that."

"You taking him too?"

"I have to. I couldn't leave him at home . . . alone," I added.

"But I'm going to make him stay outside, down the road. I won't let him come in."

Mr. Goceljak nodded approvingly. "He's too young for it. Come to think of it, so are you."

He wiped the knife on his apron. He'd gotten all of the meat he was going to get from the leg. The bone gleamed white. "You can change out in the shed if you like."

I took the pants and cap down from the peg where I'd hung them.

"Good luck then," Mr. Goceljak offered.

Martin hurried away from the door and pretended to be admiring the bicycle when I came out.

"He saw you," I said. "I told you to stay out of sight."

"I just wanted to look in a little."

"Didn't I tell you not to?"

"Yes," he conceded.

"If you do it again, if you disobey me when I tell you to stay hidden, then I'll take you home. I'm not fooling, Martin."

"All right."

"Promise."

"I promise."

"Swear to God."

He let out an exasperated sigh. "All right, I swear to God."

"Good."

"Now can we eat?"

"Go ahead, you eat. I've got to change." I held up the pants and cap to show him what I meant.

"You're going to put on boy clothes?"

"I do it almost every day."

"What does it feel like?"

"No different than my regular clothes." Martin considered the statement as he took a bite of his sandwich. "I'll be right out," I told him, slipping the latch on the door to the curing shed.

"Okay, I'm not going anywhere. Not moving. Not an inch," Martin attested between bites. "Swear to God."

The shed was pitch black. There was no light, no electricity. I clumsily slipped on the pants and tied the rope belt. As my eyes adjusted, I could make out the shapes of hanging sausages, thick and fingerlike, as well as a half-dozen pigs' legs, all lined up, like they were marching. I wound my hair into a tight knot on the top of my head just as my mother would do with hers, then I pulled the cap down firmly.

"You do look like a boy. Kind of," Martin said when I stepped out of the shed.

"Kind of?"

"It's just 'cause I know you're not."

"I guess we're ready then."

"Do you ever get to ride this?" he asked, tracing the curves of the bicycle's seat with his finger.

"I could if I wanted. I told Mr. Goceljak I knew how."

"But you don't."

"I know that."

"So did you try?"

"It was hard. Much harder than you'd think."

Martin gazed at the bicycle with a mix of awe and apprehension. "Really?"

"I almost fell down. And I wasn't even moving yet."

"Oh," he replied, a little put off. "Do you think, maybe, sometime I could try?"

"I don't know. I could ask Mr. Goceljak."

"Would you?"

"I will, but only if you really promise not to sneak a look at where I'm taking you."

"But I already swore to God."

That no longer seemed like enough. It hadn't for a while, and I feared it never would again.

"Just remember, you look and no bicycle."

"Fine. Can we go now? It smells back here."

"It does?"

"You don't smell it?" Martin pinched his nose and made a face.

I didn't smell a thing. Then I remembered the first day I'd gone to work for Mr. Goceljak. The sweet, pungent scent of smoked meat blending with the tinny odor of the raw was so overpowering I'd worried it would cling to my clothes. Until Martin mentioned it, I hadn't even realized that I'd become acclimated to it.

"Come on," I told him. "It's a long walk."

WE MADE OUR WAY OUT of town and along the dirt road to Mr. Beresik's house. The muddy ruts in the road were deeper than usual and marred with tire tracks. Several cars had passed that way. Martin hopped from one side of the tire tracks to the other, playing.

"Aren't you hungry?" he asked.

"Not really."

"I'm cold."

"Do you want to run?"

"Not really."

"It'd make you warmer."

"I'm not that cold," he said. "How much farther?"

"It's just up over the hill."

"Thank God."

I hadn't heard those words in a while, hadn't said them myself, and they sloshed in my ears like icy water.

More than a dozen cars and trucks were pulled up around Mr. Beresik's property, all parked at different angles. We'd never seen so many cars in one place besides the lot outside the steel mill.

"Look," Martin marveled, running ahead.

Most were beat up and rusted, the paint dull with dust. Nevertheless, together they made an impressive sight.

"Look at that one," Martin said, racing up to a crystal-yellow Mercury that looked like one long sweep of swelled metal. He ran his hand along the side, petting the car the way he had petted Ragsoline's horse.

"Don't touch, Marty."

"Why not?"

"It's not yours."

"Who's going to see me?" He patted the plump girth of the front wheel's hull.

I was about to scold him when I realized that the cars would keep him busy and they would keep him away from the house.

"All right. You can touch the cars. But you have to stay out here. You can't come inside. You can't come on the porch. You can't even go near the door."

Martin saluted me. "Yes, sir," he chimed, and I frowned. "What? You're supposed to be a boy, right?"

"Just stay out here. If anybody comes out that door, you hide. You hide by those bushes over there. And don't go near that fence," I ordered, pointing to the dog pen.

"Why? It's empty."

"No, it's not. It might look like it, but it isn't. Marty, I'm serious. Don't go near the fence." The gravity of my tone scared him, so much so that he took a step away from the pen.

"You can eat my sandwich. And here. Take my mittens." I pushed my mittens onto Martin's hands. I still had the bandages on. "I'll be out as soon as I can. But no matter what, don't come inside."

I mounted the porch and could already hear the din of voices from below the house. I turned back and Martin waved, my mitten doubling the size of his hand.

A handful of men were in the kitchen, taking bottles of beer from the icebox and popping off the caps. I tried not to make eye contact, but one of them nodded as I passed, a silent greeting. Then another man stopped me. "Ey boy," he said in Polish. "Bring a few of these bottles down, will you?"

"Okay," I grunted, keeping my head low as I let the men fill my arms with beer bottles. I teetered down the basement steps behind them, bottles clanking, fearful of letting one slip.

The basement was packed, crammed to the walls with more men. Chairs from upstairs had been brought down and lined up along the pit. Some of the men milled around while others had staked out their seats and wouldn't budge. Most were smoking, bottles in hand. A cloudy layer of cigarette smoke hung at the ceiling, nowhere to go.

When one man spotted the beer I was carrying, he approached and pulled one from my arms. "Thanks, kid," he mumbled. Other men were soon doing the same.

"Didn't know you hired a waiter, Walt?" someone called out.

Mr. Beresik appeared from alongside the pit. He saw me holding the bottles and cracked a grin. "Didn't know I'd hired one either." He helped me set the bottles down on the floor. "Don't mind these old bastards. They'll give you a hard time if you let 'em. But I won't let 'em, okay?"

I shook my head. It was all I could do because my arms were aching from carrying the bottles.

"You ready to win some money?" Mr. Beresik asked.

"I hope so."

"Hope ain't got nothing to do with it. Just luck. And unfortunately, that's worse." He nudged me playfully. "You'll do fine. I'll find you when it's a good bet. Help you put your money down with Vic. He handles all the bets 'cause I'm too busy with the dogs."

Mr. Beresik gestured toward the far corner of the pit room where a thick-nosed man in a squarish hat sat on a stool. Two crates were stacked in front of him as a makeshift betting table. I didn't realize I'd be giving my money to anybody but Mr. Beresik and my apprehension showed.

"Don't worry. Vic's good with the numbers, but his fingers aren't slippery."

Mr. Beresik melted back into the crowd, greeting the men, shaking hands and slapping backs. I scooted over to the far side of the pit and hid in the corner, wedging myself in where the wooden slats that formed the railing met the wall.

Boisterous laughter boiled up from one end of the basement, then blended in with the murmur of men discussing bets. Most had fallen in along the handrail encircling the pit. Some put out their cigarettes while others lit them in anticipation. A few were chewing tobacco and spitting it into empty beer bottles or down into the pit.

The man beside me shook his head when he saw someone spit tobacco juice into the pit.

"Means he'll spit on the dog when it's fighting," the man said ruefully. He was a heavyset older man with an uneven beard and fat forearms that fanned out when he leaned on the railing. "Better not be my bet he's spittin' on."

A bell sounded from Vic's corner and the room settled. Mr. Beresik cut through the crowd on one side of the pit and lifted up two cards with handwritten numbers on them.

"Nineteen versus forty-one. Nineteen versus forty-one."

A door opened into the pit and a man in shirtsleeves came out holding a cream-colored pit bull on a tight chain leash. The dog had reddish eyes and a healed scar running the length of its shoulder. The man positioned the dog in the far corner of the pit, unhooked the leash and straddled the dog, then grasped it by the jowls, preparing to rein it back. Spit flung from the dog's mouth as it worked itself into a frenzy.

"Nineteen," Mr. Beresik shouted. Then the door swung open again. "Forty-one."

Another man entered the ring. He was clean shaven and wore a dress shirt and brown trousers with a matching hat. His clothes gave him an air of affluence, which rendered him utterly out of place in Mr. Beresik's basement and especially in the middle of the pit. His dog was mottled with black and brown speckles, and its fur was so ravaged with scars that it looked mangy. The man held his dog back in the same manner the other had, pulling on the dog's face and exposing its teeth.

Mr. Beresik nodded to Vic and the bell sounded again.

What followed was a blur of movement. Both men released their dogs simultaneously, and Forty-one darted across the pen and tackled the cream-colored dog, pinning it to the ground.

The men backed into the safety of the corners while the crowd went wild, hollering and leaning over the railing to get a better look at the fast start to the fight. The dogs' heads were whipping from side to side, each trying to get a better angle on the other's neck. Nineteen dove low and hooked its jaws onto the other dog's shoulder, but Forty-one bucked and managed to wrangle free. The man chewing the tobacco spit on Nineteen, hitting it on the rump.

"See," the heavy man said to me. "What'd I tell you."

The tobacco juice dribbled off Nineteen's pelt while Forty-one nipped at its face, then ripped into the dog's ear. Nineteen yelped and tried to pull away, but Forty-one yanked back, hind legs jerking. The ear was hanging, bloody, with a piece partially severed.

I dropped my head and pretended to cough from the smoke, but I was covering my eyes with the brim of the cap. A few fervent yowls rose up from the ring and I clamped my eyes tight. Soon I heard only one dog barking. I didn't need to look to know it was Forty-one.

"Glad I didn't bet on that one," the heavy man next to me huffed. "Nineteen *used to be* my lucky number."

When I allowed myself to look, Forty-one was standing in the center of the pit, wagging its stub of a tail. The man in the matching hat and trousers whistled twice and Forty-one trotted to his side, then together they disappeared behind the pit door and into the bowels of the basement.

Someone from the crowd handed the man in the shirtsleeves a big sack cut along the seams.

"What's happening?" I asked the heavy man.

"Winner took his dog back into the pens to wait for the next match. Winner always gets another match."

The other man covered the cream-colored pit bull with the sackcloth, hoisted it into his arms, and carried it through the same door.

"Loser's got to bag his 'un up," the heavy man informed me.

Three more matches came and went. Before each fight, I would look to Mr. Beresik across the pit, but he would shake his head, telling me not to put my money down. As soon as the owners and their dogs entered the ring, I fixed my eyes on the railing. With the brim of the cap covering my eyes, I hoped I looked like I was watching, at least from Mr. Beresik's vantage point. Listening was almost worse. A constant snarling, the click of teeth biting air then biting flesh, and the barks or howls that followed mingled with the cheers and booing from the men.

The fourth match was a draw. Both dogs had injured each other so badly that one limped out and the other had to be carried. The dirt pit was muddy with blood. Dust kicked up by the dogs during the fights clotted the blood into muddy pools.

"Here we go," the heavy man said. "This is the one I been waiting for."

Mr. Beresik held up the number cards: Seven and Forty-one. He gave me the nod and gestured for me to hurry over to Vic's table.

Vic spoke in a gnarled Polish accent, making it hard for me to understand him. "How much?" he said. He had to ask me twice.

"I don't know."

Vic frowned. Men were waiting in line behind me, impatient to place their bets before the dogs were let out and the betting was closed.

"All of it," I heard Mr. Beresik say from behind me. He put a hand on my shoulder. "How much you got there anyway?" I showed him the quarters and the five-dollar bill. He grinned.

"Six dollars, eh? Freddy Goceljak must be getting generous. Put it all on Sally."

"Sally's fighting?"

"Yup. And she's going to beat that bastard Szymkewicz's bitch."

"Is that Forty-one?"

"Yeah. And Szymkewicz's as nasty as his dog. He's lucky I still let him fight here."

"Why?"

"Doesn't train his dogs right. Doesn't treat 'em right." Mr. Beresik got a look on his face like he'd eaten something bitter. "He hits 'em with sticks or burns 'em to make 'em meaner. You can see the welts on the dogs when they come out. It's bad business."

"Full six?" Vic asked Mr. Beresik, attempting to speed the line.

"You want to do it? Bet it all?"

"What happens if Sally wins?"

"Odds aren't in her favor," Mr. Beresik said in a hushed tone so the men behind us wouldn't hear. "People think she can't beat

Forty-one. But I know she can. She'd more than double your money in one match. You could take home a little over fifteen dollars."

The number chimed in my ears, ringing out over the din, irresistible. I tentatively laid my money on the crate, setting the quarters on top of the bill in a neat pile. Vic swiftly scooped up the money and it hurt to see it go. He handed me a scrap of paper with a string of numbers on it.

"You turn that back in for your money. When you win, that is," Mr. Beresik explained. He glanced at my newly bandaged hands. "Not a bad job. You rewrap those yourself?"

"No, my brother did it for me," I told him, then I realized I shouldn't have.

"You should bring him next time."

"Next in line," Vic shouted.

"I got to get back to the pens and get Sally into the pit," Mr. Beresik said. "I'll see you out here in a minute."

"Good luck," I called after him.

"Remember what I told you about luck," he chided as he slid into the crowd.

When I returned to my spot, the heavy man had a scrap of paper of his own and was massaging it between his thick fingers.

"Who'd you take on this one?"

"Number Seven," I told him.

The heavy man scoffed. "You crazy, boy? That old Sally couldn't lick a house cat. Walt's been running her so long everybody knows not to lay money on her. See all these men holding tickets?" Most of the men around the ring held their betting scraps in their hands. "Don't none of them have money on Seven. It's all on Forty-one. Beresik knows he's gonna get cleaned out on this match. Have to pay up for all these guys. I'd like to see that stack of money." The heavy man shook his head, marveling at the vision. "You got a sucker's bet there, boy."

I didn't understand. Had Mr. Beresik tricked me? I gripped the scrap of paper as the door to the pit swung open.

Sally strode out into the center of the empty ring, unhurried, with Mr. Beresik holding her leash. Men along the railing booed. The heavy man folded his arms. "She's done this so many times she looks plain bored of it."

Out came Szymkewicz with Forty-one straining at the leash. Both men grasped their dogs by the jowls and unhitched the leashes. Vic held up the numbers for Mr. Beresik, then rang the bell. My heart leaped as Forty-one bounded out at a full sprint and hurled itself into the air at Sally. But Sally countered. She was already up on her hind legs, anticipating the move. She bashed Forty-one in the face with her head, grazing its nose with her teeth.

Forty-one backpedaled momentarily and the men hissed in disappointment. Sally was forcing Forty-one toward the pen door, twisting and biting at its haunches. Mr. Beresik and Szymkewicz positioned themselves in opposite corners of the pit to wait out the fight. Szymkewicz chewed his bottom lip intently as he monitored the match with hands on hips. Even at that distance I could see that his eyetooth was cracked and broken in half.

"Just look at him," the heavy man said.

"Who?"

"The guy with Forty-one. Runs his dogs at any match that'll have him. But not many will. Don't know why Walt still lets him come. Gets the bets up, so it's good for business, I s'pose."

"I heard he beats his dogs."

"That and more," the heavy man retorted. "That and more. But a winner's a winner." He held up his scrap of paper as if it were a gold coin, then he began to cheer. "Go on, Forty-one," the heavy man hollered. "Go on and kill that bitch."

The dogs were locked in battle, heads swiveling back and forth in fluid bursts. Then Forty-one lunged, catching the bottom end of Sally's front leg in its jaws. Forty-one shook its head ferociously, ripping the thin flesh that covered the bone. My stomach lurched. I didn't want to look but couldn't tear my eyes away.

Sally writhed yet was unable to free herself from Forty-one's grip. Blood was streaming from the wound and as they scrambled around each other, the dogs kicked up more blood, flinging spurts onto each other's coats. The man with the tobacco spit at Sally, sending a trickle of tobacco juice onto her head.

"Bastard," I shouted, surprising myself as well as the heavy man. However, the curse simply melted in with the rest of the cheers. "He spit on her," I said.

"Don't bother me if it's not my dog," the heavy man replied.

Forty-one pulled hard on Sally's leg, dragging her across the ring and gnawing at the bone, unwilling to let go. Sally continued to nip at its face and haunches, anywhere she could get in a blow, but she was slowing, losing steam.

"Bet that leg's broken," somebody behind me said. "Bitch's done for."

Mr. Beresik folded his arms tightly. His lips were moving as though he was praying, then I realized he was talking to Sally, spurring her on. Forty-one momentarily released its jaws from

Sally's leg and Sally tried to step back but stumbled. The leg was indeed broken.

She faltered and got to her feet just as Forty-one reared high, driving its teeth into her face and forcing her to the ground.

"No," I shouted.

The men began roaring and waving their scraps of paper and pushing in tighter around the railing. The heavy man bounced on his crate. Szymkewicz pinched his bottom lip between his fingers, his shoulders tense and high, scrutinizing his dog's every move. Forty-one dug its teeth under Sally's chin, trying to get to her neck.

Mr. Beresik was mouthing words to Sally, willing her to get up. Blood began to flow from under Sally's jaw, streaming down her chest.

"Go, damn it. Go!" the heavy man cheered. "Kill her. Kill her."

Forty-one bore down on Sally, snapping at her in a ferocious rhythm. Sally bobbed her head, trying to fend off the dog. With a sudden strike, Forty-one got hold of Sally's neck. Blood poured from the wound. The men cheered louder. Sally blinked, long and slow, tired and perhaps dizzy from blood loss. I clutched the scrap of paper in my hand, balling it into my fist in spite of the pain of the blisters.

Forty-one was lurching back and forth violently, then Sally tilted her chin, as if to give the other dog full access to her neck. But when Forty-one went in, she opened her massive jaws wide and caught the side of the dog's head between her teeth.

An almost human wail went up and the men looked around, wondering if it had been one of them. It was Forty-one. Sally had driven her top teeth into the other dog's eye, blinding it. Her bottom teeth snared Forty-one's mouth, sealing it. Sally got to her feet, holding her broken leg up limply and balancing on three feet. Then with stunning speed, she threw Forty-one to the ground, hammering the dog against the pit floor.

The men went quiet as Sally began to shake the dog relentlessly, gashing its snout and biting off the end of its tongue. The heavy man cringed. Szymkewicz pinched his own lip brutally. Mr. Beresik was frozen, eyes riveted on his dog. Forty-one tried to free itself from Sally's grip, but couldn't and was left lying there at Sally's mercy, of which there was none.

She shook and shook and shook, blood flailing from the wound on her neck as Forty-one whimpered and let out a gurgling yowl. Then a nerve-jangling crack resounded in the pit. Forty-one went limp. Sally had broken the dog's neck.

The crowd of men began to jeer and curse, ripping their scraps of paper into shreds and throwing them into the ring at the dogs. Szymkewicz stared down at his dog's body, seething. Sally wouldn't let go of its neck.

"You won, kid," the heavy man sneered as he wadded up his scrap of paper and tossed it into the pit.

Mr. Beresik gave a sharp whistle and Sally dropped the dog instantly, then her legs gave out and she fell to the ground. Mr. Beresik rushed to her side and picked her up in his arms. I slipped under the railing and jumped into the pit with him.

"Kid. Don't," the heavy man called out.

Mr. Beresik held Sally in his arms as her head lolled. He was about to yell at me for getting in the ring, but gestured for me to open the pen door instead. I followed him into the pen room. The ceiling was so low he had to hunch over. Tiny wooden pens with iron gates lined both walls. A handful of dogs waited, one to a pen, barking viciously at the smell of Sally's blood.

Mr. Beresik laid Sally on the ground. Her blood had seeped into his shirt, causing it to hang off him, wet and loose. I knelt at his side.

"I'll get the cigar box. I'll get it and you can bandage her up, right?"

"No," Mr. Beresik answered. "Not this time."

Sally's chest heaved and more blood poured from the gaping wound on her neck. The cut on her leg was so deep that the bone showed through, a glint of white beneath the torn fur. Mr. Beresik tenderly inspected the gash on Sally's neck and a torrent of blood flowed from it.

In anguish, he whispered, "Jesus."

"No," I yelled. "Fix her. Get the bandages. You can fix her."

"You're a good girl," Mr. Beresik hummed, stroking Sally's back. "You're a good girl."

Sally blinked at the barking of the other dogs, instinct prevailing even as she lay dying, then her eyes fell on me.

Don't die, Sally. Don't die. Not for me.

"Fix her," I shouted, pushing Mr. Beresik's arm. He continued to hum to her, saying she was a good girl as her eyes rolled closed.

"Fix her," I demanded, shouting over the barking of the other pit bulls. I was beating on him with both fists. My bandages were soaking up the blood from his shirt and turning red in my hands.

Mr. Beresik pushed me away from him and I went sprawling on my back, dust rising around me. He hadn't intended to push me that hard, but he had, hard enough to knock the cap from my head. A long lock of my hair fell onto my shoulders. Mr. Beresik stared for a long moment, then he squinted, pushing back tears.

"Get your money and get out of here," he said.

I got to my feet and pushed my hair back under my cap. "I'm sorry," I said. I was sorry for everything, more than I could even imagine.

He didn't reply, only kept stroking Sally. I rushed out of the pen and back into the ring, where Szymkewicz was picking up his dog. He'd rolled the body in a long sheet of paper like the butcher's paper Mr. Goceljak used, then hefted the dog into his arms and pushed past me into the pens. I was alone in the pit, staring up at the room full of men, all swilling beers and arguing bitterly over the match.

One man called out to me. "Ey, boy, get out of there. Next match is about to go."

Soon other men were yelling at me as well.

"Can't stay down there forever," the heavy man said, holding out his hand to me from ringside.

I climbed up out of the pit, my clothes stained with patches of blood.

"Better get your money," the heavy man warned. I uncurled my fist and found the bet sheet netted in the web of the bandage, the one spot that was unsoiled.

Men stared as I wove through the crowd. They wouldn't move aside to let me pass, so I had to push by them to get to Vic's table. He glanced up at me from under the brim of his hat.

"That'll be fifteen and change. You want it in ones?"

"I don't know. Whatever."

He crisply shucked off fifteen single bills and a few dimes, then piled them in front of me.

"I'd leave if I were you, boy. Too many men here that'd take that money from you in a heartbeat."

I shoved the money into the pocket of the trousers. Vic watched me do it, as did the other men behind me. The odor of spilled beer and cigarette smoke had thickened and become ominously dense. I ran for the stairs, bumping into men as I went, then took the steps two at a time. I flew from the house at a full run, dodging the men lingering in the kitchen, and out onto the porch.

There were even more cars than before. The pack had grown, stretching out onto the road and boxing in the house. Martin was nowhere to be seen.

"Martin," I shouted. I couldn't hold back any longer. Tears began to boil over. "Martin."

"I'm here. Over here."

From behind the hulking tail of a black pickup, his face appeared, just the eyes at first, cautious, then his whole face.

I tore off the porch, grabbed Martin's hand, and started sprinting. "Run, Marty. We've got to run."

Frightened, he did as I said, but dropped the lunch tin and scrambled to retrieve it. He kept up for a while, far enough that Mr. Beresik's property was long behind us, then he slowed, exhausted.

"I can't," he panted. "I can't run anymore." He bent over to catch his breath. "Why are we running?"

I slowed a few steps ahead of him. "We've got to get back," I lied. "We've been gone too long."

"You're crying," Martin said, approaching. He studied my face inquisitively. Tears had taken on a whole new meaning for him. "Why? Because you saw the dogs fighting?"

"How did you know that?"

"I heard some men talking when they got out of their car. It was a blue car. Not as nice as some of the others. They said they were going to bet on the dogfight." Martin was proud of what he'd discovered. "Did you see it?" I nodded. "And it was sad?" I nodded again. "Very sad?"

"Yes, Martin. Very sad."

"And that's why you're crying?"

I was crying for too many reasons to count, so many I'd lost track. "Yes," I replied. "That's why I'm crying."

Martin handed me my mittens back. He saw the blood on the bandages and was about to ask about it, but stopped himself, a small gesture of kindness. I put the mittens on, but couldn't feel them. The cold had gone too deep and nothing would ever be enough to warm me up, not for a long time.

MY BROTHER PUT HIS HAND in my coat pocket as we walked back to Hyde Bend. The sun shone but the wind blew on, gusting against our shoulders, pushing us to return and to not look back.

Saturday Mass had let out and Field Street was full and humming.

"I've got to return the clothes," I said.

Martin stood behind the butcher's shop, outside by the bicycle, holding the handlebars and maneuvering the front wheel over the dirt.

"Do you promise to stay out here?"

"Promise. And swear to God," he moaned, more interested in the bicycle.

Mr. Goceljak was helping customers up front. He didn't hear me come in the back door and I was thankful for that. I didn't want to tell him what had happened. I took the wad of money from the pocket of the pants. The bills were wilted, thin and wrinkled, as if they'd been through a thousand hands. It was more money than I'd ever seen, but it couldn't compare to the weight of the quarters the first time Mr. Goceljak had set them in my hand. This money felt like nothing.

I folded the bills into my skirt. They were so light I had to pat my pocket again and again to reassure myself that they were still there. I pulled off the pants and cap and hung them on the peg as usual. The pants seemed so limp, the rope flimsy, the cap hollow.

"Have a nice day," I heard Mr. Goceljak tell the customer, then I slipped out the door before he had time to realize I had returned.

"Come on," I told Martin. "One more stop."

Through the front window, I could see that the Savewell was busy, bustling with women in line and women at the registers.

"I'll be right back," I told Martin, leaving him outside before he could argue.

There were women in their church clothes buying tablecloths, perusing magazines, picking up skillets to check the price on the bottom. The scent of perfume and powder sweetened the air. I'd never felt so dirty. I could feel the dust from the pit between my fingers, on my neck, my face. My hair was matted from wearing the cap and my face was swollen from crying. I didn't resemble these women, not even vaguely.

I made my way to the back room and the door was open. Mr. Sekulski was inside, sitting at the desk, glasses perched on his nose as he skimmed a stack of papers. The little painting of the Black Madonna was right where it had been before, unmoved, unchanged, waiting. The only difference was that there were more things piled around it. The baby Jesus was obscured by a lamp, while the Black Madonna peeked over the side of the shade with one eye, ever watchful.

"I've come for the painting," I said, standing in the doorway.

Mr. Sekulski looked up from his papers.

"The painting." I pointed.

"You have the money to buy it back? Don't waste my time if you don't."

I took the bills from my pocket and Mr. Sekulski's eyes locked on the money.

"Fourteen dollars. Like you said."

"Is that what I said? I thought I said sixteen."

"No, you said fourteen." Panic made my voice tremble. "I remember, you said fourteen. You said fourteen."

"Then I guess that'll have to do." He whisked the bills from my hand, counted them out on his desk, then folded them into his shirt pocket. "I'll get it down for you."

He stood on a step stool and pulled the painting from the shelf, sending a shower of dust down on himself. "Damn thing," he cursed, then he blew off what dust was left and handed it to me. "See. Good, eh? Like new."

I took the Black Madonna in my arms. I hadn't remembered just how small it was. The frame was narrow and light. It was like holding a soap bubble. If I clasped it too close it would break, too loosely and it would float away. I put the faces of the Madonna and child to my chest, shielding their eyes.

Mr. Sekulski noted the bloodied bandages on my hands. "I told the lady who sold it to me that it was a good piece. Nice, I mean."

"What?"

"That it's a sweet picture. Not too gaudy or anything."

"No, what did you say before that?"

"The lady who came here to sell it—"

"It was my father. My father sold you this painting."

Mr. Sekulski shook his head resolutely. "No, it was a woman. Pretty. Her hair in a bun. Don't know her name, but she brings me things from time to time."

"That's a mistake."

Annoyed that I didn't believe him, he anxiously dug around behind his desk to prove his point. "Here, I'll show you. I locked it up with the jewelry. Too nice to leave it laying around."

Mr. Sekulski took out a tiny lockbox and opened it with a key. Inside lay a lump of jewelry, gold chains and pearls knotted in with rings and bracelets. Like a hidden treasure, all of Hyde Bend's riches sat there, sold off, biding their time until their owners could reclaim them, if ever.

"Here. See." He held up a silver pocket watch with a thickly roped fob as evidence. "She sold me this 'un. Said it was her father's."

My heart faltered. I knew the watch. My mother had shown it to me when I was younger and told me it was her father's. It was the one thing he had left her.

"Why? Why did she sell it to you?"

"Said she owed some money," Mr. Sekulski explained. "Must

have been a lot for all of the times she's been here." He held up a thin gold band. "This is hers too."

It was my mother's wedding ring. An aching horror descended on me like a sheet being pulled over my head. Once, after church, Martin had asked her why she didn't wear a ring like other women did. She told us she was afraid of losing it. She told us that her hands were always in water when she was working and that she didn't want it to fall down the drain or slip off.

The realization of what my mother had done came hurtling at me, then went careening off again. I tried to hold it down in my mind the way I'd tried to hold myself under the water in the bathtub, fighting all the way.

"She usually comes around every few weeks or so," Mr. Sekulski added, shutting the lockbox. "She'll sell a brooch or some candlesticks. Sometimes little things. Depends." He waved to a pair of brass candlesticks sitting on the shelf, still nestled in a small cloth sack. It was the same sack my mother had tried to hide from our view two weeks earlier.

"Haven't seen her in a while though. Maybe she finally paid off that money after all."

The truth poured over me in one long, awful cascade. I gripped the painting to my chest.

"Careful," Mr. Sekulski warned. "That's a delicate thing. You'll break it if you don't watch how you hold it."

I wheeled around and bolted from the back room only to run right into Martin. He had heard everything.

"You didn't make me promise. You didn't make me swear. Not this time."

I pushed past him and he chased after me. "Let me see it."

"It's just the painting."

"But she sold it. That man said she sold it. Why'd she sell it? Why'd she sell all of our things?"

I was racing through the aisles with Martin hard on my heels.

"I don't know."

"Yes, you do."

"Martin, I said I don't know."

"I know you do. I can tell. Don't lie to me."

We were tearing through the store, making a scene. "Don't talk so loud," I told him. "We've got to go home."

Martin pulled me to a halt outside the Savewell. "Why did she sell all of those things? Tell me." He was trying to order me, the way our father did, to stand his ground, but it was desperation that flooded the plea.

"Tell me," Martin implored.

"She needed the money to pay for Papa's—"

I stopped myself, the word *Papa* tingling on my tongue. My heart bloated with a new kind of pain. "For his drinking," I lied.

Martin struggled to read my face. "That's all?"

"That's all."

Martin's face twisted. He wanted to believe me so badly that for a while I think he did. But over time, the lie I told that day festered. Martin would never forget it and neither would I.

As we headed home, Martin put his hand in my pocket again, ambling after me a half step behind. It wasn't the last time he ever did that, but I remembered it as if it was. I can't recall the path we took or who or what we passed. I pushed everything out of my mind so I could hold on to the memory of what it was like to have Martin's hand in my pocket. I tried to memorize the feeling of his fingers against my hip, to fill my head with the heft of his hand and the tug of my coat as he walked alongside me. The feeling was so sweet it hurt, but I wouldn't let it go.

Martin paused before we entered the apartment. "Can I touch it?"

My mother would never let us near the painting of the Black Madonna. Once Martin had stood on a chair to admire the painting close-up and my mother scolded him for breathing on it. I'd felt the temptation myself to wake in the night and run my hand over the painting, but I was too frightened to do so, afraid that somehow the marks of my fingers might show.

I lowered the painting away from my chest. I'd been holding it so tightly that the frame was driving into my ribs, leaving an ache with edges as square as the frame. Martin studied the painting, then laid his hand at the top of it and drew his fingers along its surface.

"It doesn't feel like I thought it would," he said. "Now you."

Martin waited, yet I was reticent. "It's okay," he assured me. "It won't hurt. Better take those off first," he cautioned. I was still wearing the bloodied bandages. "I'll help you."

I held out one hand, then the next while he delicately unwound the bandages. The hands that were revealed beneath were mangled. They didn't seem like my own or even real. The welts were nearly black and were dotted along the edges with red clots. The blisters had turned white. The pile of bandages was overflowing in Martin's arms. "What should we do with them?"

"Put them in my pocket."

He stuffed the bandages into the pocket where his hand had been and I almost stopped him, but couldn't explain why I didn't want them there.

"Okay," Martin said, urging me on. The painting was waiting.

With a tentative touch, I ran my finger over its surface, tracing the outline of the Black Madonna's burnt robes, lingering along the folds, soaking up the texture of each shadow and line.

"Can I touch her face?" I asked. Martin was as unsure as I was.

I brushed my fingertip along the Black Madonna's cheek, caressing it from one side to the other, then pulled away.

"I don't want to do this anymore."

"All right," Martin replied. "Do you want me to open the door?"

"Yeah, you open it." I cast a glance down the alley. Swatka Pani's house stood hunched where it had always been. Only now the fallen limbs of the rosebushes were gone, blown away. No sign of life remained. I gave Martin the key and he unlocked the apartment door.

"You want me to go first?"

"No, I'll go."

"Are you scared?"

I didn't have to answer. Martin opened the door and my mother was sitting at the table, stitching up the collar on the shirt she had been mending for my father. The note we'd left was nowhere to be seen. She didn't look up from her sewing. She kept drawing each stitch in and out in a sweeping rhythm. When she did finally glance up, the needle froze in midair.

The painting lay in my arms, its back to her, yet there could be no mistaking what it was. The needle quivered in her hand, then my mother let out a sigh so brief but so full of agony that I heard every secret in it, every untold truth.

She did it all for you.

THE GRAVE OF GOD'S DAUGHTER | 279

With unfeeling legs, I moved across the apartment and pulled a chair alongside the wall. I stepped on the seat and came face-to-face with the shadow the painting had left in its absence. That faint spot was everything I was, the product of darkness and sunlight and the proof that a presence, no matter how slight or small, still leaves its mark. Hands shaking, I rehung the painting of the Black Madonna and covered the shadow for good.

THE DAY I BROUGHT HOME the Black Madonna fell from memory, gone but not excised from any of our minds. My mother never asked how I had gotten the painting back or what I had done to pay for it. I believe the thought of what I might have learned in the process terrified her. It was easier to pretend that nothing had happened, for her as well as for me. What was not spoken was not real. To say anything aloud would have made it too true to bear.

That spring passed, and a year later, the man I knew as my father was sent to war. The National Polish Alliance drafted all of the able-bodied men in Hyde Bend and shipped them to France to fight the fast-encroaching German army. The steel mill closed briefly, as did the salt plant, then women began to take their husbands' jobs and the work went on. Hyde Bend became a town of women and children. Men were scarce and those who were around were old or infirm, useless.

Two months after he was sent away, the man I knew as my father was shot through the back of the skull in a forest in the middle of the night as his regiment trekked north to fortify the front. His body was buried in an army graveyard outside Pittsburgh along with thousands of others. A stark, granite headstone listed only his name, date of birth, and date of death. Once a month we would make the journey to his grave, taking two buses and making a mile-long walk to get there. At each visit, Martin and I would stand silently and watch as my mother meticulously weeded the plot, ripping up stray dandelions and pulling out the dying grass. Afterward, we would leave and return to what we knew.

The war went on. Food that had once been scarce grew scarcer. People prayed more and went to church less. Time worked against us in every way. There was too little to the day to make enough money and too much night to consider what we didn't have and what we'd lost. My mother continued to work at Saint Ladislaus. Father Svitek was diagnosed with cancer of the stomach and grew ill. My mother tended him in his sickbed until he was moved to a hospital, where he too died. Another priest was brought in and my mother became his housekeeper. He soon left, then another priest arrived, then another. The priests came and went while my mother remained the only constant.

After that day, I never went back to the butcher's shop. Mr. Goceljak knew where I lived and, early on, I worried he would come to the apartment and inquire as to why I hadn't returned. He never did. Though I was only partly thankful that he didn't. I never saw Mr. Beresik again either, except once I glimpsed him driving a truck down Field Street, heading out of Hyde Bend, toward his house. The truck was piled high with bales of hay, for the dogs' bedding, I guessed. The bales were stacked neatly one on top of another, the yellow straw glimmering as strands blew from the bales and fluttered through the air, lost in the truck's wake. I put the pain of missing both men away, tied it up tightly and hid it in the back of my heart.

A year into the war, I overheard women gossiping by the laundry lines and saying that the woman from the house on River Road had died. It was Mr. Goceljak who had found her. She hadn't answered the door for any of her deliveries. Worried, he went to her house and discovered her body in bed, tucked neatly under the covers. She had died in her sleep, a peaceful death, the only peace she'd had in years. I wondered if the woman had ever thought about me, about the boy who came to her door to make deliveries, the one she chose to talk to. I wondered if she missed that person. There were times I would try to picture her face and all that would come to mind were memories of her disheveled hair, her loose sweaters, her house heaped high with refuse. They were the only images I had of the woman who was my grandmother. Later I learned that she was buried out of town. No one knew where, or if they did, they wouldn't say. I assumed that Mr. Goceljak had paid for her burial. It was a feeling, never confirmed, and even years later, when I would pass his shop and pause, I debated whether to go inside to ask. The truth was something I didn't trust myself with. It was better that I didn't have it.

I never told Martin what I had learned about our mother or about what she had done, but Martin sensed I was holding something back from him, like he sensed every other lie, and for that, he never forgave me. I came to believe that the man I knew as my father must also have known the truth, maybe not all the details, but enough.

My mother had been an unparalleled beauty and there could be no doubt that he would have married her for that and that alone. Perhaps she'd lied to him about being pregnant and made him believe that I was his. Eventually he must have figured out that I wasn't. I pictured him studying me as an infant and as I grew, not seeing himself in my face. I imagined his doubt rising and swelling, so much so that he drank to keep that doubt at bay.

In the absence of truth, my imagination was all I had. I tried to piece together my mother's life, to envision her with the priest. I concocted a love story out of nothing and embroidered it with fictional details of stolen glances and tender moments. They would have met when she was a teenager, when she'd first taken the job at the church after her father had died. I could see her cooking meals for him at the rectory, pots steaming, mending a lost button on his sleeve or making his bed. I imagined that the spot where we always sat in church might have been the spot where she first saw him or the spot where they first spoke. I could never know the truth, but the romantic tale I'd fashioned in my mind gave me solace.

Imagination also let me piece together how my mother had fallen prey to Swatka Pani. When the old woman from the house on River Road refused to pay, Swatka Pani sought my mother out and threatened her with exposure. I pictured Swatka Pani hissing about how she would let her secret loose if my mother didn't pay her off. I decided that was how it had all begun. My mother sold everything she had, yet it would never be enough. I surmised that she'd even started stealing things from the rectory to pawn, then finally, she'd had to sell her beloved painting of the Black Madonna. Still, Swatka Pani wanted more. When the man who I believed was my father started using most of our money for alcohol, my mother could no longer make her payments. Then Swatka Pani must have grown impatient and upped her threats. The truth about my identity would shame us all. It would have ruined me. But my mother wouldn't let that happen.

That night when Leonard knocked on our door, it was not a visit, but a reminder. Swatka Pani had sent him to make sure my mother met her to deliver the money. And they did meet that night, out by the laundry lines. It was my mother I'd overheard arguing with Swatka Pani while I was trapped in the outhouse. My mother must have told her that she would have the money later, but that Swatka Pani would have to meet her at the river to get it. Money was the only thing that would have gotten Swatka Pani there. In my heart, I knew my mother planned to kill Swatka Pani. She thought God had closed His eyes on her for what had happened with the priest and that there was little she could do to save herself. She could save me.

I could image countless things about that night when she met Swatka Pani at the river, the dark moon, the stairway, the bright shadow of the cross shining on the water. But the only thing I chose to believe was that in that moment, my mother loved me more than she could ever say or show or even feel.

CHAPTER THREE

THE PRIEST HAS BROUGHT THE FUNERAL to a close. I have heard nothing he has said, nothing except the sound of the wind blustering against my coat, flickering the grass and sending a hushing rustle through the trees. The other mourners step back, away from my mother's grave, preparing to take their turns in line to throw dirt on the coffin, but they are waiting for Martin and me, courtesy for kin.

"Do you want me to go first?" Martin asks quietly.

I can only manage to nod.

Martin scoops up a handful of dirt from beside our mother's coffin and clutches it in his fist, then opens his palm and lets the dirt drop in one heavy torrent.

"It's your turn," he says, moving aside, away from the coffin, leaving it all to me.

I fill my hands with dirt and the soil feels as solid as stone, the cold giving it heft. I spread my fingers and the dirt falls away, sifting and catching on the breeze, refusing to come to rest on the coffin. A few granules of dirt skitter over the top and glance off the wood, making brief contact, but that is all. This was how my mother knew love, only in passing. It was a thing that never stayed, lingering just long enough to make you miss it once it was gone. Her father, her mother, her brother, her husband, her God, and the one man she cared for, they had all left her, and their departure twisted her heart inside out. There was no room inside, no place to put Martin or me.

"You have to let them go now," Martin tells me, touching my arm. The other mourners are waiting.

I step back, giving them room, and each man and woman toss their handful of dirt onto the coffin, then they head off down the rutted path from which they came.

"Do you want to stay for a while?" Martin asks.

"I don't know."

"You can," he offers. "They can't make you leave." He is trying to joke, then he realizes the vague irony in his choice of words. After a moment, he adds, "I'm not going to stay. Not unless you want me to."

"No, not unless you want to."

Martin furrows his hands deeper into his pockets. "No, I'm going to go."

"All right then."

"Are you staying in town over night?"

"No, no I hadn't . . ." I let my voice trail off.

Disappointment dulls his reply. "That's okay. It's a long drive back."

My brother knows I have a family now, a husband, children, another life, a life that is waiting for me somewhere else.

As we stand there in silence for a moment more, I yearn to lean over to him and take his hand from his pocket and put it in mine.

"I'm gonna get going," he tells me and I don't stop him. "I'll be down . . . well, you know where to find me."

Martin looks around one last time straining to come up with something else to say. "Don't stay too long. Looks like rain."

With that, my brother turns from me and hastens along the path toward town. I watch him walk away then vanish down the road into nothing. In the distance, beyond the high point of path, lays the potter's field. The rows of headstones stipple the land in wide, uneven arcs. I vaguely wonder which one was his, which one belonged to the priest, my father. There are so many, too many to count.

The cemetery's caretaker appears, plodding up the path with a shovel slung over his shoulder, a wool scarf wound around his neck.

"Oh," he says, surprised to see me. "I thought everyone had gone. I'd come back later, but . . ." He gestures to the sky and the looming clouds.

"No, it's fine. I'm done here."

"You sure?"

I nod, but don't make a move to leave. "What do you do now?" I ask.

"What? With the grave?" He is hesitant to answer. "I've got to lower the casket and fill it back. Then I have to relay the grass. Put a little fertilizer on so it takes."

"Are all of the plots here sold?"

"No, not all of 'em. But most. This is an old cemetery, you know."

"What about this one?"

An empty stretch of grass waits next to my mother's grave, a so-far-unclaimed plot.

"What? Right here?"

"Yes, right here."

"These are good spots. Most been bought a long time back. I can tell you this one was bought over forty years ago. Bought and paid for by—" The man motions at my mother's grave and stops himself, embarrassed. "I don't know if the one next to 'ers been bought," he replies. "Have to check."

"Could you do that?"

"What? Right now?"

My silence is my reply. A gust of wind surges over the ridge, thick with the scent of impending rain, and the man's face sours. He glances back at the open grave ruefully.

"All right, I s'pose," he huffs, hoisting the shovel back onto his shoulder. "I'll check."

The man trudges toward the cemetery's front gate, disappearing down the path as Martin did.

I am alone as the first raindrops fall, landing softly on my mother's coffin and rolling lazily down to the dirt. I was wrong. The rain has come. Not a downpour or a deluge. Just a simple rain falling in the only direction it has to go.

THE GRAVE OF GOD'S DAUGHTER | 289